Inside
DUMONT

Inside DUMONT

A NOVEL IN STORIES

MICHAEL CRAFT

QUESTOVER
PRESS

INSIDE DUMONT

While dressing for dinner on New Year's Eve, the last thing Marson Miles expects is to fall in love that night—with his wife's nephew. But when Brody Norris arrives from California to join his uncle's architectural firm, Marson finds his life turned upside down. And the quirky little town of Dumont, Wisconsin, will never be quite the same.

Inside Dumont is a reflective exploration of Marson's later-life journey, set against a loving portrait of the place he and Brody will call home. This impressionistic chronicle of their growing relationship—and the orbit of events leading up to it—is told from a variety of viewpoints within a fluid timeline. The novel's dozen episodic narratives range from tender to suspenseful, from romantic to mysterious, all of them brightened with a good measure of humor.

Design and typography: M.C. Johnson
Author's photo: Questover Press
Cover image: modified from a photo by Yinan Chen

Library of Congress Cataloging-in-Publication Data

Craft, Michael, 1950–
    Inside Dumont : a novel in stories / Michael Craft
    ISBN: 978-0-692-72303-6 (hardcover)
    ISBN: 978-0-692-71604-5 (paperback)
    BISAC: Fiction / Gay
            Fiction / Literary
            Fiction / Short Stories (single author)

First hardcover and paperback editions: September 2016
Questover Press
    California

Prior working versions of several narratives
from *Inside Dumont* were published as follows:

"Frog Legs"
Chelsea Station Magazine, May 2014, Chelsea Station Editions,
    New York NY
Badlands Literary Journal, Fall 2014, California State University,
    San Bernardino, Palm Desert Campus
Outer Voices Inner Lives (anthology), November 2014,
    MadeMark Publishing, New York NY
Off the Rocks: Vol. 18 (anthology), December 2014,
    NewTown Writers Press, Chicago IL

"In the Fridge"
Chase the Moon Magazine: Issue 1, September 2014,
    Manchester UK

"Upstaged"
The Outrider Review: Vol. 2, Issue 1, January 2015, Omaha NE

"The Transit of Venus"
Glitterwolf: Issue 7, January 2015, Manchester UK

ACKNOWLEDGMENTS

While writing is often a notoriously solitary pursuit, I could not have brought *Inside Dumont* to publication without the help of numerous friends and associates, including Gina Bikales, David Grey, and Timothy Hess, for their guidance with various plot details; and Nancy Cunningham, Barbara McReal, Annelies Pocovi, and Larry Warnock, for their attention to the words on the page. My heartfelt gratitude goes to both Michael Nava and Patricia Nell Warren for endorsing this volume with their kind words of advance praise. As always, my agent, Mitchell Waters, was generous with his enthusiasm and wise counsel. And my husband, Leon Pascucci, has not only served as the trusted first reader of all my written work, but has also been a font of patience, support, and good cheer. My sincere thanks to all. — *Michael Craft*

CONTENTS

PART 1

ONE

Frog Legs

Amateur night—that's what they called it back in college, back when he was learning to drink. New Year's Eve—the night of resolutions and fresh beginnings. Now, though, in the last year of his fifties, there would be far less drinking, tepid interest in resolutions, and no chance whatever that he would be awake for the ritual flipping of the calendar.

Marson Miles, AIA, an architect at the height of his modestly esteemed career, stood in his dressing room, his sanctuary, in the house he had designed but hated. Were it not for his wife, their home would reflect the clean, disciplined aesthetic that had inspired his design of the local performing-arts complex. Questman Center had wowed critics and public alike at its dedication the prior spring and had been featured as a cover story in the autumn issue of *ArchitecAmerica*, the first such coup to be scored during the thirty-year practice of Miles & Norris, LLP.

"Marson?"

"Yes, Precious?" He turned from the framed magazine cover, which was not permitted to be displayed in the public areas of the house, and offered a feeble smile to his wife, who had banished the hard-won trophy to his closet.

"Zip me," she said with a clumsy pirouette, showing him her back, from which sagged the glittery flaps of a too-tight cocktail dress.

"Yes, Precious." He called her Precious; friends called her Prue; her parents had called her Prucilla. He zipped her, lamenting her choice of couture, which might have looked comely on a woman half her age—a woman old enough to be their daughter. But there were no children. They had tried, at first, but the lack of offspring had been met with little more than a mutual shrug, so they gave up. And in time, without rancor, without even much discussion, they had fallen into their arrangement of separate beds—in separate bedrooms.

His suite was a tranquil island of minimalism, with spare, contemporary furnishings and a subdued, neutral palette, while her suite wallowed in a florid outpouring of the posh Tudor aesthetic that enshrouded the mini-mansion she had badgered him into building for her. One day during the construction phase, in the offices of Miles & Norris, he had glanced over the floor plans, shaking his head. "It's a Disney monstrosity, replete with turrets," he said to Ted Norris, who was not only Marson's business partner, but also Prucilla's brother. "All that's missing is a drawbridge and a moat."

Tonight in Marson's closet, Prucilla eyed her husband askance. "You're wearing *that*?"

"I think so, yes." For their New Year's Eve dinner with Ted and Peg Norris, Marson had dressed in classic, understated good taste—black cashmere blazer, charcoal flannel slacks, white spread-collar shirt, and *the* tie. Of the hundreds of neckties arranged by color and pattern, hung from carousel hooks on both sides of a full-length mirror, his trusty old Armani provided the finishing touch for most special occasions. Silvery gray damask, with a subtle pattern of jaunty geometrics, it was both dressy and sporty, coordinating with almost anything. He couldn't recall exactly when he had bought it, at least twenty years ago, but it had cost some two hundred dollars, even then. A shameless extravagance, to be sure—but oh, the silk, the hand, the way it tied—*this* is what they meant when they spoke of investment dressing.

She watched with a snarky frown as he stood before the mirror, looping and sliding the sinuous tails of silk, which began to form the distinctive V-shaped Windsor knot beneath his throat. She said, "If you insist on wearing that old thing, can't you at least have it cleaned?"

"It's clean, Precious. I take good care of my things. Besides, you can't dry-clean a necktie."

"Don't be ridiculous."

He glanced over his shoulder at her. "Have you ever tried it?"

"Well, *no.*"

"I have." He returned his attention to the mirror, explaining, "They come back clean, but the body or the sizing or whatever—it's shot. They never tie right again. No, the only thing to do with a soiled necktie is to throw it out." Marson gave a final tug, pinched the knot with a perfect dimple, and watched as the tip of the Armani dropped precisely over his belt buckle. He spun on his heel to face her and raised both palms, intoning, "Tuh-dah!"

She mimicked his gesture, then scowled as she tossed her palms toward him. "Don't forget," she said, marching out of the closet and into the hall, "we're five tonight."

"Don't remind me." He followed. "I'm not sure what to think of your nephew's arrival."

She halted under a velvet-swagged iron chandelier and turned. "You *hired* him."

"The job offer was your brother's idea. Things are picking up, and we could use the help, so I went along with it."

"See? Everything's hunky-dory." Her tone turned menacing: "So what's the problem?"

He shrugged. "It's just that I hardly know Brody. How old was he—like *fourteen*?" The Brody in question was the son of Inez Norris, older sister of both Marson's wife, née Prucilla Norris, and Marson's business partner, Ted Norris. Something of a black sheep, Inez had followed her hippie leanings to California and, even now, remained estranged from the family, although she had returned for Marson and Prucilla's wedding thirty-five years ago, single and pregnant—with Brody. Marson's only other, postnatal, sighting of Brody had been fourteen years later, when Ted married Peg.

Recalling this, Marson realized that Ted's wedding, his second, had been the occasion for which Marson had bought his pet tie, the Armani. He had stood as best man. And at the reception, he'd met Brody.

"He *was* fourteen," Marson said to Prucilla, astonished by the passage of time. "And now he's an architect . . . and he's coming to work for me . . . and we've barely met."

She leaned close, speaking low. "You'll meet him tonight. Think of it as a family reunion." Her breath smelled of cucumber as she fingered his tie. "Happy New Year, Marson."

A drop of something hot and acidic slid to the pit of his stomach.

A star-pierced sky arched over the frigid night. There'd been a dusting of snow for Christmas, but it was gone now, and the dry, thin air felt clean and invigorating to Marson as he crossed the restaurant parking lot with Prucilla. He hadn't bothered with a topcoat; she huddled into a black mink cape while pecking across the asphalt, sputtering puffs of steam, churning her arms like the pistons of an old locomotive.

As they entered the restaurant lobby on the stroke of eight (Marson was nothing if not punctual), diners from the early-bird seating doddered out, while those who would be reveling at midnight were still at home dressing, drinking, or both. The hostess looked up from her computer and stepped over to greet them. "Don't you look *special* tonight. Happy New Year."

"Thank you, Ginger," said Prucilla, pivoting her shoulders so Ginger could remove the fur.

"Same to you, Ginger," said Marson. "Have the Norrises arrived?"

"About two minutes ago." Ginger draped the mink over one arm; with the other, she gestured toward the far end of the dining room. "You've got the prime booth tonight, number twenty-two. You folks enjoy." And with a bob of her head, she hustled the fur away.

Marson took Prucilla's arm to guide her past the bar and through the crowded room, but she pulled it back. Though they had often dined here and always liked it, New Year's could be an ordeal. Booked to capacity, the room was not only noisier than usual, but decorated with a cloud of gold and silver balloons that floated about the ceiling, trailing Mylar streamers that swayed at eye level. And there would be a special menu—overblown, overpriced.

Prucilla gave a demure wave as they plodded through the crowd. From the side of her mouth, she told Marson, "I don't know *what* Ted sees in Peg. Talk about mousy."

"Now, now—she always speaks kindly of *you*," he lied.

Booth twenty-two was horseshoe-shaped, with a round table, surveying the entire room from the far corner, backed by mirrored walls. The combined effect of the mirrors and the fluttering Mylar made Marson feel unsure on his feet—

and he hadn't had a drink yet. Brody had not arrived, but Ted and Peg were seated together at the back of the horse-shoe, watching and smiling. As their friends drew near, they began to inch toward the ends of the booth, sliding and squeaking on the leatherette, preparing to stand.

With a laugh, Marson waved them down. "Stay put—it's 'just us.'" Greeted with cheery handshakes and air-kisses, the new arrivals settled in at the ends of the horseshoe, Marson next to Ted, with Prucilla next to Peg. It was a tight fit. Marson wondered if Brody was not joining them after all—or if he was, where he would sit.

Prucilla was telling Peg, "Love your little frock . . ."

Marson asked Ted, "Did Brody's flight get in okay?"

Ted nodded. "Last night. He did some exploring today. Moved a few things into a temporary apartment—hell, he's starting a whole new life. He'll be here soon." Ted flashed Marson a quiet smile that transcended four decades. Their wives dished the dirt.

A round of drinks arrived. They had known each other so long, Ted had already placed the order: bourbon for himself, a dry gin martini for Marson, chardonnay for Peg, and a champagne cocktail for Prucilla. They were in the middle of a generic toast, something about "us" and "the future" and "new beginnings," when Marson's eye drifted to the mirror behind Ted, in which he saw Ginger approaching with a chair hoisted overhead, leading someone to the table. Before Marson could turn and stand to greet their guest, Ginger had planted the chair in the opening of the horse-shoe and—bang—there sat Brody.

Amid the clatter of arranging a new place setting and ordering the fifth drink, amid the welcomes and the mus-ings about the passing of years, Marson marveled at the transformation of the gangly fourteen-year-old he had met so long ago. Now in his mid-thirties, Brody Norris had flowered into an intelligent and affable young man who also happened to be an architect of considerable promise—and jaw-droppingly handsome. Peg's jaw did in fact drop as she hung on his every word, while Prucilla listened with a look of forced enthusiasm, as if miffed that *this* had sprung from the loins of her sister non grata.

As Marson studied Brody's *beauty*—which was indeed the right word—he was struck by the conspicuous resemblance to Ted Norris in his earlier years. That tousled shock of sandy-blond hair . . . the crooked grin . . . those arresting green eyes. With Brody to the right and Ted to the left, Marson glanced back and forth, seeing two men, nephew and uncle, who looked more like twin brothers at different ages. Yes, there were some knockout genes in the Norris family. To Prucilla's misfortune, though, their transmission had been restricted to the Y chromosomes.

Brody wagged his hands in a halting gesture. "Before we say another word"—the chitchat subsided—"I just need to tell Marson that I could *not* have been more impressed with Questman Center. Sure, I'd seen the piece in *ArchitecAmerica*, but the photos didn't begin to capture what I saw this afternoon. I took the tour—"

Marson interrupted, "Thanks, Brody, but—"

"I took the tour," Brody continued, resting his fingertips on the sleeve of Marson's blazer, "and I couldn't help thinking, My God, this is right up there with the best of Mies, Corbu, Neutra—you name it. Iconic. The term has gone threadbare, but Questman truly *is* iconic."

"Agreed," said Ted, raising his glass. "Bravo, Marson."

Marson reminded his partner, "Your name's on it, too. We're a team."

Ted told his nephew, "Don't listen to him. Marson's the

designer. I mind the business and the engineering."

Marson laughed. "I need *somebody* to make sure the roof stays up."

Brody touched Marson's arm again. "Well, I was totally blown away, and so were the docents this afternoon when I told them I was coming to work for you."

"Frog legs!" said Prucilla.

All heads turned to her.

She waved the evening's menu card. "It's a prix fixe, and the appetizer is frog legs."

"Ish," said Peg. Prucilla was right — Peg *was* mousy. She spoke little, so when she did, people took note.

"I think that sounds rather *festive*," said Ted, nudging his wife.

"I've never had them," said Marson, "but it's New Year's, and there's a first time for everything."

By the time the appetizer arrived, the table was on its second round of drinks, and any squeamishness Marson might have felt about the frogs was quelled by the gin.

"Tastes like chicken," said Peg.

"They say the same thing about rattlesnake," said Prucilla, chowing down.

Ted brought the focus back to Brody: "So . . . when did things fall apart with Lloyd?"

Brody set a bone on the plate and dabbed his lips with his napkin. "It started a year ago. I knew something was up when he needed to be traveling over Christmas. I mean, his kids are *my* age, and they'd always come to California, but last year — supposedly — he needed to visit *them*. Turns out he went to Vegas, to meet this guy we'd done a beach house for in Malibu. Five years younger than me, lots of bucks — catnip for Lloyd. It took six months to get everything out in the open, then another six to get it settled. But it's over."

Marson asked quietly, "You made out all right?"

Brody nodded. "We were married in California. Now we're divorced. And the firm is closed. Fifty-fifty."

"That's tough," said Marson, "but I'm glad you had those protections in place."

Brody smiled. "And I'm glad I landed here."

"How nice," said Prucilla, licking her fingers. "Everybody's glad and happy." The sauce was Asian, sweet, and sticky.

Ted said, "Amazing, isn't it, how times have changed? The whole 'gay issue' is so mainstream now."

"How modern," said Prucilla. "Everybody's so open and evolved."

Ted turned to Marson. "Remember, back in college? The topic was sort of . . . *radical*."

Marson's brows arched. "Was it ever."

With a quizzical look, Brody asked, "You guys went to college together?"

"Sure," said Ted. "Architecture school—that's how we met."

Marson added, "We were roommates."

The table went silent for a moment.

Prucilla cleared her throat, then leaned to tell Peg in a stage whisper, "It makes one wonder if there might have been some antics in the dorm."

Peg's eyes bugged.

Brody laughed. "Nonsense, Aunt Prue. I have special powers—that gaydar thing? And I can tell you with absolute certainty that Uncle Ted is utterly, *incorrigibly* heterosexual."

Ted lifted his hands in surrender. "Guilty as charged."

"*I'll* tell the world," said Peg, nuzzling him.

And at that moment, under the table, a table that squeezed five people into the space for four, Brody's knee drifted a microscopic distance toward Marson's, and as the woolen fibers of their slacks approached each other in the dry air of a January's eve, a spark—an actual spark of static electricity—leapt from one leg to the other with a sharp, audible snap that shot through Marson's thigh and made him gasp.

"Gosh, sorry," said Brody, moving his knee. Then he eased it back again, letting it rest against Marson's.

Breathless, Marson dared not let his eyes meet anyone else's. Staring down at the plate of stripped-clean frog bones—long, thin, and delicate, they didn't resemble chicken at all—he felt suddenly nauseated by the thought of having eaten this swamp thing, and he saw the array of bones circling the table, circling the entire dining room, and he wondered what they did with the *rest* of the frogs, and he envisioned a dumpster behind the restaurant brimming with these bloated, legless swamp things, and he wasn't feeling well at all, and he regretted that second martini, and he was *very* concerned about that egg-and-spinach thing for lunch, and—

"Marson!" said Prucilla, aghast.

"Precious?"

"You're white as a sheet. What's *wrong* with you?" Her tone was more scolding than concerned.

Brody touched Marson's hand and looked into his eyes. "Are you okay?"

"Um"—Marson blotted his forehead, then his lips, and set the napkin on the banquette—"sorry. I just need a bit of air. Excuse me, please."

Brody got up and moved his chair aside.

Marson edged out of the booth, composed himself, and mustered a nonchalant air as he made his way across the dining room toward the lobby. Passing by Ginger, he explained, "Forgot something in the car," and went out the front door.

In the parking lot, he found a quiet corner, leaned over a bush to brace one palm against the wall, and took a long, deep breath of the night air. For a moment he thought the nausea might pass. But he was wrong. And dangling beneath him in the cold breeze, directly in the path of the gushing, greasy frog bile, was his favorite Armani necktie.

New Year's morning, the house was quiet, save for the lullaby rumble of the furnace.

Marson awoke with a clear head and a calm stomach — the silver lining to his purge the prior night. Having had no appetite for dinner, he was now hungry, so he decided to spiff up for a nice brunch somewhere. He showered and shaved, made a few phone calls, and dressed for the day in velvety corduroys, a comfy lambswool V-neck, and smart Italian loafers.

With the folded, sullied necktie in hand, he went down to the kitchen. Its walls had the texture of rough-hewn stone (faux, of course), like a dungeon from some cheesy production of *The Pit and the Pendulum*. But this morning the room seemed bright to him, bright with the prospect of change.

Prucilla sat with a cup of coffee in a shaft of sunlight at the breakfast table, reading a newspaper, nibbling toast. She wore a tentlike flannel housecoat and a spongy pink turban. Facing the window, she made no acknowledgment that Marson had entered the room, despite the distinct clack of his loafers on the limestone floor.

He stepped to the sink, opened the door to the trash bin, and tossed in the Armani, where it settled among the coffee grounds. Closing the door, he asked, "Why did you marry me?"

Her head made the slightest turn in his direction. Her lips

sputtered; toast crumbs darted through the beam of sunlight. Then her gaze returned to the paper.

He moved to the table and sat across from her. His voice was soft but sure: "It was a serious question. It deserves an answer."

She set down the paper, sipped her coffee, and paused in thought, eyes adrift. "What's the stock answer—'love'? Let's just say I married you for the same reasons you married me."

"I doubt that," he told her. "You see, I married *you* because I was deeply—and impossibly—in love with your brother."

For the first time that morning, she looked at him.

He continued, "I married *you* to keep Ted in my life. The business came later."

Her features pinched, then relaxed. "Feel better? Get it off your chest?"

"Prucilla"—he never called her that—"I want out."

She laughed. "Want out? I'll suck you dry and *spit* you out."

He looked about, whirled his hands. "It's all just . . . *stuff*. You can have it."

"Then it's true what they say: there's no fool like an old fool."

"Maybe." He knew it was an odd moment to be smiling. Patting a pocket for his keys, he said, "I need to be going."

"Where?"

"Brunch. At the club."

"How dreary. Why would you go to New Year's brunch *solo*?"

He paused. "I'm not."

And beneath the table, Marson relived the sense memory of Brody's knee touching his.

And he felt the spark.

❑

Just a Gigolo

Opening night of the new performing-arts center was possibly the biggest event to hit sleepy little Dumont since the town's founding some two centuries ago among the pristine lakes and timbered moraines of central Wisconsin.

Way back when, not long after the territory was admitted to the union, there'd been a hanging in the town square, which drew a crowd of early settlers from as far off as Green Bay. The botched and gruesome execution took twenty minutes to strangle the condemned man, whose thrashing and writhing horrified onlookers to such an extent that a movement was born, banning capital punishment in the state. But generations had since come and gone, as had direct memory of the hanging, with little else through the intervening years to stir the collective soul of the townspeople — until tonight. No one now alive could recall a singular event of more pride and import to all Dumonters than the dedication and opening of Questman Center.

Mary Questman, widowed heir to the paper empire that was the town's raison d'être, sat front and center. A kindly matron with a taste for music and theater, she had bemoaned Dumont's make-do performance facilities in the local high school and had felt a tinge of umbrage every time she drove over to Appleton to enjoy more suitable venues at the university. So when an ad hoc fund-raising committee was formed to rectify the situation, she was ripe to be tapped as its honorary chair. She had the clout to exact generous pledges from the upper crust, and within a year, she herself wrote a three-million-dollar check, putting the campaign over the top—and putting her name in lights.

She'd spent her money well. The complex included a large concert hall, a traditional proscenium theater, and an experimental "black box" performance space, all state-of-the-art. A vast common lobby on the upper level covered scenery and costume shops, classrooms, and rehearsal spaces below. What really set the facility apart, however, was its progressive design and its flawless integration with its setting among the rocky ravines of an old city park that had fallen into disuse but now buzzed and thrummed as the town's new crown jewel.

Bucking the consensus of the committee, Mary had insisted on recruiting homegrown talent to design the project. The selected lead architect, Marson Miles, founding partner of a long-established local firm, had surprised the skeptics and risen boldly to the challenge. It was rumored that the architecture critic from the *Chicago Tribune* had flown up for tonight's festivities, and photographers were on hand from design publications based on both coasts. Not since the opening of the Calatrava addition to the Milwaukee Art Museum had the eyes of the architectural world turned to the Badger State with such a unified and focused gaze. Everyone now seemed to agree that building Questman Center would not only energize the town's cultural life, but would, in fact, put Dumont on the map.

" . . . put Dumont on the map!" said the mayor, speaking from a podium on the stage of the concert hall, backed by the tuxedoed forces of a full symphony orchestra that had been bussed over from the university. "So this evening, we celebrate the heroic contributions of two extraordinary Dumonters. First, Marson Miles . . ."

Seated in the front row next to Mary Questman, Walter Zakarian touched her hand and leaned to whisper in her ear, "I think they're saving you for last."

She whispered to her escort, "Quiet, Walter."

He had often invited her to call him Wally, but she never did, since the nickname struck her as better suited to a much younger man. He was well into his forties—much younger than she, by some twenty years—but *Wally*? She thought of that cute, slim, curly-headed Cleaver boy. Walter Zakarian had a distinct paunch and was beginning to bald, but he cleaned up well, danced light in his loafers, and provided a reliable source of companionship, both social and intimate.

Some called him an opportunist. Some said he had a shady past—there were rumors that his long-ago ancestors had dabbled in the slave trade with Persians and Turks. His version of the story was different—his forebears had built their wealth as honorable traders of spices, then silk, and finally rugs. To this day, he carried on that tradition in Dumont, where he owned the region's largest flooring and carpeting business. In his TV commercials, he called himself the Karastan King. Others called him oily. But Mary just called him Walter.

He had never married—another topic of ample gossip—but in the three years since Mary Questman's widowing, he had proposed just such a union on numerous occasions. She took wry satisfaction in pointing out to him that she didn't need his money; she had far more. And she was amazed to discover that she enjoyed her independence, freed from her forty-year tenure as wife of Quincy Questman, a man she had loved but now remembered as pompous and overbearing.

What's more, Quincy had been twenty years her senior. At first, the age difference hadn't mattered, but it didn't take long for the sex to peter out. Ever the realist, Mary now felt that time was no longer on her side. So Walter served a purpose.

Despite her best efforts to be frank with Walter, telling him point-blank that their relationship was "just for fun," he continued to laugh off her caveats, insinuating himself further and further into her life. His overnight stays had grown more frequent, and he had begun to leave a few things—clothes, toiletries—in anticipation of his next nocturnal performance. She realized she was sending mixed signals by permitting this, but she had to admit, he really knew his stuff, and his stamina was off the charts.

So that evening in the concert hall, there he sat, posing as a couple with her, basking in her limelight, sharing her glory. It was all a bit *much*, she thought. Decisions, decisions.

A hearty round of applause drew her attention back to the stage, where the mayor had just presented a plaque to the center's architect, Marson Miles. She joined the others in clapping, and within a moment, they were all on their feet.

"Please, everyone," said the architect, "please be seated. I'm humbled by this reception, but I'm grateful, too, because without the faith shown by one woman, I would never have had the opportunity to design the building in which we are gathered, and Dumont would never have achieved such a magnificent goal. I speak, of course, of our neighbor and dear friend, Mary Questman."

At the mention of her name, the crowd again rose as one, calling her to the stage, where the musicians joined in the ovation, then launched into the stately opening strains of Beethoven's "Consecration of the House" overture. And there at Mary's side stood Walter Zakarian, raising her hand in victory as the room sparkled with the flash of cameras.

After the concert, the crowd made its way across the lobby, through the doors, and out to the front plaza. A sweet scent of lilacs drifted through the warm spring night. Beneath each lamppost, clumps of forsythia pierced the pools of light with spears of yellow-flowered branches. Everyone mingled and gabbed, delirious with the fine weather and the big event and the dawning of a new era in Dumont.

Mary moved through the crowd like small-town royalty, stopping every few steps to acknowledge the adulation of her subjects—the bouquets, the gushing thanks, the handshakes from strangers, the kisses from friends, and still more flowers, all of which she passed off to Walter, who was ever at her heels.

Predictably, every reporter on the scene wanted to nab her for a few words, all of whom she tried to accommodate—*noblesse oblige*. Though gracious as always, she noticed a pattern develop during the interviews that left her, in a word, pissed. Each time a reporter leaned near, notebook poised, asking a question, and she paused to formulate a thoughtful response, Walter would jump in and attempt to answer for her—as if she needed guidance, as if he wanted to protect her from a misstatement, as if he were her flack, as if he were her *husband*.

When this occurred for the third time, she interrupted him, saying, "I'm not addled, Walter. I can speak for myself."

"Of course, my dear. Do forgive me." Though he had been born on these shores, as had his parents before him, a certain old-worldliness colored both his manner and his speech, surfacing at times in ticks and superstitions that Mary dismissed as genetic leftovers from a heritage that was foreign to her.

She turned to the *Tribune* reporter. "Walter has a habit of putting words in my mouth."

The reporter asked, "And Walter is . . . ?"

Good question. It seemed to be popping up more and more. Everyone in town already knew Walter Zakarian as the Karastan King, but now they were wondering, Who is he, exactly, *to her*? Mary told the reporter, "A friend."

Walter grinned as if they were hiding a secret—a filthy little secret.

Next in line was Glee Savage, features editor for the *Dumont Daily Register*. Something of a fixture in town, she'd been with the paper for decades, weathering the *Register*'s succession of owners through good times and bad, through the recent bloodbath of cutbacks as print gave way to digital. But she was the consummate survivor, all that was left of the features department, and tonight was one of the rare occasions when Dumont's "society beat" actually warranted ink.

Glee leaned close, touching Mary's arm. They had been on a first-name basis for many years, having attended all the same club meetings and fund-raisers. She asked, "Could I have a word with you alone, Mary?" Her eyes slid in Walter's direction.

"Oh," said Mary, turning to Walter, as if remembering something. "Could you find that magazine writer again? I wanted to mention that the classrooms—the educational aspect—that was all Marson's idea. They should talk to him about that."

"Of course, my dear. Good thought." Walter began weaving his way into the crowd with his armload of flowers.

Mary pivoted toward Glee. "What?"

The reporter hesitated.

Mary waited. "Glee, love, I've *never* seen you at a loss for words."

"It's just that I hate bringing this up tonight—*your* night. But I need to run something past you that Walter said to me."

Mary nodded. "I'm listening."

Glee took a deep breath. "You and Walter are seen everywhere together, and this has been going on for quite a while. In the eyes of many, the two of you *are* a social unit. But you're not married, and as far as I know, you're not engaged."

"Yes," said Mary. "I mean—yes, we're *not*."

"Which leaves open the question of how to refer to him. I mean, he's popping up in stories with you all the time, and he's even taken the lead in initiating a few. Last week he suggested that I refer to him as your 'partner,' and I know you didn't like it."

"No," Mary agreed, "I did not."

"So earlier this evening, he cornered me in the lobby, and this came up again, and he asked me to refer to him as"— Glee pinched her lip in her teeth for a moment—"as your 'consort.'"

Mary's eyes bugged. "*What?* Don't you dare."

"Of course not. But 'friend' is lame. 'Boyfriend' is worse. 'Escort' sounds, well . . . *dirty*. And I've just about run out of options."

Mary was fuming—and not at Glee. "Consort, my ass. By any objective measure, he's just a gigolo."

The two women froze for a moment. Then both burst into laughter.

"Well," said Glee with playful understatement, "I probably shouldn't print that."

"Probably not. Look, love. You're one of the few people in the world I can level with. I'm getting older now, and it's hard not to wonder how much time is left. Don't get me wrong—everything's working just fine. And that's why this . . . 'interlude' has its appeal. But that's all it is, and he doesn't seem to get it. So maybe, in print, you could refer to him as my 'companion for the evening.' It's simple, it's true. And it has *no* implications for the future."

"Gotcha. Perfect. Thanks, Mary." Glee leaned in for a quick lady-hug and then took off to get a few extra quotes from Marson Miles.

Walter returned. His flowers were starting to droop. The crowd had begun to thin. "Mary, my dear, it's been a glorious evening. Shall I take you home?"

Though his question, on the surface, was innocuous, she noted that he had now appropriated the word *home*—her home—for his own use as well. It was a foregone conclusion that he would spend the night . . . and wake up with her . . . and then what? Would the whole cycle begin again? And again?

As they crossed the outer plaza toward the parking lot, her weighty thoughts were interrupted by the approach of a small boy, who asked in a tiny voice, "Mrs. Questman?"

"Yes, honey?"

He was black, no more than four years old, shirtless, wearing puffy satin shorts and a sprightly little cap with a long white plume. "Thank you, Mrs. Questman," he said, presenting a Tiffany-blue box, some five inches square, adorned with a white silk bow.

Mary and Walter stood hushed for a moment.

Crickets chorused in the night. A dragonfly circled the lad's feather.

"Sweetie," said Mary, crouching to look into his eyes, "how lovely. Thank you."

The child handed her the box.

Walter also crouched low. "What's your name, sonny?"

With a shy smile, the puckish creature turned and skipped away. The dragonfly droned after him, and both disappeared beyond the glow of a lamppost, under which grew a perfect half-circle of mushrooms.

In rapid succession, Walter kissed the tip of his pinkie finger, touched it to his forehead, then touched it to his ear—a frequent, absentminded ritual that must have invoked some form of supernatural protection. Helping Mary to her feet, he asked, barely above a whisper, "What was *that*?"

Mary mumbled, "I have no idea . . ."

In the car, they laughed about it.

"Someone went to a lot of trouble setting that up," said Walter, steering his Lincoln Navigator like the captain of a schooner. At every turn, the flowers in the rear swayed and bobbed, gassing the cabin as acridly as church incense.

In the passenger seat, Mary covered a dainty cough with a frilly handkerchief that had been hiding in her bosom. "Well, he was cute as a *bug*," she said. "I wanted to gobble him *up*." The blue gift box sat in her lap.

Walter's eyes glanced from the road to the box. "Aren't you going to open it?"

"Nope," she said. "That would spoil the mystery. And I like surprises. Later."

The hulking SUV lumbered around a corner and turned onto Prairie Street, near the center of town, where Dumont's old money had built their grand homes among the oaks and the arching elms. They passed a landmark Taliesin house built by the original publisher of the local paper, then pulled in next door, under the porte cochère of the Questman mansion, built by Quincy Questman's great-grandfather, who'd been the entrepreneurial son of a lowly lumberjack.

"A man could get used to this," said Walter, killing the engine and surveying the grounds.

Don't hold your breath, thought Mary.

The bouquets reminded Mary of her husband's death, and she was sick of the smell, so they left them on the porch. "I'll phone around in the morning," she said, "and see if a nursing home wants them."

Indoors, they switched on a few lights and by habit (egads, they had habits!) ended up in the kitchen. Mary still carried the blue gift box, which she set atop an ornamental cake stand that served as the centerpiece of a large kitchen table. She plumped the bow, then stepped back a pace to admire the tribute that had been so enchantingly presented to her. It seemed to glow—with a hint of mystery, she thought—in the puddle of light that was cast from an elegant old fixture of hobnail milk glass hanging low over the table.

Walter stepped to the end of the counter where a selection of liquors was always at the ready. He poured himself a splash of cognac in a snifter, turning to ask, "Something for you, my dear? You deserve it."

"I suppose, just a drop or two." With a suggestive lilt, she added, "I'll want my wits about me—later."

He poured her a stiff two-finger slug, waltzed across the tile floor, and handed her the snifter. With intertwined arms, he toasted, "To us."

Saying nothing, she took a tiny sip.

He drained his snifter in a single gulp, exhaled, and smacked the glass on the table. With a clap, he rubbed his hands together and purred into her ear, "I must take a quick shower, my dearest, but I won't be long—don't keep me waiting." He pecked her cheek, then bounded out of the kitchen, across the front hall, and up the wide mahogany staircase, taking the stairs by twos.

Within moments, the hiss of his shower drifted through the quiet of the house. He was obsessively clean when it came to their lovemaking, thank God—one of his few ritualized fussings that did *not* annoy Mary.

She pulled out a chair and sat at the table, swirling her cognac. Immersed in thought, she took an occasional sip, and before long, the glass was empty.

She got up, carried both glasses to the sink, and rinsed them. After tending to a few other kitchen tasks, she switched out the lights, except the one over the stove, since Walter sometimes had late-night cravings. Ever since childhood, he had feared entering a darkened room.

In the entry hall, she tapped in the code to set the security system, switched on a little lamp at the base of the stairs, and started the long flight up. The stairs, she knew, would one day pose a challenge, but to date they hadn't fazed her, and she liked the notion that they would help keep her limber for the workout ahead.

Upstairs, all was quiet, and a shaft of lamplight spilled into the hall from her bedroom doorway. Entering, she found Walter sitting up in bed, watching her, lounging with his hands behind his head. Tufts of chest fur sprouted from the top edge of the covers. Beneath, the mound of his belly led to the pup tent of his readiness.

Her pupils widened. *This* was Walter's special talent. *This* was why she put up with him. She undressed without a word, and in a twinkling, she was there beside him in bed.

"Can Wally come out and play?" she asked, peeping under the covers. Though she had steadfastly refused to address Walter himself as Wally, she coyly relented when summoning his "little brother," as he sometimes referred to it.

With a hearty growl, he whipped back the covers, releasing Wally.

With a girlish shriek, Mary eyed it in mock horror.

With an operatic guffaw, Walter took her in his arms.

And with singleminded purpose, Wally did what Wally did best.

Finally, when the sheets were thrashed and the deed was done, all three of them fell into a deep, deep sleep.

An urgent whisper broke the stillness of the room: *"Walter!"*

From the far side of the bed came a burbled "Hngh?"

"Walter," she whispered again, shaking him. The bed squeaked. "There's someone in the house!"

Walter sat bolt upright, though Wally was down for the night. "What?" he asked, rattling his head.

"Shhh."

"What time is it?"

"I don't know—two?"

Wild-eyed, Walter stretched his neck toward the door, listening. "I don't hear a thing."

"I don't either, but it woke me up. I heard breaking glass. And then crying. Like a woman . . . or a child . . . *weeping.*"

In the dimness of the bedroom—little night-lights glowed from three baseboard sockets—Walter began rummaging in the drawer of a bedside table. Sex toys bounced on the carpet.

"Not *now*, Walter."

"I'm looking for a *flashlight.*"

In a testy whisper, she reminded him, "I left lights on all over the house." Then she got out of bed and slipped into a robe.

Hesitating, Walter also got out of bed, wrapped himself in a loose sheet, and moved to the doorway with Mary.

They both peeked out into the hall. Nothing looked unusual. Nothing was heard.

They moved to the top of the stairs, peering down into the unknown. Walter kissed the tip of his pinkie, touched it to his forehead, then his ear.

They took one cautious step downward; the stair creaked in the gloom. Then another. They took a full two minutes to reach the landing, from which they could survey much of the first floor. Nothing looked amiss, so they descended the remaining stairs at a normal pace.

Standing in the entry hall, Walter shrugged. In a normal voice, he said, "Everything looks just fine."

Mary went to the keypad. "The alarm is still set—just as I left it."

"Maybe your imagination got away with you. In the dark, well, your mind can play tricks."

Mary crossed to the kitchen and stepped inside, followed by Walter. In the light from the stove, nothing seemed wrong—no forced entry, no broken glass. But when she flipped the light switch, she drew a sharp gasp.

"What?" said Walter.

With trembling hand, she pointed to the cake stand in the center of the table.

The Tiffany-blue box was gone.

Walter kissed the tip of his pinkie—

"Stop that," said Mary, swatting his hand.

Walter cinched the sheet tighter around his belly and moved across the kitchen to a phone on the wall.

"What are you doing?" said Mary.

"Calling nine-one-one."

"Good idea." Then, "Wait." She moved to the counter, opened a drawer, and fished out a slip of paper. "Call that *nice* Sheriff Simms. He was here just last week. I made a contribution to his re-election, and he told me to call if I ever needed anything. Here's his cell."

Mary handed over the number, and Walter placed the call.

Sheriff Thomas Simms rapped at the back door within five minutes, which had given Walter scant time to rush up to the bedroom and throw on a shirt and pants. In his hurry, he had dropped his sheet near the bottom of the stairs. When he returned to the kitchen and opened the door, he was rumpled, unshaven, and barefoot.

Simms, on the other hand, looked picture-perfect. Tall and fit—black and lithe—he wore a dark blue business suit, white shirt, snappy necktie, and a shoulder holster. Still in his thirties, he had risen fast through the command of the Dumont County Sheriff's Department, attaining the rank of detective before being elected to the top job. Assured by Walter on the phone that Mary was in no immediate danger, Simms had arrived with neither sirens nor backup.

Walter shook hands as Simms entered from the porch. "Thanks for coming so quickly, Sheriff. Are you always so . . . 'put-together' at this hour?"

Simms laughed. "Not often. I had a late dinner meeting, then decided to catch up with some paperwork. I'm only a few blocks away, so here I am."

Mary breezed into the kitchen with the dropped sheet in her arms, still wearing a robe, but nicely spruced. "*Thomas,*" she warbled, "how good of you to come. Shall I put the kettle on?"

"Thank you, Miss Mary. That's not a bad idea."

She plopped the sheet over one of the chairs at the table, then fussed with a kettle and teacups. Over her shoulder, she said, "Do make yourself at home, Thomas."

The sheriff took a seat at the table, as did Walter. Pulling a notebook from inside his jacket, the sheriff said, "Now, walk me through this. What happened?"

Walter did most of the talking, even though it was Mary's story—the mysterious gift had been given to her, not him, and the disturbing noises had been heard only by her.

Simms said, "I did a quick walk-around, and there were no signs of a break-in. The blue box—have you looked for it?"

"It's not in the refrigerator," said Mary. She closed the refrigerator door and brought a creamer full of milk to the table.

Simms leaned back, mulling the situation. "Crazy, huh? Sounds like something out of Agatha Christie—one of those 'locked room' whodunits."

Walter said, "I think the key to all this is the little boy. It shouldn't be too hard to figure out who he was. I mean, there just aren't that many blacks in Dumont." The kettle whistled. Walter added, "No offense, Sheriff."

"None taken."

Mary filled the teapot from the kettle and brought it to the table to steep. "The breaking glass, the weeping—it must have been a dream, but it was so *vivid*."

Walter never reacted well to talk of dreams. He hugged himself with both arms, as if fending off a chill.

Mary arranged three cups on the table, then circled around to join them, standing at an empty chair. "I can't help wondering if Quincy . . . if Quincy might have . . . "

Simms hesitated. "Your late husband?"

"Yes, Thomas." She pulled out her chair, preparing to sit.

"You see—" But she stopped short with a terrified gasp.

"Miss Mary?" said Simms. "Are you all right?"

Walter asked, "What is it, my dear?"

Mary's unbelieving stare was fixed under the table.

Simms leaned down to have a look. "I'll be damned," he muttered, lifting from the floor a long white plume.

Walter kissed the tip of his pinkie, touched it to his forehead, then his ear.

Mary slumped into her chair. "Quincy died in that bed, you know—our conjugal bed. That night, I think he drew his last breath under this very sheet." She reached to pat the sheet that sagged over the back of the adjacent chair. From a certain frame of mind, it might have been seen as a withered little phantom seated next to her. But it was just a sheet—perhaps her husband's shroud, desecrated by Walter that night as a makeshift toga.

The sheriff looked at Walter, and Walter looked at the sheriff.

Mary raised both arms, gazing through the ceiling toward the heavens. "Oh, Quincy," she keened, sounding guttural and unearthly. "Are you *angry*, Quincy?"

Walter looked at the sheriff, and the sheriff looked at Walter.

After the impromptu séance, Mary pleaded deep fatigue, drained by the tête-à-tête with her dead husband. Sheriff Simms promised to check on her in the morning; then she took to her bed in a swoon.

Alone in the bedroom, she turned out the lights and padded to the door, cracking it open. On high alert, she listened to Walter and the sheriff conversing in muffled tones in the kitchen. The sheriff left—the back door closed—and Walter raced up the stairs.

She inched away from the bedroom door as he shot past and beelined to the guest room, where he had begun to store his things. She heard the rattle of hangers, the hurried gathering of toiletries from the bath, the frenzied zipping of bags. Then he raced past in the opposite direction. She poked her head into the hall to watch him tiptoe down the stairs with garment bags thrown over his shoulder like a stealthy Santa. His footfalls receded into the kitchen. The back door opened and closed.

Mary flumped into bed and listened as the rumble of the Navigator disappeared into the night. Then she closed her eyes and slept the dreamless sleep of a drugged, happy baby.

"Good *morning*, Thomas."

Sheriff Simms stepped into the kitchen from the back porch, beaming a smile. "How you doing this morning, Miss Mary?"

She mirrored his smile. "Never better, Thomas."

Birds trilled beyond the wide-open windows. Bacon crackled in a skillet. English muffins popped from the toaster.

Simms said, "He left pretty quick, didn't he?"

"You were watching?"

"Yeah. Glad it all worked out. But as I recall, your husband died in the hospital, not home in bed."

Mary winked. "He was there for months."

"I'm still sorry for your loss."

"Thank you. For everything. Care to join me for breakfast? Won't be but a moment."

"I'd love to, but can't—expected downtown."

"Ah," she said wistfully, "the law never rests . . ."

He chuckled. "You got that right. Not much rest last night. Well, I should get going." With a respectful nod, he moved back to the door.

"Oh!" she said, stopping him. "I almost forgot—just one more thing."

Curious, Simms returned to the middle of the room as Mary stepped over to the stove. She opened the oven, bent low, reached in past her elbow, and pulled out the blue gift box.

"This was never meant for me," she explained, handing it to Simms. "It's for little Tommy. Could you take it home to him?"

Simms eyed the box askance—lifted it to his ear—jiggled it. With a grin, he asked, "Tiffany? For a four-year-old?"

"It's a little clock, something to help Tommy learn to tell time. I thought he might enjoy it."

"Thank you, Miss Mary. We just started teaching him—he'll love it." Simms tucked the box under one arm, then paused in thought.

"Wow," he said, shaking his head, "four years old. He's got all the time in the world."

"Know what, Thomas?" Mary flipped the bacon. "So do I."

❑

THREE

Glee Savage

She reached across the table to tap my hand. "Don't eat those," she said with a roguish grin. "They're castor beans."

I dropped the shiny brown pod with its bright, delicate swirls of color into the festive little Chinese bowl, which held several dozen specimens. About the size of chubby lima beans, they reminded me of a nun's rosary beads. An adjacent bowl held almonds, which I nibbled instead. "Castor?" I asked, loosening my tie. "As in ricin?"

"Precisely!" she said, pleased I had made the connection. "*So* toxic—and yet *so* beautiful."

To my eye, they looked more sinister than lovely, perhaps even evil, like some unknown species of tropical roach. I had reached for one out of mere curiosity, with no intention of putting it in my mouth.

It was an August afternoon in central Wisconsin, smack in the middle of the dog days, but the air had turned cool on that Tuesday, the sky a breezy blue rather than steamy white. Glee Savage had run into me at a party the prior weekend and suggested that I come to her home for an interview. She had been pushing this idea for several months, wanting to run a story about me in the "Inside Dumont" column she wrote for the local paper, where she had served as features editor for many years. I myself had lived in Dumont only since that past winter, but Glee Savage—

with her big hats and her big purses, with her ruby-red lips and her high-heeled strut, with her flair, her bounce, her pizazz—Glee was the long-established fashionista of these timbered hinterlands, a clarion voice of culture sounding in the wilderness. And although she was at least twenty years my senior, maybe thirty, she seemed to treat me as a kindred spirit.

When she'd pitched the interview again last weekend, I'd protested. "That's flattering, Glee, but I doubt that your readers would find me of any interest whatever."

"Are you kidding? Brody, love—tongues have been *wagging* since your arrival."

"Hardly."

"You think not? It's not every day that a talented—and *handsome*—young architect leaves the glamour of Southern California to put roots down here, of all places."

"Young? I'm thirty-*six*."

She slid her glasses down her nose to eye me over the rims, reminding me, "You're young enough to be my son."

"Even so—"

"Plus," she interrupted, "you're gay. Brody Norris—we need to talk."

So I had arrived that afternoon at the appointed hour, parking at the curb in front of her tidy bungalow. The house was a vintage example of the Craftsman style, which she had perked up with fuchsia trim and a riotous front garden, mostly green. Potted pink geraniums lent pops of color on the steps to the front porch. Flanking the gate at the sidewalk, huge bushy stalks, at least ten feet tall, sprouted spectacular palmate leaves variegated with sinuous veins of maroon, a conspicuous, exotic look for this small Midwestern town; these, I now realized, were Glee's castor plants.

Sitting with her in the sunny inglenook of her living

room, separated by the bowl of castor beans, I noticed that she wore a string of them around her neck and another looped around one wrist—primitive, homemade accents to an otherwise chic ensemble of dressy gray slacks and a red blouson top. Had the necklace included a few bones or animal teeth, the getup would have gone voodoo, but if anyone could pull off such a look, it was Glee Savage. Still, I couldn't help thinking that castor beans provided dubious raw material for a crafts project. Stringing them—one slip of the needle—and sayonara.

"Care for some iced tea?" she said. "I brewed it fresh this morning."

"Sure, thanks. But you didn't need to bother—we could've met at your office."

Standing, she explained, "I do most of my work from home now. The newsroom is dead. Skeleton staff, no photographers—we shoot our own pictures with our phones, if you can believe it. They don't even *print* the paper here anymore. It gets trucked in overnight as a local wrapper for the national edition."

I gave her a sympathetic nod. "More and more, it's a digital world."

"That it is, Brody. That it is." She breathed a little sigh, turned, and stepped to the kitchen.

After a moment, I called to her, "Can I help?"

"Don't be silly," her voice lilted over the clatter of ice and glassware, the slosh of poured tea. Then she paused. Appearing in the doorway, she said, "Let's go out back. Too nice to be stuck indoors."

A fine idea. It had been a hot, sticky summer, so the cool afternoon felt like a gift from higher powers—perhaps Glee had charmed a benign voodoo god that morning.

Picking up the bowl of almonds, I joined her in the kitchen, which gleamed with pink and gray tile and classic white appliances so perfect I thought they must be reproductions. She suggested I leave my sport coat, so I hung it on the back of a chrome dinette chair before following her out to the back porch.

While her front garden was green and leafy, the back-yard was filled with flowers, fruit trees, and a manicured vegetable patch extending the length of a side fence. The opposite fence backed a tall stand of more castor plants in a colorful range of species to which she had apparently devoted some study—little tags were spiked in the ground at the base of each plant. At the back of the property stood a large shed attached to a vine-covered carport, under which was parked the ancient fuchsia hatchback in which I'd often spotted her zipping about town.

As I surveyed all this from the porch, Glee arranged on a low table the tea, the nuts, a plate of cookies. "Please, Brody, get comfortable," she said, indicating I should sit on the cushioned glider bench. She sat across from it in a deep Adirondack chair, placing her iPhone on one of its broad wooden arms and her steno pad on the other. She would take notes the way she had long ago learned, in shorthand.

I settled onto the glider, stretched a languid arm along the back cushion, and crossed my left ankle over my right knee. It took but the slightest flex of my foot on the porch floor to set the glider in motion. Lulled by the rocking, I began to hear sounds emerge from the quietude of the afternoon. From beneath me came the slow, rhythmic squeak of the glider. Nearby, paper rustled as Glee paged through her notebook. Locusts buzzed lazily as if from everywhere and nowhere. Out in the yard, on a low branch of a fruit tree, a robin warbled, puffing his ruddy breast, fat with a lunch of worms and cherries. Next door, beyond the fence, the flutter of a push mower's blades made halting progress through thick turf. From somewhere down the back alley, a basketball pinged on the asphalt. And overhead, the far-away, muted roar of a high-flying jet drew my eye to the pristine blue, where a tiny glint of metal led a long, straight vapor trail from west to east. At such an altitude, it wasn't landing anytime soon—I thought it might be heading from California to New York. And there I sat, a world away from either coast, weary of the queries from friends old and new who fretted over my ability to survive culture shock.

"Are you still on speaking terms with Prucilla?"

Glee's question yanked me from my reverie. Silence—birds, locusts, lawn mower—nothing. I blinked, snapping back to the moment, turning to Glee, bringing her words into focus. I must have looked dismayed.

"Sorry," she said with a gentle laugh, "I didn't mean to be abrupt—or indelicate."

"Uh, not at all," I said, echoing her laugh, but it sounded forced. I reached for my glass of iced tea and took a sip. She was asking about Prucilla Miles, born Prucilla Norris, my aunt Prue, who had been married to Marson Miles, the architect for whom I now worked, who also happened to be the new love of my life.

Tongues were wagging, as Glee had noted, not only because my arrival last winter had led to the breakup of Marson and Prue's marriage of three decades, but also, and perhaps even more tantalizing, because Marson was old enough to be my father. As an added plot twist to this local soap opera, Marson's business partner at the Miles & Norris architectural firm was Ted Norris—my uncle and also the brother of Marson's ex-wife, Prue. Last but not least, the remaining offshoot of this contorted family tree was Inez Norris, sister of both Ted and Prue, who had fled the Midwest during the hippie era and settled in California, where, unwed, she had given birth to me. She had also given me her Norris surname.

Setting down the tea, I told Glee, "It's complicated."

"That's *one* way of putting it." She burst into laughter.

As did I. Then I said, "It's amazing. Aunt Prue seems fine with everything—now. Marson was good to her, so she can enjoy her new independence. I didn't know her before, but Marson thinks she was never very happy."

With a thoughtful nod, Glee said, "That was always my impression—not a happy woman."

"You've known her quite a while, then?"

Glee had set aside her steno pad; I was pleased to assume this conversation had gone off the record. She said, "Prue and I grew up together."

"Really? You're *from* here?"

Glee shrugged. "Born and raised. I've known both Prue and her brother, Ted, since grade school. And I went to college—at Madison—with Inez."

"You know my *mother*?"

"Not anymore, Brody. But back then? Thick as thieves." The trace of a smile crossed Glee's face, then faded. She reached for her tea, drank, and cleared her throat.

I leaned forward, elbows propped on my knees. "She's never said much about college. I knew she went to Madison, but that's about it."

Glee leaned back in her chair, eyes adrift. "I was in journalism, which is all I ever wanted to do. Inez majored in women's studies, which was the latest thing. Those were times of huge social change—Vietnam, civil rights, women's lib—and we were both staunch progressives, but for her, it wasn't just politics. It was her life. Once I called her a bra-burner, just joking, and she thought it was funny, but not long after that, she went to a rally and *did* it. I wrote about it, and the story made the front page of the campus paper. She loved it."

"That sounds like Mom," I said. "She hasn't changed much."

Glee looked me in the eye. "May I make a pointed observation?"

"Please do."

"Your mother was a lesbian."

"Still is, mostly." I leaned to whisper to Glee, "But I was not immaculately conceived."

"No kidding?" said Glee with a wry expression. "That's just my point. Inez was a *feminist* lesbian — it was a *political* statement as much as a sexual preference. But now and then, let me tell you, she got the itch. She had no problem making occasional whoopee with the right man."

I chuckled. "Still the same. She brags about being 'truly bisexual.'"

With a low chortle, Glee said, "Then she's softened her thinking, as well as her phrasing. She used to call bisexuality a cop-out. I remember verbatim a quote she gave me for another story: 'There's no such thing as half-gay. Ask anyone who's half-black.'"

I sat back. "Yikes."

"Yikes is right. My editor loved that quote — ran it in big italics in a sidebar with her picture. Letters poured in for a month."

I began to ask, "Were you . . . ," but I hesitated.

Glee moved from her chair to sit next to me on the glider. Resting the fingertips of one hand on my knee, she said, "What would you like to know?"

"You said that you and Mom were thick — thick as thieves. Were you lovers?"

"No, sweetie. I'm not gay, never was. I've never *married*,

either, which sets some folks to wondering. But I did come close once. It didn't work out."

"Sorry."

"So am I. But that was *very* long ago." Her hand left my knee and reached for the tea. Gazing out toward the wall of castor plants, she drank.

This was not the interview I'd expected. Not a word had been spoken regarding art or design, my prior work, or my adjustment to small-town life—all topics I had anticipated. Instead, we'd explored some wistful memories of *her* past life, and I noticed that the open page of her steno pad was still blank.

Bringing our conversation back to the present—and, obliquely, to the topic of architecture—I said, "Marson suggested that I invite you over for dinner. The place isn't finished yet, but I think you'll like what we've done. Interested?"

That caught her attention. "Am I ever! I've been *dying* to see what you guys have been up to. When?" She reached for her steno pad.

"Thursday—night after next?"

"Perfect." She made note of it.

We set the time, tussled over what to bring, and then I sensed that our interview, which had never quite begun, had ended. She rose from the glider, gathered her things, and led me back into the kitchen. I carried both glasses of tea and set them on the counter.

"Take a cookie," she said. "They're good." She wrapped one in a paper napkin, slid it into my shirt pocket, and patted my chest.

"Thanks."

She paused, squinting, her features twisted in thought. "Do you ever talk to your mother?"

"Of course. All the time."

"Of course you do. I'm wondering, Brody—could you maybe tell her I said hello?"

"Happy to do it."

"Awww, thank you, sweetie. But she never knew me as Glee Savage—she wouldn't know that name."

"It's your pen name, right? I had a hunch. I mean, who would name a kid Glee Savage?"

She countered, "Who would name a kid Glee *Buttles*? I'll tell you who—Mr. and Mrs. Russell Buttles. God, isn't it *awful*?"

I thought it judicious not to answer.

She saved me the trouble. "As a little girl, I couldn't stand that name. You can imagine the jokes. But at least, growing up in the fifties, I had the comfort of knowing that a Prince Charming would come along to rescue me with some other name. Smith, Jones, Johnson—it didn't matter which prince, so long as it wasn't Prince Buttles. But things didn't go as planned. So when I got my first job out of school, right here with the *Dumont Daily Register*, the paper's founder, Barret Logan, asked me, 'And what byline will you be using?' That's all it took. And to this day, I have happily been known as Glee Savage."

"You tiger, you." I growled.

"That played into it, I admit. Back then, reporting was *still* dominated by men, so I felt it would be to my advantage to juice up my byline. And you know what, Brody?"

"What?"

"It made me more aggressive—as if I were living up to the name."

I hadn't talked to Mom in over a week, so I phoned her in California the next day. "By the way," I mentioned after the usual pleasantries, "a woman here, a Miss Savage, asked me to say hello to you."

The line went silent for a moment. "Who?"

"Oops," I said, playing along, "that's right—she changed her name. You'd have known her as Glee Buttles."

The line went silent again, longer. "Glee is *there*? She ended up back in *Dumont*?"

"She's worked for the local paper since she got out of college. You didn't know?"

"I guess we lost track of each other."

"She said you two were pretty close."

"We were. But I made the move to California after my junior year."

"And you never followed up with her?"

"Never." Mom paused before adding, "She wanted to kill me."

With an uncertain laugh, I asked, "That's a figure of speech, right? Hyperbole?"

But Inez Norris changed the subject: "Good news, Brody. That mountain conservancy? We've just managed to protect another twenty square miles as bighorn habitat."

I have always been attracted to older men. Raised by a single mother, I had perhaps been searching for a father figure—that would be the easy analysis. But my life as a boy had never been wanting, either materially or emotionally. Inez had parlayed her progressivism into a lucrative career as executive director of various action groups, and from my earliest days, she had surrounded me with a circle of vibrant friends that included men who were brainy, arty, passionate, and hip.

So I had never lacked male role models, though some might have judged them the *wrong* role models. In fact, one of my mother's lesbian chums—of the lipstick variety—had cautioned her during my eighth birthday party that I needed someone in my life to teach me the rudiments of softball rather than the finer points of zapateado. She was dismissed before the cake was cut; her Prada pumps never crossed our threshold again. And I am still an excellent dancer.

As is Marson Miles.

On the night I met him as an adult (there had been but one earlier encounter, at a family wedding, when I was fourteen), I recognized a soulmate at the dinner table who had not yet seen clearly into his own soul and had not yet imagined the potential for happiness beyond his dormant marriage to my prickly aunt Prue. But that very night— New Year's Eve—a seed was planted that would flourish fast in the hothouse of his repressed druthers.

And now we were building the next phase of our lives together. We were also building a home—or more precisely, we were gutting, rehabbing, and "repurposing" a former commercial space on First Avenue, Dumont's historic main drag. The erstwhile haberdashery was undergoing a quick transformation into loft-style living quarters, with an open plan on the ground floor and a sleeping area up on the mezzanine, connected by a spiral metal staircase. As two architects with a shared dream, we saw this as a temporary solution to the needs of our recent cohabitation—we would take our time and savor the process of designing, and later building, the perfect house, the statement of our vision. So we had sped through the structural changes to the loft and moved in as soon as the permits allowed. What was left of the project boiled down to decorating, and that too was all but complete. It was a predictable, minimalist scheme, predominantly black and white, furnished mostly with leather, chrome, and glass. In any major city, this style would be humdrum, but here in Dumont, it was the height of off-the-charts sophistication.

Marson was a designer to the core, and his incisive sense of visual grammar informed every aspect of his life—this was but one of the reasons I respected him as well as loved him. Thursday evening, he stood at the center island in the kitchen area, whisking his vinaigrette, its ingredients arrayed in strict formation on the black granite countertop.

Not only fastidious, he was also the kindest, most gentle man I'd ever met. He told me, "It's been rumored for years that she *did* kill a woman."

"Huh?" I had just mentioned what my mother had said about Glee Savage on the phone.

Marson's tone was matter-of-fact: "Nothing was ever proven." He tasted the vinaigrette with the tip of a finger, then reached for the pepper mill.

I shut the oven door—the chicken looked fine—and stepped to face Marson across the island. "*What* was never proven?"

He added a dab of Dijon mustard and resumed whisking. "This goes back a while, at least ten years. You know that flashy house on the other side of town, the big one with an elliptical library, two stories?"

"I think so. Rather nice—of kind."

"Right, not bad—*of kind*." The expression had become our code for any style not quite up to our snuff. Marson continued, "The woman who built it, a Mrs. Reece, was a corporate bigwig and an absolute terror. But she was also something of a publicity hound, so she invited Glee over to tour the place just as it was being finished, hoping to get a photo feature in the *Register*. Turns out, they discovered there was some past connection—bad blood, so to speak—and they got into a cat fight, right there, witnessed by a small crowd of tradesmen and decorators. The confrontation was limited to verbal zingers—until Glee hauled off and landed a bitch slap, then turned on her heel and left."

"In a huff," I suggested.

"Yes, in a huff." Satisfied with the vinaigrette, Marson put the bowl in the refrigerator and rinsed the whisk in the sink. "The next day—take a guess—Mrs. Reece met her demise, found cold as a day-old mackerel on the stone floor of the library, where she had fallen from the second-floor balcony. The evidence suggested she was pushed over the railing during a tussle. No witnesses, but plenty of suspicions."

"Hmmm," I said, lifting a stack of plates to be set on the table, "sounds like a game of Clue."

"Doesn't it? But the pieces of the puzzle never did fit, and the investigation was inconclusive, so no one was ever charged. Trouble is, Glee was never flat-out exonerated, either."

Good God, I thought. Glee had told me that her pen name had made her more aggressive. Was there more to it? Had it triggered a latent taste for devilry?

"But Glee's a total sweetheart," said Marson, wiping down the counter. "I never believed any of it, not for a minute."

Then why, I wondered, had my mother felt threatened by her?

Glee arrived at seven sharp. As Marson led her from the front vestibule into the main space of the loft, she screamed.

Fussing in the kitchen, already on edge, I nearly pissed myself.

"Fabulous!" she gushed, flailing both arms as she spun to take it all in. Her voice seemed amplified as it echoed from the twenty-foot ceiling. The pods of her necklace rattled as

she came to a stop and planted both hands on her hips, nodding serious approval.

Marson carried her huge red purse in one hand and her bulging tote bag in the other. I carried a dish towel, wiping my hands, as the three of us met in the center of the room, near the dining table. She removed a broad-brimmed straw sun hat, bright red, as we leaned to kiss cheeks. "Brody," she cooed, "Marson," she bubbled, "you boys are *such* a breath of fresh air — one of the nicest things to happen to dusty old Dumont in a long, *long* time."

Marson reminded her, "I've been here forever."

"But not with *this* one." She gave me a wink while telling Marson, "I think Brody's been good for you."

"I think you're right." Marson gave me a quick kiss as he brushed past, moving to the kitchen. He set Glee's tote bag on the island and her purse on the floor. "You don't exactly travel light, do you?"

"Never have, m'dear. Life is but one long, elegant caravan. Might as well bring full provisions and enjoy the adventure." She reached into the tote bag and removed a hamper, which she set on the counter and opened. It contained a beautiful, glistening cherry pie.

"You shouldn't have," said Marson.

She flicked a hand. "Just a little something I whipped up this afternoon. Such a bumper crop of cherries this summer. If *we* don't eat'm, the birds will."

Then she reached into her tote again, removing two boxes. They were both the same size, about as big as a brick, but one was wrapped as a gift, in pink paper with a bow, while the other was wrapped to be mailed, in brown paper with postage and a return-address label already affixed. She slid the pink package toward Marson. "This is for you two."

"How lovely," he said, lifting it, giving it a rattle, a sound

I recognized. "Should we open it?" He handed it to me.

Glee said, "Later, perhaps." Her tone was coy.

I rattled the box, confirming my hunch—I had no doubt she'd been harvesting some more of her prized castor beans.

Glee slid the brown package toward me. "And this one's for your mother. I wonder if you'd mind mailing it to her. I have no idea where to send it."

I fixed drinks in the kitchen while Marson gave Glee the tour. She *loved* everything—effusively. When they began their way up to the mezzanine, with Glee's chunky heels clanging on the metal stairs, I waited till they were out of sight above the kitchen, removed the two packages from the center island, and set them at the far end of another counter, well away from the food. Then I stepped to the sink and gave my hands a good washing.

By the time they spiraled down, I had moved to the conversation area, near the front of the building, with a tray holding our drinks and the clever little appetizer that Marson liked to concoct from chorizo and goat cheese. Arranging these items on a low, square marble-topped table, I announced, "The bar's open."

"And not a moment too soon," said Glee, beelining for the frosty cosmo that awaited her. "August has a tendency to leave one so *parched*."

"I'll drink to that," said Marson, ready for his martini.

I was on a Tom Collins kick. How retro.

Before long, we had settled into a relaxed gab session, lounging around the cocktail table, sipping and nibbling as we drifted from topic to topic—the weather, a local election, modernism, postmodernism, the digital divide—and on and on.

Then an angel of silence drifted through the room. In

awkward unison, the three of us reached for our drinks. When Glee set down her glass, she asked me, "Did you, uh, talk to Inez?"

"I did. Yesterday. I said hello for you."

Glee's brows arched, prodding me to continue.

"She was surprised to hear you were back in Dumont."

"Well, we did lose touch. Did she, uh, *ask* about me, anything at all?"

"Actually, no. She changed the topic." I glanced at Marson, who looked back at me over the rim of his empty martini glass. Turning to Glee, I asked, "What happened between you two?"

But now Glee changed the topic. "When you were growing up, was it difficult, not having a father?"

With the slightest grin, I reminded her, "I may have my mother's name, but I also had a father—even though he was never acknowledged. Inez referred to him as 'the sperm donor.'"

"That's *so* Inez," said Glee, returning my grin. And once more, we fell silent.

Marson stood with his empty glass. "Anyone for another?"

Glee and I declined.

"I'll just check on dinner." Marson stepped over to the kitchen.

Glee pivoted toward my chair. "I meant: Was it difficult not having a father *around*?"

"I have nothing to compare my experience to, so I can't say whether it was difficult or not. It didn't *seem* bad at all—I had a happy childhood."

Through a warm, wide smile, she said, "That's wonderful, Brody. So glad to hear that."

In the kitchen, Marson had removed the chicken and roasted vegetables from the oven. He began uncorking a bottle of wine.

I moved over to the sofa to sit next to Glee. As I shifted to face her, the leather squeaked and our knees touched. "It's sweet of you to be so concerned."

"I guess I can't help it."

Her comment struck me as strange, which must have shown on my face. In the kitchen, Marson rummaged in a drawer for serving utensils.

"Did you ever meet him?" asked Glee. "Your father."

"Oh, sure. I saw a lot of him. But I didn't know he was my father. He seemed like sort of an uncle."

Marson was unwrapping the pink package at the end of the counter.

"Nosy me." Glee's hand drifted to a stray wisp of hair. "May I ask his name?"

"My father? Gordon Harper."

Glee's eyelids fluttered, then closed for a moment.

Marson had picked one of the shiny little pods from the box and held it just beyond the tip of his nose, examining it.

I told Glee, "Gordon died about ten years ago. I didn't learn he was my dad until later."

She opened her eyes and peered into mine.

Marson ate the pod. My eyes widened with panic. He said, "Glee, these are delicious!"

"Brody?" said Glee. "Whatever's *wrong*?"

I pointed to Marson. "He just ate one of the castor beans."

"Castor beans?" Glee laughed. "They're candied cherries."

"I'll put them out later with the pie," said Marson, tossing the salad.

Glee again studied my face. "I'm sorry you never knew your father—*as* your father."

I said, "He was an astronomer."

She corrected me: "An astrophysicist."

"Ah, that's right, of course." I blinked. "You *knew* him?"

She rolled her eyes. "You look just like him."

Marson was carving the chicken and arranging it with the vegetables on a platter.

I asked Glee, "You knew Gordon—back in Madison?"

"That's right."

And suddenly, I didn't need another word of explanation. It all made sense: Glee had told me she'd once found her Prince Charming, but it hadn't worked out. That was Gordon Harper. And Glee's best friend, the radical lesbian Inez, stole him on a whim, ran off to California with him, and bore his child. Glee may have wanted, may even have threatened, to kill Inez. But she didn't. And now, here she sat—sixty-something, single, and childless.

With a pained sigh, I said, "I'm sorry for what Inez did to you."

"Oh, sweetie"—Glee shook her head—"don't be crazy. If she hadn't done that, you wouldn't be here. And wouldn't *that* be a tragedy?" Glee reached to wrap me in a tight embrace.

Marson had brought the salad to the table and was pouring wine.

Though I could not see Glee's face, I could tell she was crying. And oddly, I sensed that her tears were happy ones. Though she said nothing, I understood that she saw in me the son she might have had with Gordon.

A dainty bell interrupted the sniffles—mine as well as hers.

"Dinner," announced Marson, "is served."

❑

Like It Never Happened

Ted Norris knew he was in trouble. The special that evening was knolselderijstamppot.

The waiter explained, "It's a mash of potatoes and celery root."

"Ish," said Ted's wife, Peg, whose tastes were pedestrian at best.

"It's one of the quintessential recipes of the Netherlands," the waiter continued. "It makes a lovely side dish with any of our entrées. If you'd prefer it as a main course, we serve it with smoked pork sausage."

"How *intriguing*," said Ted's sister, Prucilla Miles, who fancied herself a foodie. "I wonder — could we get a serving of it, with sausage, for the table to share as an appetizer?"

"Certainly, madam."

Ted said, "Whatever you want, Prue. You're the birthday girl."

The waiter withdrew to place the order.

"Birthday girl, indeed," said Prucilla with a little hoot. "I applied for Social Security last week." Primping her steely helmet of hair, coiffed just that afternoon, she added, "Early benefits." She was sixty-two.

"But, Prue," said Ted, "you've never had a job."

Again the hoot. "Of *course* not."

The birthday dinner was Ted's idea; Brasserie Hollandaise

was Prucilla's idea. The restaurant had opened in Green Bay only a few months earlier, getting some buzz for its fusion of French, Belgian, and Dutch cuisines. "I know it's rather far," Prucilla had told her brother, "but it sounds just *mah*-velous. Do you mind?"

Ted did mind. It was at least an hour's drive from their home in Dumont, Wisconsin, and while the adventurous menu was alluring to his sister, he was sure his wife would not enjoy it.

But Prucilla deserved—and demanded—some extra coddling these days. Her recent divorce from Marson Miles, who was Ted's business partner, had endowed Prucilla with a handsome settlement and, just as important, the bonus of bragging rights as the wronged woman. "Not only was I *dumped*," she would tell anyone who'd listen, "but he dumped me for a younger *man*. Can you imagine?"

Ted could, in fact, imagine why Marson had decided to begin a new life without Prucilla. Earlier that year, in February, when Marson had sat down with Ted to confide the heavy news, Ted had soaked it in, nodding, and then, rather than rising to his sister's defense, he'd asked, "What took you so long?"

Nonetheless, Ted recognized that Prucilla's birthday— her first as a single woman in thirty-five years—deserved some accommodation. So when she asked if he would mind driving to Green Bay, he replied, "Of course not, Prue. Whatever you want." And now, on a Saturday in late September, there he sat with his sister on one side and his wife on the other, wanting to drink himself silly, but thinking it imprudent, as he still needed to haul everyone back to Dumont that night.

" . . . broadens our perspective and keeps us *young,*" Prucilla was saying, whirling a hand as her eyes drifted to the ceiling. "Trying new things—seeking out the zest of the unknown—it expands the *mind*!" She turned to her sister-in-law. "Don't you think so, Peg?"

"I guess so."

Prucilla's gaze turned to her brother. The arch of her brow, though subtle, spoke volumes, as if saying, Do I need to remind you, Ted? Haven't I always said so? Before you were married, you made the mistake of asking me what I thought of her, and I gave it to you straight. Peg is mousy.

Prucilla, on the other hand, was *not* mousy. She had some heft, some meat on her bones, and she didn't hesitate to squeeze into some gold lamé when the occasion called for it—such as a birthday dinner at a trendy continental restaurant in bustling Green Bay. And unlike Peg, she was never at a loss for words.

Peg was a good fifteen years younger than either Ted or Prucilla. Ted had found a measure of macho pride in this age difference when he took Peg as his bride—his second—some twenty years earlier. Prucilla, however, had not minced words. "She's a *child*," she'd told her brother, "a child bride with a child's mind."

The waiter returned with a bottle of Dom Pérignon, which Ted had ordered in advance as a surprise for his sister. Marson Miles, Prucilla's ex, had suggested it—in fact, he had already paid for it—but he'd asked Ted to tell the ladies that dinner would be charged to the company credit card that night, as he did not want to intrude on the festivities with a reminder of the divorce that had left Prucilla so operatically, yet gleefully, disgraced.

The knolselderijstamppot arrived with a flourish, presented in a shallow earthenware pot by the head waiter as a phalanx of bussers descended on the table to remove the chargers and set the dinner plates. When all was ready, Prucilla was first to be served. *"Merci, monsieur,"* she trilled, and the waiter moved to Peg. Ted watched the slits of Prucilla's eyes slide to Peg's eyes, which bugged with apprehension as the waiter scooped a big, steaming heap of the stuff onto her plate. Except for the crude slabs of sausage, it looked like baby food. Ted was served last.

"Bon appétit." And the waiter disappeared.

Prucilla dug in, making piggy sounds as she slopped up the mashed vegetables, then chomped on a gnarly brown chunk of sausage and washed it down with a goodly slug of Dom, smacking her lips.

Ted took a timid forkful and tasted it, finding it distinctive and peculiar, but bland—neither awful nor wonderful. Judging it much too heavy as an appetizer, he picked at it, spreading it about his plate. And he kept an amused eye on Peg, who was still working up to her first bite.

She gave the mash a slow swirl with her fork, which she lifted to her nose for a cautious sniff. While smelling it, her features went through a series of transformations, first conveying dread, then curiosity, and finally pleasure. Her eyes fluttered. She gave her head the slightest shake, as if to dismiss a thought and clear her thinking. She took a taste, then set down her fork.

"It's *good,*" she said, astonished. "Nice choice, Prue."

Prucilla looked even more surprised than Peg, confirming Ted's hunch that his sister had ordered the strange dish not because she wanted it, but to annoy her companions. She'd been that way since childhood—her passive-aggressiveness had destroyed dozens of friendships. No one had been more surprised than Ted himself when, so many years ago, his friend Marson had announced he was marrying this woman.

She flashed Peg a thin smile, then covered it with a gulp of champagne. Setting down the flute, she huffed a petite belch.

Ted raised his glass to her. "Glad you like it. Marson said it was your favorite."

With fallen features, she asked, "I beg your *pardon*?"

"The Dom Pérignon — it's a gift from Marson."

She pronged her fingers on the base of the glass and slid it an inch or two from her plate. "It's burnt."

Peg gave Ted a quizzical look.

Prucilla told Peg, "The bottle once froze."

"Tastes fine to *me*." Peg took a long sip, then continued to enjoy her mash.

The waiter appeared. "Is there a verdict on the knolselderijstamppot?"

Ted quipped, "It's a mouthful."

"Magnifique!" declared Prucilla.

Peg raised a finger, pausing in thought. "Say. See. Bone."

Prucilla and the waiter exchanged a glance.

"Sorry," said Peg. "I don't remember much of my high-school French. And I don't think they taught it so well in Montana."

With a soft chuckle, Ted reached to pat her hand.

The waiter pressed a hand to his lips. Prucilla sputtered. Then they both burst into laughter and a cascade of French. Prucilla spoke it with gusto, à la Julia Child. *"Quel accent déplorable,"* she said, shaking her head, brushing away an imaginary tear.

Because Prucilla had decided she didn't like the champagne, and because Ted needed to drive, mousy little Peg ended up drinking most of the bottle. Not that she guzzled it. The meal lasted some three hours, so it was easy to polish it off by the final course—a chocolate marquise laden with prunes, infused with cognac, and topped with a candle.

Although Peg's drinking was temperately paced, it nonetheless packed a wallop, as she never had more than one. And the boozy birthday cake didn't help.

When the check arrived, Ted made quick work of the tip and the total. He signed the slip, pocketed his copy, and patted for his keys.

"You're a genius," said Peg, who had watched his every little move with awe.

Ted shared a grin with his sister and asked his wife, "Why's that?"

"The way you just zip-zip-zip." Peg mimed signing the check. "I mean, all that *arithmetic.*"

Ted shrugged. "You mean the tip? Nothing to it. You just lop off one decimal place, double what's left, and that's your twenty percent. Easy-peasy."

Peg leaned toward him on her elbows. "Genius."

Ted leaned toward her on his elbows. "I'm an architect, not an accountant." But in truth, he really did have a head for numbers. In his architectural firm, Miles & Norris, design duties fell to his partner, Marson Miles, while Ted oversaw the engineering and the details of running the business.

Peg's head wobbled. "Easy-peasy, lemon-squeezy."

Prucilla told her sister-in-law, "Why, Peg sweets, I do believe you're shit-faced."

It was a quiet drive home, save for the snoring—Prucilla lay beached in the front passenger seat, head lolled back, mouth agape, while Peg slept fitfully, curled up across the backseat, sucking her thumb. Driving the back roads that led to Dumont, Ted was sober, alert, and focused on his task, but there was little traffic, so the lack of conversation gave him ample time to ponder the roles played in his life by three women—two of whom were there in the car. Each had predominated for about twenty years.

First was Prucilla. His sister's presence was so command-ing that Ted's memories of boyhood through high school focused more on Prucilla than on their mother, not to men-tion their older sister, Inez, who still seemed distanced from the entire family. Prucilla—always Prue to family and friends—had a knack for getting her way. She was an early master of a full spectrum of techniques, ranging from sweet talk to conniving to brute force, which had allowed her to enforce her will with the satisfaction of victory, but without the reward of happiness. She worked her way through wave after wave of friendships, some lasting longer than others, but most abandoning her. Family, however, didn't have the luxury of estrangement that could be exercised by friends, not when living in the same small town, so Prue was simply a fixture in Ted's life. Though he still found her unpleasant, her bite had lost its sting, defanged by the passing of years.

The next woman to play a central role in his life and in his psyche had been his first wife, Jill, whom he had married fresh out of college and had divorced at the cusp of forty. Those years were a busy blur. He was building a career. So was she. They built a house, but not, as they say, a home. In the rush to achieve the good life, they never got around to children—until, near the end, when Jill's pregnancy be-came obvious. At that point, she and Ted had not bothered having sex in some five years—or rather, no sex of the sort involving the mechanics of procreation—so that was that. Jill started a new life, as well as a family, with the red-head-ed chiropractor who'd been sleazing around with her, and Ted found himself single again.

Act three. Enter Peg.

Within a year of the divorce, while visiting Chicago for an AIA convention, Ted met his bride-to-be when he stopped for a pre-dinner cocktail in the lobby bar of his hotel. She was nursing a glass of chardonnay, reading Ann Landers in the *Sun-Times*. As Ted reached through the crowd at the bar to take delivery of his bourbon old-fashioned, he glanced over the young woman's shoulder and said, "Don't tell me — Ann says to wake up and smell the coffee."

"Don't you just love her?" said the young woman, turning to Ted with a broad smile. "She's so down-to-earth."

And so it began. Ted and Peg introduced themselves. Six months later, Ted and Peg married. It was as if she had been sent by providence to put his life back in order, to fix the misstep of his first, failed marriage. His second time around, in his early forties, he wasn't much interested in fathering a baby, telling Peg, with a good measure of angst, "By the time the kid graduated from high school, I'd be pushing sixty." To Ted's relief, Peg didn't mind; she just wanted him to be happy. She was like that—year after year—accommodating and loyal.

Ted recognized that Peg's docile personality came with a certain price. Her tastes were limited. She had little intellectual curiosity. She showed no interest in travel or extravagance. Making the best of this, Ted decided to count himself lucky, and when talking about Peg to others, he often praised her "unassuming nature." Prucilla called her "simple."

A few years after their marriage, on a crisp October weekend, while the Matthew Shepard murder in Laramie was the headline of the day, Ted and Peg were having a cookout with Ted's partner, Marson Miles, who was then married to Prucilla. It was just the four of them, gabbing on the patio, enjoying a round of drinks while a Weber full of ribs tanged the autumn air with vinegar and molasses.

"Did you read about it?" said Marson. "The people who found him—tied up on that fence post—at first they thought it was a scarecrow."

"How awful," said Peg, bowing her head.

Ted said, "It's a hell of a sad story, unbelievable."

"Well," said Prucilla, "that kid must've been sort of dense—a practicing pansy in Laramie, of all places. Some people might say he was asking for it."

"*Stop* that," Marson told her sharply.

Peg looked up, somber-faced. "Prue has a point—some people in Montana aren't too open-minded." She reminded them, "I grew up there."

The others got quiet. "Uh, honey," said Ted, "Laramie is in Wyoming."

"Duh," she said, thumping her forehead, "right next door—it's been a while."

Marson said, "Easy mistake. Have you ever noticed? People not '*from* here' always seem to confuse Wisconsin and Minnesota. I'll bet it's the same with Wyoming and Montana."

Prucilla noted, "But Peg is '*from* there.'"

Later, in the kitchen, Prucilla cornered Ted, pinning him against the open refrigerator as he reached in for some ice. "See?" she said to her brother, gleaming. "I told you. She's not only mousy. She's dumb as a *rock*."

While Ted would never, ever concede that his affable wife was dumb, he himself, on occasion, had found her a bit airheaded whenever the topic turned to her past. She rarely mentioned her childhood, and she spoke of her parents only when asked. In fact, Ted had met her parents only once, when they came to Wisconsin for the wedding. They then returned to Montana, with little subsequent contact other than the occasional Christmas or birthday card, sent from a box number. When asked about this, Peg explained, "They're out in the sticks."

It was as if Peg's prior life didn't matter. Or even exist. She seemed perfectly fulfilled by her life with Ted and happy with her life in Wisconsin. Not long ago, they had celebrated the twenty-year mark, and Ted felt secure in his hopes that they were good for another twenty—at least if the fates smiled upon him, allowing him to live that long.

Now, back in Dumont from their dinner in Green Bay, Ted pulled into the driveway of his sister's Tudor-style McMansion, shifted into park, and got out of the car. It was after eleven, and the night air carried a whisper of the hard frost that would arrive within a week or two. He took a deep breath, invigorated by the chill. Stepping around to the passenger door, he opened it and roused his sister. "We're home, Prue."

He helped her out of the car and escorted her up the walk to her door, which she fumbled to open, still groggy. Stepping over the threshold without thanking him, she turned to offer her cheek, which he pecked. Then she disappeared into the house, bolting the door.

"You're welcome," he mumbled to the lion-headed knocker, inches from his nose. With a roll of his eyes, he turned and walked back to the car.

Opening the back door, he shook his wife's shoulder. "Peg, honey? We'll be home in a minute. Why don't you get in front, get some air?"

She stirred, then groaned. "I've got such a headache."

He tried not to laugh. "I'll just bet you do. Poor baby."

The next morning, a Sunday, Ted rose early to get ready for a golf game. The greens were still in good shape, and the turning leaves were spectacular, but there would be few playable weekends remaining, so this was perhaps his last game of the season.

When he got out of bed, Peg was sleeping soundly with her back to him. She'd had a rough night, complaining again about the headache when they switched out the lights, then thrashing through her dreams in the wee hours. So Ted slipped out of their bedroom, shut the door behind him, went downstairs to the kitchen for coffee, and then tended to his morning routines in one of the guest rooms.

When it was time to get dressed, he returned to their bedroom and saw that Peg hadn't moved. He wanted to let her rest, but he would soon need to tell her he was leaving, so he said, "Morning, honey!" while moving past the bed and through the bath to their dressing room. Two or three minutes later, he emerged in his golf outfit—Peg always liked to kid him about the argyle sweater and socks, but hey, he offered no apologies for being a traditionalist, at least when it came to golf. But his wife had still not stirred.

Curious, he stepped around to her side of the bed, crouched, and fingered a shock of disheveled hair from her face. "Peg? I need to go now."

She didn't respond, so he gave her a shake, and she flopped onto her back like dead meat. Ted's initial, panicked reaction was that she was, in fact, dead. But he felt under her chin, and she was warm. She was breathing. "Peg!" he shouted, then shook her again, harder, but he could not wake her.

And a moment later, he was pacing with the phone, calling nine-one-one, describing Peg's condition to the dispatcher, hearing that an ambulance was on the way.

And then their bedroom, their sanctuary, was invaded by emergency techs in dark blue uniforms, four of them, wearing huge black shoes, and two of them worked on Peg while two of them squawked on radios, and Ted heard the words "possible coma" and thought he might faint.

And the gurney was brought in, and the gurney was taken out. And Ted found himself riding with Peg in the boxy red van of an ambulance, choked by his fears and unable to think, let alone speak, over the din of the radios and the gadgetry and the siren.

And then they were all rushing, running, through a tunnel that led from the parking structure into the emergency room, where lights were bright and curtains were drawn and Peg disappeared while Ted fumbled with clipboards containing form after form that he could not read but signed anyway.

And someone wearing green scrubs asked him if he was all right, and he said no, and they sat him down and closed the curtain and took his blood pressure and gave him a pill.

And then a woman, also wearing scrubs, poked her head through the curtain and said, "She's coming around." And Ted followed through a labyrinth of hallways and more curtains and found himself at last in the cubicle where Peg squirmed on a padded table, moaning.

Ted asked anyone, "Can't you help her?"

"She'll be fine," said a doctor. "That was a serious blackout, but she's fighting her way through. She'll be back."

Peg started to mumble. Her voice was weak, her words unintelligible.

Everyone gathered near.

Her eyes drifted open. She blinked in spasms. With effort, she lifted a hand to her head. Her lips puckered. "Oooo?"

Ted leaned near and took her hand. "Yes, Peg? You gave us such a scare."

She looked into his eyes. *"Où suis-je?"*

"What, honey?"

With greater strength, she repeated, *"Où suis-je?"*

A nurse said, "Sounds like French: Where am I?" She told Peg, *"Vous êtes à l'hôpital."*

Peg turned to her, indignant, demanding, *"Pourquoi?"*

"Why?" The nurse whirled a hand. "I don't know how to say she fainted." The nurse turned to Ted. "Your wife is French?"

"No," he said, feeling he'd awoken in some screwball art film, "she's from *Montana.*"

"Qui êtes-vous?" asked Peg, trying to sit up. Ted helped her. She braced herself upright at the edge of the table, swinging her legs jauntily, pointing her toes.

The nurse told Ted, "She asked who you are."

Bug-eyed, he told Peg, "I'm *Ted*" — he tapped his hands on his chest. "Your *husband*" — he pointed to his ring.

The nurse told Peg, *"Il est votre mari."*

Peg laughed, then rattled off in a single breath: *"J'aimerais que ce soit vrai! Il est très beau, mais je ne l'ai jamais vu, et je n'aurais pas oublié ce visage."* She tweaked Ted's nose.

The nurse tossed her hands. "She doesn't know you. But she thinks you're cute."

Sitting in the hospital cafeteria, Ted slurped a cup of bad coffee and picked at the edges of a cherry Danish. The doctors had all agreed that Peg, with her apparent memory loss, was in no condition to be released, so she was being admitted to a private room for continued observation. Ted could join her again as soon as she was settled in her new quarters.

Meanwhile, Ted had phoned his partner, Marson, to explain what had happened and to ask him to take his place in the golf foursome — they were new clients and should not be stood up. Marson agreed, despite his distaste for the game, and then alerted his ex-wife, Prucilla, who now barreled into the cafeteria.

"*Ted*," she gushed, chugging toward his table, drawing a wake of curious stares, "I came the *moment* I heard."

Ted grimaced as the coffee stung his stomach. "What a surprise," he said without enthusiasm. "You shouldn't have come. It's Sunday morning."

"What else would I be doing—*church*?" She let out a hoot as she pulled out a chair and plopped into it. Its metal legs screeched on the terrazzo as she landed. With arched brows, she eyed Ted's ankles. "Brother dearest," she said, "argyle went out with bobby socks."

"For God's sake, Prue, I just had a life-or-death scare with my wife."

She picked at his Danish. "It all sounds a bit Hollywood, don't you think? Poor little Peg has a fainting spell, then wakes up speaking French? I mean, come on—her command of the language is fractured at best."

He assured his sister, "Well, she's speaking it like a Bouvier *now*."

Prucilla squinted in thought, broke off half of the remaining Danish, and chomped at it.

A man's voice, deep and resonant, asked from behind, "Ted, is that you?"

Ted turned in his seat. Prucilla looked up. They both stood.

A tall black man, beautifully dressed in a dark suit, white shirt, and a bright, striped tie, strode toward their table and extended his hand. "Heard you've had some trouble, Ted."

Ted shook his hand. "Thank you, Sheriff. It all sounds so crazy."

The sheriff extended his hand across the table. "Good morning, Miss Prucilla."

Blushing, she flapped her left hand to her bosom while shaking with her right. "*Thank* you, Thomas. So good of you to come."

Every woman in town was charmed by his habit of addressing them as Miss Mary or Miss Susan or whatever, regardless of age—a touch of Southern manners they hadn't heard much in Wisconsin. That, combined with his modest nature and his caring spirit, had helped Thomas Simms coast to an easy election as the county's top lawman, a victory he had celebrated prior to his fortieth birthday.

Ted told him, "I hate to mess up your day. I mean, it's Sunday."

"Not at all. Just brought the family back from church, checked the scanner, and here I am."

Ted said, "Please, Sheriff, have a seat." And they all sat down.

Prucilla offered, "Can we get you something?"

Simms waggled a hand. "Thanks, I'm fine. So tell me—what happened?"

Ted ran him through the story—the outing to Green Bay, the champagne, the headache, the bad dreams, the deep unconsciousness that morning, and then Peg's reawakening in the emergency room, not knowing him and speaking French. Ted concluded, "She thinks her name is Renée. The last name didn't register—it was gibberish to me."

"Renée?" said Prucilla. "That means 'reborn.' Isn't it obvious? She's faking it."

Exasperated, Ted asked, "Why would she do such a thing?"

"Beats me." Prucilla reached for the remainder of the Danish, swiped a finger through the cherry jelly, and licked it.

Simms asked Ted, "What else did she say?"

"The doctor asked her age, through a nurse who knows French, and she said twenty-two."

Prucilla snorted.

"Then they asked her who the president is, and she said François Mitterand."

"Hmm," said Simms, leaning back in his chair. "He left office when — 1995?"

"Yeah, I think that's right." Ted paused before adding, "She also said . . . she said she'd just graduated from Yale."

Prucilla's lips sputtered, shooting crumbs of Danish across the table, as she broke into a coarse laugh. "*Yale?* That mousy little snip? I'm telling you — she's faking it."

Ted brushed the crumbs from his sweater. "I don't know French, but even so, the conversation seemed to have an air of considerable intelligence."

"Hmm," said Simms, leaning back again. "It's easy to play dumb, but you can't fake smart."

Ted's phone vibrated. He checked the text message and told the others, "She's in room 306. We can see her now."

When Ted, Prucilla, and Sheriff Simms entered room 306, it got crowded. Ted recognized the doctors and the nurse from the emergency room, and he was introduced to a neurologist, a speech therapist, and a psychiatrist who had been called in. In the middle was Peg, looking regal in her hospital gown, propped up in bed by a half-dozen pillows. She had brushed her hair in an asymmetrical style that Ted had never seen before. The change of appearance was jarring — to his eyes, she didn't even look like Peg anymore. The brush rested in her hand like a revolver.

The crowd parted as Ted moved to her side. "I'm back, Peg. Do you know me now?"

The nurse asked Peg, *"Reconnaissez-vous votre mari?"*

Peg gave Ted a blank look. *"Non."* Then, with an impish grin, she tweaked his nose again.

Prucilla elbowed her way forward and planted herself at the bedside next to Ted, telling him, "I'll bet she recognizes *me*. She guzzled most of my champagne last night." Prucilla leaned toward Peg with a saccharine smile. *"Hier soir, avez-vous aimé le Dom Pérignon?"*

Peg turned to the nurse and said, *"Quel accent déplorable."*

With a harrumph, Prucilla retreated a step.

"Mademoiselle?" said Sheriff Simms from the back of the crowd.

All heads turned toward the rich, velvety voice.

He asked, *"Parlez-vous anglais?"*

All heads turned to Peg.

She paused. Her glance skipped from Simms to Ted to the head doctor and back to Simms. "But of course I speak English," she told him. "What educated woman does not? Do you consider me a fool? I was reared by an English governess."

Peg's English was fluent and rapid—as rapid as her French—though it carried the lilting inflections and prim syntax of a nonnative speaker. Everyone in the room looked peeved.

"Now, *why*," said Ted, at a loss for words, "why on earth didn't you mention this earlier?"

She gave one of those little French shrugs. "Because you did not ask."

The doctor said, "You learned English from your governess, as a girl in France?"

"Yes, but I spoke it with a British accent. Now, after four years in the States, when I telephone to my parents, they tell me they do not recognize my voice. My mother says that my English sounds like my Italian. Silly, no?" She giggled.

The psychiatrist asked, "You also speak Italian?"

"Quite well, I am told. I have always found it useful for

our summers in the south. My Dutch, however, is not so useful. We have begun to spend time there only recently."

The speech therapist asked, "You learned to speak Dutch in Holland?"

"*Ja, Nederland is een prachtig klein land.*"

Ted thought of the knolselderijstamppot—or whatever the hell they called it—how Peg sniffed it warily the prior evening, then gobbled it with delight. Prucilla, whose eyes slid in Ted's direction, seemed struck by the same recollection.

The neurologist asked, "Any other languages?"

"No," said Peg, a tad forlorn. "I began to learn Japanese, but then everyone told me it was passé, that I should switch to Chinese. There are some who believe that it will one day become the lingua franca of commerce. But I have not yet found time for it."

Ted said absently, "Yeah, I know how that goes." His thoughts, however, had drifted to the comment made by Sheriff Simms in the cafeteria: "It's easy to play dumb, but you can't fake smart."

The psychiatrist was checking his notes. "That's very impressive, young lady—four languages. How old did you say you are?"

The shrug. "Twenty-two."

Prucilla could not contain herself. She snapped open her handbag, whipped out her compact, lurched over the bed, and held the mirror to Peg's face. "Take a look, sweetie. Twenty-two, my ass."

Peg's overnight excursion to the astral plane had left her forty-some years only too apparent. With a shriek, she collapsed into her nest of pillows, out cold again.

Prucilla was banished from the room, bitching and mooing. When Peg was revived and coherent, she asked with a whimper, "How can this be?" Her face streamed with tears.

Ted sat on the edge of the bed, holding her hands. "We don't have the answers yet. It's a mystery to all of us. But trust me, Peg—we'll figure this out."

"My name is not *Peg*," she said, withdrawing her hands and pounding her fists on the mattress. "My name is Renée."

With her doctors' approval, Ted returned that afternoon with his wife's driver's license, proving that her name was indeed Peg Norris. He also brought their marriage certificate and their album of wedding photos.

Viewing these, wide-eyed, she asked the surrounding medical team, "Is this a sadistic joke, or have I gone crazy in my head? What an absolute nightmare—even worse than the others."

The psychiatrist asked, "You've been having bad dreams?"

With a shudder of deep pain, she answered in a whisper, "They are beyond description."

Before Ted left the hospital that evening, he had a talk in the hall with the psychiatrist, who said they had made a preliminary diagnosis of dissociative amnesia. "It's a rare condition," he explained, "most often associated with some traumatic past event. It could've been triggered by anything—perhaps some incidental sense memory."

Ted again thought of Peg the prior evening, sniffing the odd Dutch potato dish.

The doctor had no idea how long it might take for Peg to improve. "The good news is: the roots of her condition appear to be psychological rather than organic. But she's in no condition to go home yet."

So Ted went home alone that night and straightened up that morning's mess in their bedroom. He then fell into an exhausted sleep on the sofa in the living room with the lights on.

Monday was better. The blessings of pharmacology had allowed Peg a good night's sleep, free of dreams. And when Ted arrived at the hospital, her trace of a smile reassured him that this bizarre new reality was neither life-threatening nor permanent. Peg would get better, and things would get back to normal, and they would both have many years to joke about it.

Peg seemed to understand that everyone was as mystified by her condition as she was. They were not the cause of whatever had happened to her; they were trying to help her. And although she still claimed no memory of Ted, he made it obvious that he loved her and was worried about her.

With childlike enchantment, she discovered the powers of Ted's iPhone, the tablet computers carried by the doctors, and the high-definition TV hanging in her room. She had no recollection of Web browsers or digital photography or music collections on a microchip. Conversely, Ted was in awe of Peg's newfound intelligence, curiosity, and eagerness to learn. "What have I missed," she wondered aloud, "for so many years?" Her memories seemed to end around 1990, when she claimed to have graduated from college.

By Tuesday, word of Peg's strange amnesia case was spreading around Dumont, and flowers began to arrive from friends, some with cards and snapshots intended to nudge her memory. At Ted's suggestion, the hospital brought in a couple of large bulletin boards, and he assembled a collage of her past, which she studied with determination. Still, however, she could remember nothing of their years together.

On Wednesday, the *Dumont Daily Register* ran a front-page story on Peg's condition, which now had the whole town abuzz. The coverage included two side-by-side columns, one giving a detailed medical rundown of dissociative amnesia and the other, headlined SKEPTICS ABOUND, listing the opinions of various locals, including Prucilla Miles, who said, "Mark my words, she's faking it, and you can quote me."

On Thursday, as the flowers continued to accumulate, migrating from the windowsills to the sideboard to the floor, the ever-dapper Sheriff Simms paid a visit, wished Peg a speedy recovery, and asked to speak to Ted in the hall, where he said, "We've been checking records. The woman she claims to be—this Renée person—did indeed graduate from Yale in 1990. She soon returned to France. A year later, she took up residence in the Netherlands."

By Friday, the local paper's parent company had picked up the story, running it in the national edition, on page two, with the headline WISCONSIN WOMAN WAKES UP SPEAKING FRENCH. The hospital posted a security guard outside her room, and her doctors ordered the public-relations office to deny all requests for interviews. Ted brought a copy of the paper to Peg and said, "You're causing quite a stir." They laughed about it. Their eyes lingered on each other for a long moment. And then they kissed.

With a woozy smile, she said, "I think that I am happy to be married to you, Mr. Norris."

"That was always *my* impression, Mrs. Norris," said Ted, short of breath—and plenty aroused. He had loved Peg for twenty years and had never stopped loving her, but he now felt as if he was falling in love with her *again*. Was that even possible? She was the same woman, the same Peg. The kiss proved it. And yet, she was someone else—for lack of a better word, Renée.

On Saturday, all the wire services had picked up the story. When Ted visited Peg that morning, bringing another tote bag of her toiletries from the house, a second guard had been posted outside her room. After they kissed hello, she paused for a moment, her features twisted in thought. "Did you tell me that on the night before all of this began, we dined at a restaurant—somewhere far away?"

"Right, we went to Green Bay, an hour or so from here."

"And on the way home, did I fall asleep? Was I in the back of the car?"

"Yes!" He grasped her by the arms and gave her a little shake. "Tell me more."

"Why did I lie down in back? Was I sick?"

"No, a little drunk, but not sick. You were in back because my sister was in front. My sister Prucilla? Remember?"

"Ugh!" said Peg. "That cow—I never liked her." Then she slapped a hand over her mouth. Parting her fingers, she said through them, "I am sorry. Some things should not be said."

But Ted was thrilled. The thick wall of Peg's amnesia had cracked. At long last, she was on the mend. This would soon be over.

By late afternoon, it was past midnight in Europe, where presses rolled out Sunday editions that told the baffling tale of the woman in Wisconsin who had woken up speaking perfect French and Italian and Dutch. When Ted checked the CNN app on his phone, he noticed a feature on its home page with the headline AMNESIA STORY GOES VIRAL.

Sunday dawned bright and chilly, but there had not yet been a hard freeze, so Ted figured this was his last opportunity to get out and enjoy the golf course. He had not set up a game, as all of the previous week had been consumed by the aftermath of Peg's reawakening as Renée, so he decided to mosey out to the club, spend some time on the driving range, and hope that someone might invite him to round out a foursome. The earlier he got there, the better his chances would be, so he was dressed and out the door by sunrise.

He would of course pay Peg a quick visit at the hospital first, and he looked forward to hearing what additional memories had returned to her since yesterday's breakthrough. Before getting into his car, he paused in the driveway to pick a few mums, a tidy bouquet of orange and white and rusty maroon, to take to his wife. Not that she needed them — she had already begun doling out some of the excessive floral tributes to the nurses — but he realized that none of the flowers in her room were from him, so it was time to fix that oversight. He added a few leggy sprigs of goldenrod to the bouquet.

When Ted arrived at the hospital, the visitors' area of the parking lot was empty — no surprise at daybreak. The staff had grown accustomed to seeing him at all hours, so he knew he would have no problem being admitted that early. Bouquet in hand, he locked the car, then entered through a side lobby near the cafeteria, strolled to the end of the hallway, and took a waiting elevator up to the third floor.

The door slid open with a muffled *ding,* and he made his way down the hall toward room 306. The entire floor seemed inordinately quiet, even for the early hour. His shoes squeaked loudly on the tiles, which he'd never noticed before. Near the far end of the hall, a nurse, whom he'd often chatted up, checked her clipboard and made a sharp turn down another hall without acknowledging him. He saw no one else, and as he approached Peg's room, he realized what was missing — the security guards. Peg's door was open.

And stepping inside, Ted found . . . nothing.

The flowers had all been removed. The bulletin boards were gone, with all of their contents. The wedding album had disappeared from the bedside table, and the bed itself had been stripped, with a single sheet, starched and white, stretched tight over the mattress.

Ted heard something from the bathroom.

"Peg?" he asked with quiet foreboding. He set the bouquet on the empty bed and stepped around it to poke his head into the bath. It smelled of disinfectant. All of Peg's toiletries were gone. There wasn't even a towel or a bath mat. The noise had come from the shower, where a second languid drip trickled down the drain.

"Uh, Ted?"

Ted turned to find Sheriff Thomas Simms standing in the doorway to the hall. Ted had never seen him when he didn't look dressed for a fashion shoot, but this morning he wore jeans and an old suede bomber jacket. He was unshaven and bleary-eyed. Something told Ted that Simms hadn't driven his family to church that morning—maybe it was the shoulder holster beneath the jacket.

Ted moved a few tentative steps toward the sheriff. "What . . . what *happened*?"

Simms pinched the bridge of his nose and breathed a weary sigh.

"When did she," stammered Ted, "where's . . . did she *die*?"

Simms looked him in the eye. "That's the story." He closed the door and stepped near, telling Ted in an intense whisper, "Between you and me, no, Peg didn't die. But as far as *anyone* else is concerned, yes, she did, and here's what happened: She took a severe turn for the worse last night and died of previously undiagnosed complications. The amnesia was not a psychological condition, as first thought, but stemmed from organic causes. And you donated the body to science."

In the silence of Ted's confusion, the shower dripped.

There was so much to ask, he didn't know where to begin. "But where *is* she?"

"Sit down, Ted."

Ted sat on the edge of the bed and fingered the flowers he'd brought for Peg.

Simms pulled up a chair and sat down facing him. "She's in protective custody."

"Protective *custody*? Protection from *what*?"

"She was faking it, Ted. Not the amnesia, but everything else — the last twenty years."

Ted said nothing. The shower dripped.

Simms explained, "After Renée graduated from Yale, she returned to France, and a while later, she married into a powerful Dutch banking family."

"She was married?"

"Still is — technically. Although now she's dead — technically."

Ted winced. He fingered the flowers.

Simms continued, "This was all during the run-up to the Maastricht Treaty, which took effect in 1993, creating the European Union. It also created its common currency, the euro. Needless to say, the financial interests in this were huge. *Huge.* And Renée did something — or saw something, or just *knew* something — that could kill the whole deal and cause a major upheaval to the status quo of the world economy. Because of this — "

Ted interrupted, "*Peg?* She couldn't even balance a checkbook!"

"Don't kid yourself. The feds took an interest — *our* feds — because of the stability issues, so they agreed to get her out of there and create a new identity, not unlike a witness protection program. The danger was all too real. Her parents in France both died in a car crash — very suspicious circumstances—just before Renée went underground. The CIA gave her a makeover and landed her in Chicago, where she met this nice guy who married her and took her away to a quiet life in Wisconsin."

Ted closed his eyes. The shower dripped.

"No one planned on the amnesia episode—Renée sure didn't—it just happened. And the publicity came *this* close to blowing her cover and putting both her *and you* in mortal danger. So the feds were here overnight. She'll be in a safe place while she recovers her memory, and then the whole process starts over. Renée will become someone else."

Dumbstruck, Ted said, "I need to talk to her."

"No way." Simms pulled an envelope from inside his jacket. "Did Peg have life insurance?"

Ted pressed his fingers to his temples. "Sure."

"Good." Simms handed him the envelope. "Here's the death certificate. If I were you, I'd throw her a big-ass memorial service, and then I'd take a long vacation to deal with my grief. Somewhere tropical. Little umbrellas in the mai tais."

"But how do I—"

"This is way, *way* out of our league." Simms stood. "I'm truly sorry, Ted. But here's my best advice: Just forget it. Forget the last twenty years. All of it."

Ted looked up at him, incredulous. "Like it never *happened*?"

"Exactly."

Ted fingered the flowers.

The shower dripped.

❑

FIVE

In the Fridge

Good God, she thought when she opened the refrigerator for her morning tub of yogurt and found, instead, her shoe. The brown suede pump—a Ferragamo with a chunky kitten heel—peeped out, toe first, nestled between a six-pack of Ensure and an open box of baking soda.

Mary Questman had worn the shoes to dinner the prior evening, but couldn't remember taking them off after arriving home. She supposed she'd slipped out of them after going upstairs to her bedroom, yet here was one of them where it most certainly did not belong. Feeling foolish, she removed the shoe and set it on the counter next to the coffeemaker. Wondering what had happened to the other shoe, she checked the freezer, then slid the ice bin open. Nothing.

Mary had worried of late that her years were catching up with her. Widowed a year earlier by her much older husband—Quincy Questman had died at eighty-six—she was determined to make the most of her sixties and build a life of her own. Never too late, she told herself. As heir to a local legacy—timber and paper—she had the means to live her latter years in any manner she might choose. And thank goodness, she was in perfect health for a woman of her age. Except, she had grown forgetful.

She would sometimes walk to another room and then

not remember why she'd gone there. Or conversing with a friend, she might blank on the person's name. At times she had to think twice to recall what day of the week it was. Or what month. But these vexations were no more insidious than the need for glasses or sensible shoes. She wasn't *addled*, not by a long shot. Or so she had thought before finding one of those sensible shoes in the Sub-Zero.

What would be next—asparagus in her underwear drawer?

Sitting at the kitchen table, sipping coffee, Mary tried to focus on the *Dumont Daily Register*. Back when she married Quincy forty years earlier, the story had been front-page news in their small Wisconsin town. It had also been something of a scandal, given their age difference. But her days as a blushing ingenue were now long past, and she had stepped into the matronly role of Dumont's leading benefactress of the arts and culture.

There on page three, above the fold, was another story about her campaign to secure funding for a performing-arts complex, the sort of facility that usually graced much larger cities. When the campaign fell short, Mary had practiced what she preached and closed the sizable gap with a stroke of her pen. The design phase was now wrapping up, with the mayor extolling Mary's contribution as "a gift for the ages."

But she took no joy in the story. She could barely *read* it without pondering the riddle of the shoe on the counter. It seemed to ask, You like writing those big checks, don't you? Enjoy it while you can, sister—while you've still got the marbles to sign your own name.

"Cripes." She pushed her chair back from the table and stood. Coffee in hand, she paced the kitchen, her bare feet slapping the floor as she pieced together the events of the prior night.

Mr. Zakarian, the rug man, had taken her to dinner as a thank-you for the carpeting job just completed in her stately home on Prairie Street, where Dumont's elite marked their turf. A chivalrous escort, forty-something, with a touch of old-world charm, he picked her up at seven and escorted her back by nine-thirty. Returning home, she asked him to pull in alongside the house so they could enter through the kitchen. When he saw her indoors, she offered a nip of cognac, which he accepted with pleasure. They sat across from each other at the kitchen table, gabbing and sipping, and then he left.

At the restaurant, she'd had a cocktail upon arrival and a glass of wine with the meal, which was her custom. By the end of the evening, she was relaxed and convivial, by no means drunk, though she was grateful that Mr. Zakarian had volunteered to drive. She recalled mentioning it—"so glad you played chauffeur tonight"—as they finished their cognac at home. She remembered lolling in her chair with a lighthearted laugh and slipping her shoes off under the table.

Mary froze. She set her mug on the counter, then crouched low. And there, right where she left it, was the other Ferragamo, toppled on its side like a svelte, brown, snoozing puppy. At least that explained how the shoes ended up in the kitchen.

But it did not explain how one of them ended up in the fridge.

Later that morning—eleven o'clock on a Thursday—Marson Miles puttered at his desk in the offices of Miles & Norris, LLP, an architectural firm in downtown Dumont that Mary Questman had insisted be given first crack at presenting a proposal for the performing-arts center. The boon of this favoritism was not lost on Marson, whose firm had done good, creditable work for thirty years, but had never had the chance to design a building of such artistic significance. The theater complex was not only a dream job, but the greatest opportunity of Marson's career. He *had* to get this right. And he *had* to get it built.

So when he answered his phone that morning and the receptionist told him, sounding a bit puzzled, "Mrs. Questman is here," his heart skipped a beat.

"Here?" he asked. "Now?"

"Yes."

"Uh"—the room was spinning—"take her to the conference room. Offer her something." He hung up.

He rushed through a back office, through the drafting room where a few apprentices squinted at computers, then opened a door and told his business partner, "Mary's here."

Ted Norris looked up from his spreadsheets, ashen. He glanced at his watch. "Eleven o'clock. She's right on time—but the meeting's tomorrow."

Marson clawed the air. "I *know*."

All of the work they had done on the project—everything they had analyzed, brainstormed, polished, and drawn up in meticulous detail—*all* of it was out being laminated and mounted to make the best possible impression on the one woman who would give it a thumbs-up or a thumbs-down and thereby determine if Miles & Norris would at last make their mark on the world of architecture.

It was the biggest presentation in their firm's history, and they didn't have a goddamn thing to show their client, who was waiting down the hall.

With a plastic smile, Marson eased into the conference room and closed the door behind him. "Mary—always such a delight—and you're even lovelier than usual today." She did look good, he thought, in spite of the dread that gripped his innards. She wore a nubby silk suit of a soft, powdery blue, the color matched spot-on by stylish suede pumps— Ferragamos, unless he was mistaken. The woman knew how to dress.

"Marson, love," she gushed, bustling around the table to offer a hug. "I couldn't be more excited. I've been on pins and needles for *days*. Any longer, and I'd *burst*."

Marson swallowed. A close-range whiff of her L'Air du Temps stung his throat. "Uh, Mary," he said with a nervous laugh, "I'm afraid there's been some sort of mix-up. You see, *we* thought the meeting was scheduled for Friday at eleven."

With a curious look, she backed off a step, checking her watch. "Exactly."

"But this is Thursday."

Her expression went blank. "Oh, my heavens!"

"The work is finished, but we won't have it back until—"

Mary heaved a loud sob, then dropped her head in her hands, crying, out of control.

Marson put an arm around her and helped her to a chair. Pulling out another, he sat facing her, patting her hands. "I'm so sorry to make you wait another day."

"It's not *that*," she said, snorting a bubble of snot from her lip. "I can wait. But I *forgot*. I forgot what *day* it is."

"Awww, that's nothing. We all forget sometimes."

She gave her head a fierce little shake. "That's not the worst of it."

His tone turned cautious. "Oh?"

"I put my shoe—" She choked, then blurted, "I put my shoe in the *refrigerator*."

More confused than concerned, Marson asked, "Why would you do that?"

"Because I must be going *crazy*."

And she was lost again in a lavish torrent of boohooing.

Marson insisted he'd go to Mary's home the next day at eleven and make the presentation there. The houses on Prairie Street were set far back from the tree-vaulted avenue, with vast, manicured lawns, so he pulled well in to the long driveway, having so much to carry from the car. Opening the trunk, he leaned in, then lugged out two bulging, zippered portfolios.

"Help ya?"

Marson turned to find a slump-shouldered groundskeeper standing inches away—he'd been hacking at a viburnum hedge with a clipper that looked like a monstrous, rusty scissors. His khaki work clothes bore grass stains at the knees and elbows. He eyed Marson through a milky stare; his drooling smile lacked a full set of teeth.

Marson straightened his tie—his favorite, a silvery old Armani—and buttoned his jacket. "Uh, sure," he said. "Thanks."

The gardener dropped the clipper to the driveway; its tip chipped the cement, and its wooden handles spun a half-turn before dropping next to Marson's spit-polished blucher oxfords. A robin looked over from the turf he'd been needle-nosing, laughed, and flew off.

Without a word, the gardener hoisted the larger of the portfolios and trudged across the lawn toward the front porch. Marson followed with the remaining portfolio.

A stern-looking housekeeper awaited them at the door and offered a dull greeting: "Mary's expecting you. This way."

As Marson passed through the doorway, she took his portfolio. She also took the larger portfolio from the gardener, snapping at him, "Get back to work." She thumped the door closed with her hip, then led Marson through the entry hall and into a side parlor, which smelled of new carpeting.

Ten minutes into the presentation, Marson knew he'd nailed it. Mary was her chipper self again, focused on her dream of giving the performing arts a proper home in Dumont. She was thrilled by the vision Marson had brought to the project, and as the hour ticked by, her enthusiasm mounted.

"This is no exaggeration," she said, reviewing a series of elevations, "but I do believe this could put Dumont on the map." She gave a thoughtful nod, adding, "This will not only *house* the arts. This will *be* art."

Marson asked, "You're pleased, then?"

"Pleased? I'm *sold*. There's still the committee, but that's" — she whirled a hand — "that's a mere formality."

For once, Marson had found himself in the right spot at the right time to design the perfect project for the perfect client. And now, he had delivered. Lost in this rapture, he dared to think Questman Center might be magazine-worthy. With a bit of luck, it might even —

"Ready to eat?"

It was not Mary's ladylike trill that had interrupted Marson's thoughts, but the impatient bark of the housekeeper, who stood in the doorway, hands on hips.

"Yes, I think so, Berta." Mary turned to Marson. "I hope you'll stay for lunch."

"Delighted."

Moments later, they were in the dining room, which also smelled of new carpeting, at a mahogany table with twelve chairs, set with lunch for two. Mary sat at the head; Marson sat near her along the side, where he could see the lawn through tall windows framed by drapes of bone-colored silk. The half-witted gardener had paused in his trimming of the viburnum to dig in his nose with a handkerchief.

Berta stepped forward and removed silver domes from two bowls containing a rich, creamy-orange soup.

"How lovely," said Marson.

"But, Berta," said Mary, "I specifically suggested green pea."

"No, Mary, you didn't—you said carrot." Then Berta gave Marson a weary look, telling him, "She's getting forgetful."

"I'm sure that's not true. But I'll enjoy the soup, regardless of what's in it." With a tone meant to dismiss the woman, he concluded, "Thank you."

Berta gave him a steely look, then left the room, clanging the lids as she tromped off toward the kitchen.

Struck speechless, Marson was appalled by the woman's insubordination toward her mistress, whom she had patronized in front of a guest. He watched a tear slip down Mary's cheek as her spoon hovered over the soup. Marson reached for Mary's free hand and told her, "You needn't put up with that, you know."

Mary let the spoon sink into the soup and tossed her hands. "But she's *right*."

"Right about what?"

"I *think* I said green pea. But I might've said carrot. Who knows? It's so maddening." With a weak smile, she added, "Don't ever get old, Marson." She tried the soup.

"It beats the alternative, Mary." Then Marson also tasted the soup. It was, in fact, delicious.

But he was troubled by this Berta character—and by the air of entitlement she had assumed in Mary's home. The whole setup struck him as both sinister and cliché. Gaslighting: servants or spouses manipulating their wealthy victims into questioning their own sanity. Incentive: financial gain. Had Berta set her sights on becoming mistress of the Questman mansion?

While Marson pondered this, his gaze drifted to the lawn again, where he saw the gardener scoping out his car, moving from window to window with his hands shading his eyes from the glare. Let him look, thought Marson. Returning his attention to the soup, he enjoyed its aggressive spark of ginger.

Between spoonfuls, Mary paused to say, "If it were just the memory issue, I could handle that—I've *joked* about it. But yesterday, finding that shoe in the refrigerator? It left me feeling dotty."

"I'm sure there's a logical explanation," said Marson, imagining Berta as she skulked around the house at night, planting dirty tricks. Through the window, he noticed the gardener kneeling at the edge of the driveway, poking in the turf. Marson took another spoonful of soup, glanced out again, and saw the gardener eat a worm. Marson gagged.

Mary set down her spoon. "Are you all right, love?"

Slack-jawed, Marson pointed to the window with one hand; with the other, he wiped his soupy chin.

"Oh, good Lord," said Mary, looking outdoors. "Berta!"

Instantly, Berta stepped around from the other side of the doorway.

Marson realized she had pussyfooted back from the kitchen and had been lurking there all along. *Lurking*—the precise description for the actions of that wench.

"Berta," said Mary, pointing, "he's at it again."

Berta took a wide-eyed look, then shot out of the room, across the hall, and through the front door, slamming it behind her. She was yelling and flailing her arms as she appeared through the window, racing toward the worm-eater.

Mary flumped back in her chair, exasperated. "Snook's been a bit of a problem lately."

"*Snook?*" asked Marson, incredulous.

"Berta's husband. They've been here forever—since long before Quincy died."

Marson scooched his chair out from the table and leaned close to Mary while keeping an eye on Snook and Berta, who squabbled on the lawn. "Were they here that night?" he asked. "The night your shoe ended up in the fridge, were they here in the house?"

"Oh, *no*," said Mary, shaking her head. "They've always been day help, ten to four, Sunday and Monday off."

"Was *anyone* in the house that night?"

"Only Mr. Zakarian."

Marson flinched. "*Walter* Zakarian? The Karastan King?" The owner of the region's largest flooring business, who claimed to descend from a long line of rug merchants, always appeared in his cheesy cable commercials wearing a cape and a crown.

Mary explained how he had taken her to dinner as a gesture of thanks for her purchase. "When he brought me home, I offered a nightcap." She primped her hair. "I may have been a little tipsy."

Marson leaned in to ask the obvious question: "Have you asked *him* about the shoe?"

"Of *course* not. I may be going loony, but I don't want *him* thinking that. Such a nice man. He called earlier and suggested dinner again tonight." A tad giddy, she added, "Isn't that funny?"

Funny indeed, thought Marson. He was not alone in his hunch that Walter Zakarian might be gay. He was a finicky dresser and still a bachelor in his forties—plus, that ermine-collared cape. Discretion, however, seemed to be Zakarian's watchword. If he had a boy on the side somewhere, no one knew it. But everyone wondered.

Then again, who was Marson to judge? He was only

too aware of persistent whisperings that he himself was closeted. His thirty-two years of marriage, however, proved otherwise.

Didn't it?

Fussing at her dressing table that evening, Mary hoped she hadn't seemed too eager in accepting Mr. Zakarian's repeat dinner invitation. More pointedly, she mulled *his* motive for the second night out. The first was clear enough: gratitude for her business. But tonight felt different. It felt like a date. His voice had carried a suggestive undertone when he phoned that morning, purring through the mouthpiece into her ear.

Or was she misreading things? Mr. Zakarian often served as a walker of prominent widows at various social events. He was a clotheshorse who enjoyed spiffing up in a tux, and his escortees enjoyed the attention. Mary knew them all, and to a woman, they were coy about what, if anything, had transpired with the Karastan King after they were out of public view. Which left Mary with the impression that he was, at once, both eligible and not.

Fingering a drop of L'Air du Temps behind each earlobe, she asked herself, And what if he *is* eligible? Eligible for *what*? It's not as if I'm *looking*.

The lady in the mirror had a grin on her face. Mary wiped it off with a swipe of lipstick. She capped the tube, plopped it into her handbag, and snapped it shut. She put her watch on one wrist and a bracelet on the other, then reached for her ring in the crystal dish where she always kept it.

But it was not there.

Her wedding ring—where was it? A year after Quincy's death, she continued to wear it, and although she had begun to wonder if it was time to put the ring away and move on, she had not yet made that decision. She always wore it in public, and when it was not on her finger at home, it was kept in the little Lalique saltcellar, right there on her dressing table, next to the vintage perfume bottle, also Lalique, with its stopper crowned by a pair of frosty, kissing doves.

"Ugh!" She clenched her fists and stood. She slid each drawer open, then banged each drawer shut. She opened her handbag, dug around, then snapped it shut at the very moment when, downstairs, the doorbell sounded a single chime.

Seven sharp — Mr. Zakarian. But why had he come to the *back* door? Purse in hand, Mary grabbed her beaded evening jacket and left the bedroom. She skittered down the stairs, across the front hall, and into the kitchen as the chime sounded again.

"Coming," she called, hurrying to the door. When she switched on the porch light, the bulky silhouette of a man in a topcoat filled the gathered sheers hanging at the window. Unless she was mistaken, he was holding a bouquet.

When she opened the door, Mr. Zakarian stepped inside and presented the flowers with a bow of his head. "For you, Mrs. Questman."

"Roses," she said, taking them. *Red* roses, she thought. She recalled his purr on the phone. "Thank you — how lovely. But why the back door? You're welcome in front, you know."

He shrugged. "It may sound cornball, but there's an old superstition in my family's homeland: one must enter a house the way one left it. And we were here in the kitchen when I left the other night."

Everyone in town knew he'd been born there in Dumont, but he wore the oddities of his heritage with panache, just as he wore custom-tailored clothes. According to rumor, he bought nothing off the rack; frequent fittings took him all the way to Chicago.

Mary said, "Any door's fine, then—not smart to tempt fate." She set her purse and jacket on the table and stepped to the sink with the flowers. "I should put these in water before we go."

"But of course." He sauntered behind and helped retrieve a pitcher from the high shelf of a cupboard. "And all is well since I last saw you?"

She sighed while filling the pitcher. "It's been an odd couple of days—ups and downs, I'm afraid."

"And why is that, dear lady?" Looking troubled, Zakarian rapidly kissed the tip of his pinkie, touched it to his forehead, then tapped his ear.

Mary suppressed a laugh. Was this a quirky ethno-ritual, a bit of razzmatazz intended to ward off the goblins of misfortune?

With a pout, he asked, "Why the ups and downs?"

"Nothing serious," she said, wishing she believed it. "I've gotten so forgetful. It's upsetting." She turned off the water and set the pitcher on the counter—and there, next to the soap dish, was her wedding ring. Of course. She'd put it there while washing her hands that afternoon.

"Not to worry," he said. "There are days when I'd forget my own head if it weren't screwed on." His lips curved with a soft smile; hers did as well. Taking turns, stem by stem, he helped her arrange the flowers.

Puttering at the sink together, standing close enough to feel his warmth, she found his quaint chatter not only amiable, but charming. His manner and his bearing were as refined as his attire. And try as she might to dismiss it—good heavens—she felt a long-lost tingle of desire.

"There," he said, preening the roses, "that should keep them happy for tonight."

"Thank you again, Mr. Zakarian. They're beautiful."

"Mrs. Questman," he said with a scowl. Then he grinned. "I'd be so pleased if you would call me Walter."

"Of course — *Walter*. And please do call me Mary."

"With pleasure — *Mary*."

She noticed the ring again, mere inches from her hands, and was about to reach for it, but did not.

"Your jacket," said Walter as he helped her slip into it. Then he laughed. "I meant to ask — did you find it?"

She gave him a blank look.

"The shoe. I hope it brought a chuckle to your morning."

"Oh, *yes*," she fibbed. "I was almost hysterical."

"You stepped out of the room to check on something, and I saw my chance — and there you have it."

"And there I have it," she agreed, sharing his mirth. "Just wondering, though — another tradition of your ancestors?" She seemed to recall that certain cultures had an unsavory preoccupation with shoes.

"No, dear Mary. We could blame it on the nightcap, but in truth, I was feeling playful."

"Why, Walter," she said, taking her purse as they stepped to the door together, "I do believe you're flirting."

He purred.

She tingled.

❑

SIX

The Transit of Venus

My parents treated him as their nephew, as the son they never had, though of course he wasn't. They doted over Brody Norris, the golden boy, as if he were a member of the family, but Brody's mother—a proudly *single* mom and, just for good measure, a radical lesbian—shared not a drop of blood with us, thank God. When I was a girl, Inez Norris was always around, at least when she wasn't out organizing protests at UCLA or bussing up to Berkeley for the next conference or sit-in or whatever.

She had migrated to California from the Midwest with my future father, Gordon Harper—*the* Gordon Harper, the astrophysicist—who shared her bohemian mind-set and a quest for the unknown, hers in civil rights, his in distant galaxies. They were soul mates of the seventies, an age renowned for its sexual liberation, although logic implies that Inez's bond to Gordon was platonic, given her predilections. This was long before my mother entered the equation, while Dad was working on his second doctorate and Inez was cutting her teeth as a community activist. Around the time Dad joined the faculty at UCLA, he married Joan, a hippie potter with degrees in art and comparative religion, and a few years later, she bore their only child.

They named me Venus Allison Harper, which has always made me cringe. In spite of many proclamations from my parents' friends that "Venus is such a *pretty* name," I found it hard to ignore the coincidence that, mere months before my arrival, Joan and Gordon had adopted a huge, slobbering black Lab and named it Jupiter. I've seen photos of a christening of sorts—mine, not the dog's—officiated by Inez, who wore a gauzy goddess toga with a wreath of herbs in her hair. Since my fourth birthday, I have insisted upon being addressed by my middle name, which was made official in buttercream script on my cake.

Eyeing the *Allison* amid the four fluttering candles, Inez leaned to tell Joan in a stage whisper, "Seems the apple fell a bit far from the tree." At so tender an age, I had no idea what she meant, but everyone laughed.

Some twenty years later, my law degree, while applauded, served as further confirmation that I had indeed fallen far from the tree, with little interest in the arts or in the romance of the heavens—and even less in the countercultural zeitgeist that still shaped not only the thinking, but also the living arrangements, of Gordon, Joan, and my lesbian "aunt."

Inez had moved next door to us when I was eight because she was pregnant. I was old enough to understand that this condition represented a certain inconsistency in her avowed independence from men, and when I asked my mother about it, she explained, "Inez is proving a point." When I looked all the more confused, she added, "We're *proud* of her." But they never seemed proud of me.

On the other hand, everyone seemed *very* proud of Brody, who popped into the world when I was nine. His ear for poetry was evident by the time he abandoned baby talk and began speaking in complete sentences. By kindergarten, he developed the eye of a discerning dresser, coordinating his little sweater vests with what he termed "the right shoe." By the age of eight, he displayed precocious dancing skills, wowing everyone at his birthday party with an energetic zapateado, performed with a buff ballet master whom Inez counted among her closest circle of arty friends. Then, around the time puberty hit, Brody announced he was gay. And by the age of fourteen, when he returned with his mother from a family wedding in Wisconsin, while I was struggling to wrap up my first year of law school, he made it known he had reached two long-term decisions: his interest in men had narrowed to *older* men, and he wanted to become an architect.

No, Brody Norris had most certainly *not* fallen far from the tree, so he sucked up the affection of our communal family, filling the void of disappointment I'd created. It galled me, of course, to witness this, but in my heart of hearts I had to admit that he was, in fact, a charmer.

He was smart and inquisitive. Sensitive and polite. Plus, those looks—cute as a child, he matured into an achingly handsome adolescent who brought to mind a very young Robert Redford, with the bonus of those astonishing green eyes. Where the hell did he get those? Not from Inez. And Inez was always tight-lipped about the identity of Brody's father, who merited no more than an occasional, oblique reference as "the sperm donor."

Circling from the sidelines, buffeted by the waves of adulation that sluiced toward Brody, I took secret satisfaction in the knowledge that my so-called cousin wasn't really family at all; he was just this younger guy who happened to share with me a most unconventional upbringing. Now and then, alone together, we liked to joke about our surroundings, share our frustrations, confide our dreams. Were it not for one little wrinkle—his taste for men—I'd have thrown myself at him the moment he reached the age of consent.

It never happened, but the idea of being mounted by Brody, however delusional, became a fixation that followed me through law school and into the early years of my career. It followed me down the aisle when I married a sweet, bookish man, Bill Schimmel, who was a junior faculty member in the astrophysics department chaired by the illustrious Gordon Harper. Bill proved himself an attentive husband, loving enough, but he flat-out worshipped my father, and I never had any doubt that he had married me to ingratiate himself with the Nobel laureate. In truth, I too had entered the marriage for much the same reason. Deep down, we both understood that it was a marriage of convenience.

So when Dad died unexpectedly (Walmart, aneurysm), the pretending was over, and I left Bill before he could leave me. Besides, it had always felt borderline incestuous, tangling the sheets with the underling of my father—compared to which, fantasizing about the son of my faux aunt felt downright wholesome. Within the loony context of my extended family, I considered myself the "normal" one, but their quiet condescension made it only too clear they considered *me* the outlier. I needed to move away.

My career took me up to Seattle for a few years. Then down to San Francisco for a few more. And then it was a short hop over to Sacramento, where I was promoted to partner in my firm, which had a long-established practice among the politicos who converge there. It was a button-down life in a satisfying job that rewarded both my practical instincts and my orthodox views—but I still had that itch for Brody.

He must have been on my mind when my mother phoned a few weeks ago and pleaded for me to attend a family gathering at the clan's mountain retreat in Idyllwild, which

I had not visited for some five years. My immediate instinct to refuse her invitation was tempered by the prospect of catching up with you-know-who. I had now nudged past forty, which put Brody in his early thirties, and suddenly our age difference didn't seem so vast. Joan said, "We're having the transit party that your father started planning on the day you were born."

I moved the phone away from my ear and gave it a quizzical look. Joan had a habit of speaking in riddles. I asked, "Transit party?"

"The transit of *Venus*. It's next month, on the fifth."

"Oh. That." Anyone overhearing our conversation would have thought it deranged, but—crazy me—I now understood what she was talking about.

A transit of Venus is a rare astronomical event, a sort of mini-eclipse, during which the planet can be observed moving across the face of the sun. Transits occur in pairs, spaced eight years apart, and then the pairs are spaced more than a century apart. There had been one in 1882, and then there hadn't been another until June of 2004—during the run-up to W.'s election to a second term—but that transit wasn't visible in California. This next one, however, in 2012, would be visible on the West Coast during the afternoon and evening of a Tuesday in June—during Obama's try for a second term. By coincidence, the transit would occur on the same day as the presidential primary in California.

"That's a busy day at the office, Mom. Lots of irons in the fire."

Whining, Joan reminded me, "But there won't be another till 2117. How could you *miss* it?"

I laughed. "Oh, come on—it's no big deal." In previous centuries, it *had* been a big deal. When astronomers were still trying to determine the accurate distance from the Earth to the sun, the observable transits offered a theoretical means of measuring it. Now, however, a transit of Venus was little more than a historical curiosity, barely noted by the media, capturing the attention of only bona fide astro-geeks.

"It was a big deal to your father," said Joan. "It was *his* idea to name you Venus."

"Don't remind me."

"And the *party* was his idea. He intended to host it. He wanted the whole family to share this. Inez is already here. Brody's driving over from L.A. And I'm sure—"

"I'll see what I can do, Mom."

On the morning of Tuesday, June fifth, I took an early flight down to Palm Springs, rented a car, and aimed it up the twisting roads through the San Jacinto mountains toward the alpine community of Idyllwild, where my father had built a secluded vacation home, a retreat from the buzz and din of L.A. He had planned to retire there and, preparing to amuse himself in his dotage, had installed a sizable telescope on one of the observation decks. But alas, fate would rob him of the title *emeritus*.

With his head in the cosmos throughout his career, Gordon Harper had trained himself to think big. As a result, his mountain getaway was no mere cabin in the woods. Joining forces with Lloyd Washington, an architect on the university faculty, he had acquired a large parcel of sloping land, and together they constructed a whimsical aerie to suit the various interests of a growing communal family. In addition to Gordon's telescope, the compound featured a bright, spacious studio for Lloyd, a kiln for Joan, and a flat clearing in the timbered hills that served as a smallish amphitheater for interpretive dance, not to mention Inez's drumming circle. They named their lofty haven Zenithgate.

In the dozen years since Zenithgate had been built, I had visited there many times from Los Angeles, but not since moving away. I had driven the mountain route so often, its hairpin turns and sheer precipices failed to make me flinch, even after my long absence. Passing an elevation sign that marked six thousand feet, I lowered the car windows, which had been closed tight against the desert heat a mile below. The air carried a spicy note of pine, evoking a time when both my father and my husband were still in my life.

From the main road, I made a sharp turn into deep, blue shadow and followed the narrow strip of asphalt as it wound through the trees, over a series of crests. Then, rising to the top of a last ridge, I saw the two stone pylons that flanked a needle-strewn gravel driveway, spanned by a primitive sign of woven twigs: ZENITHGATE.

I stopped the car in a makeshift parking court, a clearing in the trees, where several other vehicles were left at slapdash angles; I recognized none of them. Having been in motion all morning, I took a few moments to absorb the stillness. A woodpecker rattled the trunk of a fat oak near the main house. A cello sang quietly in the distance, and at first I couldn't tell if it was real or recorded, but the perfection of the playing led me to conclude the latter — unless Yo-Yo Ma had dropped by for lunch, which seemed doubtful.

When I got out of the car, the setting was so tranquil that I made an effort not to bang the door closed. Stepping to the rear of the car, I opened the trunk and retrieved a few things, then paused to check my phone for messages; more than a dozen had piled up during the hour's drive. With a disgusted sigh, I pocketed the phone, slammed down the trunk lid, and there stood Joan.

"Oh, Allison — oh, sweetie — it's been *so*, so long." And she was all over me.

"Hi, Mom," I said, wriggling free from her embrace, straightening the lapels of my jacket. "You're looking well." She would soon be on Medicare, but she hadn't changed much since I'd last seen her. My whole life, she had projected a carefree vitality that I assumed to be a holdover of the Woodstock era, which had evaporated before my birth. Her Indian sandals of yesteryear were now replaced by sturdy Birkenstocks, but she still smelled of patchouli, and she still wore her hair long and frizzy, with a billowing old peasant dress, colorful but faded. Completing the ensemble, she had cinched around her waist a macramé thing that might have once been used to hang a potted plant.

"And look at *you*," she said, backing off a pace to get an eyeful. Then her smile sagged. With a curious frown, she asked, "Did you pack something more comfortable, dear?"

"I *am* comfortable." Gray flannel had become my look of choice. It traveled well from meetings to courtrooms to dinner. Matching jacket and skirt, paired with a white silk blouse and a bit of gold bling—it conveyed, loud and clear, no nonsense. In a good suit with a good label, often St. John, I was ready to take on the world.

"Well"—her tone was skeptical—"be careful walking over to the house. The manzanita berries are *everywhere*. They're sappy. Wouldn't want to ruin your heels."

"Yes, Mom." I hoisted my briefcase, my laptop, and a small carry-on.

"Let's get you settled in your room. I can help with the rest of your things."

"This is it—I travel light—and I'm afraid I can't spend the night."

She looked stricken. "What? Why not?"

"Long story, but I need to be in L.A. later."

In the years since my last visit, Joan had upped the output of her pottery projects. Whether this was a response to widowhood or boredom or a passion for her craft, Joan's heroic-scale urns, bowls, and vases exhibited an artful mix of intensity and sensitivity that surprised me. What's more, the dozens of fanciful glazed vessels — some functional, others purely sculptural — were crammed into every available space in the great room, which I remembered as sparse and uncluttered. A purplish-veined ceramic phallus in the entry hall stood taller than me by a head.

"Wow, Mom, this stuff is . . . interesting. Are you selling any?"

"I wouldn't do *that*." Her offended tone suggested that I should know better.

"I mean, maybe a gallery could represent you. I can ask around."

As if not hearing me, she said, "You can freshen up in here," and led me past the open kitchen to the guest quarters.

I followed her into the bedroom with its cozy ceiling of pine beams. Nubby blankets of red buffalo plaid draped the back of a leather armchair and the foot of the maple-framed double bed. A stone fireplace bisected a wall of windows overlooking a vista of trees and mountains and sky. By any measure, it was a special space. Setting down my things, I asked, "Isn't this where Brody usually stays?"

"He stays over in the *studio* now." Her tone again suggested I should know better. She added, "Make yourself at home. We're having lunch on the deck, maybe an hour. I'll be in the kitchen if you need me."

"Thanks, Mom," I said while digging in my briefcase. "I just want to spiff up and answer a few messages." When I looked back, she had already left the room.

In the bathroom, I splashed water on my face, patted it dry, then cupped a hand over my mouth and sniffed my breath. Finding it stale, I opened the cabinet under the sink to look for mouthwash, but found instead my father's shaving mug, brush, and straight razor. He was a finicky man who wouldn't leave the house in the morning without a clean shave, and he had often insisted that "only a *real* razor does the job." Because he always rose earlier than Mom and didn't want to disturb her, he would come downstairs to perform his ablutions in the guest quarters when no one was visiting. And now, there was his shaving paraphernalia, just as he'd left it—eight years ago—on the morning he had headed out to the Walmart in neighboring Hemet. The dried bristles of the brush had fused to the soap in the bottom of the mug. When I gave the brush a tug, its bristles split away and turned to powder, so I tossed it all into a tin wastebasket, where it landed with a clatter. The mug lay broken in two pieces.

"Everything okay?" warbled Joan from the kitchen.

"Fine, Mom."

Returning to the bedroom, I removed my jacket, sat on the bed, and opened my laptop. Another three or four e-mails had arrived, so I trashed the ones I could, filed the ones I couldn't, and saved for last the one from our firm's founding partner. It bore the subject line "Duggins v. Feinstein." The message was brief: "Duggins is asking us to draft a victory speech for tonight."

I typed: "Really? Suggest you assure him I have covered all contingencies." I was tempted to add a little yellow winky-face, but professionalism prevailed, so I closed with my initials and tapped the "send" button.

"Well, hi there, stranger."

I glanced up to find Inez Norris standing in the doorway,

hand on hip. Like my mother, she projected the air of an aging, though ageless, hippie. Unlike my mother, who had grown pudgy, perhaps from endless hours at the potter's wheel, Inez was still svelte and sinewy as a cat. Barefoot, with her graying hair twisted in a knot and bound with a beaded headband, she wore a simple black leotard that sported large sagging circles of sweat beneath her arms and her breasts, suggesting she had just sprung from her work-out at the ballet barre or the yoga mat.

I shut my laptop. "Hello, Inez."

She strolled into the room. "You brought homework?" With a wry expression, she added, "It's a holiday."

"The transit of Venus—whoopee." I twirled a finger in the air.

"Well"—Inez sat on the bed with me, separated by the computer—"Gordon wanted us to do this."

I rolled my eyes. "He still rules the roost. And Mom is still duped."

"That's not fair, Allison. It's not even true."

"Isn't it? Other than Mom's pottery, *nothing* has changed here. It's like a *shrine* to the great Gordon Harper. Nothing's been *touched*. I found his shaving crap in the bathroom—and threw it out."

Looking alarmed, Inez got up, stepped over to the bath, and peeped inside the wastebasket. "You shouldn't have done that," she mumbled. "Joan won't like it."

"See? She still *worships* him. She worships his *relics*. She's deluded."

With a soft smile, Inez reminded me, "She was married to him for thirty-three years."

"That may be, but he wasn't much of a husband—or father."

Inez returned to the bed, moved the laptop aside, and sat next to me again, so close I could smell her sweat. She said,

"Now, what do you mean by that?"

I paused, reluctant to say it. Through the window, I saw that Joan had stepped outside to pick berries from a patch on the sunny side of the deck where a long table was set for our impending lunch. Beyond, on the highest deck, my father's telescope was aimed toward the western sky. Then I looked Inez in the eye, telling her, "Dad cheated on Mom." Looking down at my hands, I added, "A lot. I'm sure of it."

"He was a man, Allie. That's what they do. They're wired that way."

I groaned. "He was my *father*. It shouldn't *be* that way."

Inez shrugged. "Says who? Besides, what makes you so sure of this?"

"I just sorta figured it out." Closing my eyes, I recalled, "I was maybe nine or ten and beginning to understand things. I'd see it in movies—a husband with a girlfriend. And I started to wonder about the nights he was away, supposedly giving lectures. The awkward pauses when I'd walk in on a phone call. The weekends when he was never *around*. So I asked him."

After a long pause, Inez prompted, "And?"

"And he told me. No specifics, but he confirmed my suspicions. You know Gordon—he could rationalize anything. He even managed to convince me not to bother Mom with it. He managed to *recruit* me to protect her from the truth. And ever since, I've felt like an accomplice—against my own mother."

Inez patted my knee. "Allison. Let it go."

"I'd like nothing better, but *Joan* won't let it go. After five years away, I thought she might've moved on. But she *still* hasn't gotten over him."

"She loved Gordon. You don't 'get over' that."

"Fine. But she still carries on like he walked on water.

And he didn't. Honest to God, I'm tempted to burst her bubble."

Inez drew a sharp breath, clicking her tongue in her mouth. "Don't go there, Allie." She combed a finger through my hair.

I tensed, then stood. Watching Joan through the window as she fussed with the table, I told Inez, "You're probably right. It would only upset her. It might even crush her."

"That's not the point. Joan is tougher than you think." Inez got up, moved to the bathroom, lifted the plastic liner from the wastebasket, and tied the top of the bag. Then she walked back through the bedroom, heading out toward the kitchen. But she stopped in the doorway and turned to face me.

"The point is—and you may not believe it—Joan is tougher than you are."

Joan stood at the kitchen counter whipping a big bowl of cream with a hand-cranked eggbeater. Merry as a mother elf, she whistled while she worked. I stood next to her at the sink, cutting the stems from an early crop of strawberries, big as babies' fists. Inez prepared a batch of green slop in the blender, pulsing the switch as she added more kale, spinach, and yogurt. Her latest dietary kick may have been healthy, but it looked like something the cat had spit up. She dipped a spoon into the swirl, then tasted her concoction. "Perfect," she declared. "The kale doesn't taste at all like dirt."

"Then why bother?" I asked with a sputter of a laugh.

"Oh, *you*," she said, offering her spoon. "Try?"

I shook my head and rinsed my berries.

"When I finish with this," said Joan over the clatter of her eggbeater, "I need to find the solar filter for Gordon's telescope. Can't watch the transit with the naked eye —

you'd go blind."

I suggested, "Maybe that's why this never quite caught on."

Joan ignored me. "He left a tackle box full of whatnot at the back of the hall closet. The filters ought to be in there. I haven't touched *anything*."

My eyes slid toward Inez. My expression asked, See what I mean?

Joan said, "Look who's here—Brody's back with the ice."

My gaze snapped from Inez to the window over the sink, through which I saw Brody Norris on the deck, crouching to dump several bags of ice into a Coleman cooler. From behind, the tendons of his thighs flexed beneath his khaki shorts. His biceps stretched the sleeves of a frosty green polo shirt. He looked as fresh and tasty as a scoop of lime sherbet. Standing, he clapped his hands dry, turned, and walked off toward the parking court.

The strainer of berries landed with a splash as I dropped it in the sink. "Be right back." Then I darted through the house and out the front to the driveway.

Brody turned at the sound of the slamming door. "Well, hi there, Sis!"

Tripped by the word, I slowed my run to a normal pace as I crossed the gravel toward the A-frame studio. During Brody's early years of grade school, while I was in high school, he had started calling me Sis. In light of our living arrangements—and the parallel relationships he saw at school—it was only natural for him to think of me as a big sister, though he was bright enough to understand the distinction. At the time, I had found the moniker endearing. Now, however, as he stood there looking hunky and blond and good enough to eat, I found the term about as appealing as a cold shower. In fact, it creeped me out. "We're both grown up now," I said, "so can we drop that? Great to see you, Brody." And I offered a hug.

Birds gossiped in the pines as he pulled me into an embrace, pecked my lips, then held me at arm's length. "Bigtime lawyer. You must be knockin'em dead, Allie—you look fabulous."

I felt the heat of my blush.

His eyes, his lips. Then he squinted through a frown.

"What?" I asked.

In reply, he asked, "St. John? The outfit?"

I gave a tiny, fearful nod.

"You might"—he made an effort to control his grimace—"you might consider something a little less stodgy. Michael Kors would be a good look for you."

Go to hell, I'd have said if anyone else had suggested it. Instead I asked, "Take me shopping sometime?"

"Well, *yeah*." He trotted up the steps to the studio and opened the door. "Come on in."

I followed. The large room on the ground floor was an architect's work space as well as living quarters. I presumed the loft that was nestled in the peak of the building was meant for sleeping, though I had never been up there. I had rarely been inside the studio at all, as it belonged to Lloyd Washington, the architect who had designed the Zenithgate compound. In the early years after it was built, Lloyd and his wife, Susan, came up to the mountains often. A biracial couple—Lloyd black, Susan white—they provided the perfect sort of mash-up that was nectar to Inez and my parents. Lloyd and Susan's children were in college by then, and the studio was meant as a refuge and reward for the parents. With a lascivious wink and his baritone laugh, Lloyd liked to call it their "love shack," a crude phrase evoking an image that I always found, at some primal level, unsettling.

But that had been years earlier, before Dad died, so I

thought perhaps the Washingtons no longer spent much time at Zenithgate and had offered the studio to Brody, who had begun his own architectural practice—an arrangement that would allow him to work away from the office when he came up to visit Inez.

Brody was in the galley kitchen pouring two glasses of lemonade. I asked, "Lloyd's not here, I guess?"

"Nope."

Hmm. Just us. I asked, "Nothing stronger?"

He peered at the lemonade for a moment, chagrined. "I guess this *is* sorta tame. Wine?"

"Thought you'd never ask."

He dumped the lemonade, set out a pair of good crystal stemware, and poured chardonnay from an open bottle he retrieved from the refrigerator. Handing me one of the glasses, he lifted his own, toasting, "Welcome back."

I admitted, "It's been a while," then drank.

"I understand," he said, setting his glass on the counter. "Not much here for you."

I thought, Are you *kidding*? I wanted to ask, Don't you get lonely up here? I know you like guys, but come on, there's a lot to be said for our shared history. Aren't you even curious about taking things to the next level? I'd go there in a heartbeat.

We gabbed about nothing, as if avoiding *the* topic, but he must have seen that I was flustered. Christ, with him standing there in the kitchen, pleasant as pie, hotter than hell—and literally within reach—I was on the verge of a swoon, so I steadied myself by planting an elbow on the countertop. It was a clumsy, inelegant pose.

With a note of concern, he said, "Everything okay?"

"Must be the altitude." With a weak smile, I added, "Sorry. I feel so foolish." I touched his hand, then looked away, embarrassed.

"Not at all. I think it's cute."

And that's when I knew: it was now or never. "Brody," I said, choosing my words with care, trying not to stammer, "this is a bit awkward. It may come as a surprise, even a shock, but I—"

The front door slammed. "Brody!" shouted a husky baritone.

We both turned as Lloyd Washington rushed through the studio and into the kitchen, waving a magazine overhead. Stuffed under his other arm was a pile of mail. Though I was standing right there, he didn't seem to see me—or couldn't be bothered. He let the mail drop to the floor and slapped the magazine on the counter, opening it to a dog-eared page. "We made it!"

Brody screamed like a girl and knocked over his glass as he lunged forward to take a look. "Oh. My. *God!*"

Lloyd grabbed him from behind, spun him around, and planted a big wet kiss on Brody's gaping mouth. Brody flung his arms around the other man's shoulders and held tight as Lloyd dragged him to the center of the room and spun him in circles like a limp doll. I stared bug-eyed. Brody laughed with wild abandon. Lloyd's chortle rumbled through the cavernous space. Though old enough to be Brody's father, Lloyd was as massive and fit as a quarterback. He could easily have crushed the life out of Brody, but there was unmistakable tenderness in the way he nuzzled the younger man's neck and stroked his blond hair with a beefy black paw.

"Must be really good news," I said as a reminder of my presence.

"Hi there, Allie," said Lloyd, panting to catch his breath, never taking his eyes off Brody. His offhanded tone suggested we had seen each other just yesterday—but it had been at least five years.

Brody slipped out of their embrace, joined me at the counter, and turned the magazine in my direction. "*Western Design Digest*. Hot off the press. It's a beach house we did in Malibu."

"'We'?" I asked, glancing at the magazine.

"Washington & Norris," said Lloyd, beaming. He joined us at the counter and drummed his huge hands on the butcher block. "Didn't you know? Brody and I started a firm to-gether—and it's going gangbusters."

Confused, I asked, "How do you manage that? I mean, with your teaching."

"That was my *former* life, Allie. I took early retirement, climbed down from the ivory tower, and decided to see if I could make it in the real world. A little scary at my age, but hey, I've got an awesome design partner." He mussed Brody's hair.

Brody tapped the magazine. "We knew the *Digest* was considering a feature—they spent two days shooting the place—but we had no idea if it would make the final cut." With wistful understatement, he said to Lloyd, "Business has been good, but it's about to get *way* better."

Flipping through the eight or ten pages, I said, "Nice." In truth, I thought it looked severe. If you've seen one white, angular multimillion-dollar beach house, you've seen them all.

"Thanks," said Lloyd. "Palmer Ross loves it. An ideal client—and the 'celebrity thing' might've tipped the scales with the *Digest*."

The name was familiar. "Palmer Ross?"

Brody explained, "The whiz kid who invented that blog-ging platform—sold it for gazillions, and he's still in his twenties."

"Not only that," said Lloyd with a low, lecherous laugh, "but Palmer is every bit as sweet and innocent as he looks. One smokin-hot, baby-faced nerd. Sugar *and* spice—wouldn't you love to try a taste of that?"

"Now, now," said Brody, reminding Lloyd, "you're married."

"Speaking of which," I said, eager to change the subject, "how's Susan?"

Lloyd shot Brody a bewildered glance. Brody shrugged. Lloyd turned to me, saying, "Susan was *also* part of my former life. Lots of changes, Allie."

"Uh"—my head was spinning—"did I miss something?"

Brody raised the back of his left hand and waggled his fingers.

I gasped. Saw the ring. It matched Lloyd's. I asked, "Married? Where?" With a smirk, I added, *"Denmark?"*

"No, Miss Smarty-ass," said Lloyd, "we were married right here in California, four years ago this fall—during that brief window when gay marriage was legal, before the last election, when Prop 8 shut it down. Surely you heard about it."

"Prop 8, yes. You guys, *no*. I'm stunned—why didn't anyone tell me?"

Brody said, "We sent you the announcement."

Lloyd added, "We were married that October, and the announcement did double duty as our Christmas card."

Brody corrected, "New Year's card."

"New Year's card," said Lloyd. "I designed it myself."

I felt weak. "May I sit down?"

"Sure thing, Missy. Step into my parlor." Lloyd led us from the kitchen to a conversation pit near the fireplace. He and Brody shared a love seat—how touching—with me, solo, in a second love seat, facing them across a low square table. In the center of the table, one of Joan's huge bowls held a mound of pinecones.

Trying to make sense of the unexpected news, I asked, "You're *sure* you sent me the card?"

"Positive," said Brody. "We wondered how you'd react."

Talking it through, we determined that I had doubtless received the announcement but had overlooked it. To the best of their recollection, the envelope had borne only their return address, not their names, which would have caught my attention. What's more, the months leading up to and immediately following the last election had been hectic for me, so the niceties of social correspondence had not been high on my list of priorities. I had just made the move from San Francisco and was still getting settled in Sacramento. I was doing some volunteer work for the McCain campaign. And my firm had taken on a good deal of pro bono work in support of Prop 8—which Brody and Lloyd did not, of course, need to know.

I tossed my hands. "Sorry, guys. If I got your announcement, I must have pitched it without opening it. My belated congratulations."

Lloyd said, "We thought it was sort of strange that we never heard back from you."

"Actually," said Brody, "we thought you didn't approve."

"Don't be ridiculous." But I did not, in fact, approve. I found Lloyd's second marriage even more troubling than his first. It was a gut thing; it didn't work for me. And having Brody messed up in Lloyd's midlife crisis made it all the worse. What's more, it vexed me to realize that Lloyd's lack of commitment to Susan was on par with my father's disloyalty to Joan. No wonder Lloyd Washington and Gordon Harper had gotten along so well for so long—they'd had far more in common than their star-faculty status at UCLA.

"What's wrong?" said Lloyd. "I was going to pop a bottle of Veuve Clicquot, but you look perplexed."

"It shows, huh?"

Brody told me, "The expression 'death warmed over' springs to mind."

"It has nothing to do with *you*," I lied. "I've had Gordon on my mind today," which was true enough. "Being away for so long, I thought I'd already put some old issues to rest, but this morning, everything came rushing back."

Brody looked baffled. "What issues?"

Lloyd took a stab: "Politics?"

I shook my head. "Long before he died, we agreed to disagree. No, it's much deeper—and far more hurtful."

Lloyd's caring tone took me by surprise. "Allie," he said, "if you don't want to talk about it, I respect that. But if you *don't* talk about it, we can't be of any help. And truth is, I'm a pretty good listener." He nudged his husband. "So is Brody."

I lolled my head back and groaned. The sound reverberated from the studio's peaked roof. I told the rafters, "Dad cheated on Mom." Then I sat up straight, facing Lloyd and Brody. "There. I've said it."

Lloyd's tone was matter-of-fact: "He was a product of his age."

"That's total bullshit—it doesn't excuse a thing."

Brody said, "You don't know for sure if he—"

"He *told* me, Brody. Not in so many words, but he didn't deny it either. And if I could figure it out—if this stupid *kid* could figure it out—Mom had to know as well. And it absolutely fries me that she still lives this crazy fantasy that he was some sort of god."

Lloyd heaved a little sigh. "In the world of astrophysics, he *was* some sort of god. I mean, Jesus—he won a Nobel

Prize."

"He was my *father*," I yelled. "I deserved better. Joan deserved better."

"I've never heard Joan complain," said Lloyd.

"That's my point. She's delusional."

Lloyd leaned forward. "Joan Harper is the most level-headed woman I've ever known. Crazy fantasies? Not her style."

With unnerving certainty, Brody said, "And she's *never* been delusional."

"Period," said Lloyd.

There was something in their tone, in their unity and surety, that gave me pause. Still, I protested, "She's my mother. I think I know her better than you do."

Lloyd noted, "You haven't seen her in years. You've barely spoken to her."

I crossed my arms. "I've been busy, okay?" Quietly, I added, "I've been busy forgetting what Gordon did to her."

"Allie," said Brody, "they were married more than thirty years. They were happy. Even though things might've been unconventional, they had an understanding. Let go of it."

"Let *go* of it? For all I know, he was fucking his *students*."

"Never," said Lloyd. "I was Gordon's best friend. If that ever happened, I'd know it."

Stewing in silence, I pondered my father's evils and the many years of deceit. Then I looked Lloyd in the eye. "You're every bit as blind to Gordon as Joan was. There were other women. It's a fact."

Both Lloyd and Brody drew a breath and held it. They glanced at each other—then at me—then again at each other. Lloyd's raised brow seemed to ask a question. Brody nodded.

"Allie," said Lloyd, "their gig was unusual, but it's not

what you think."

My lips parted, ready to rebut him, but something told me to shut up and listen.

He continued, "Gordon loved Joan with his whole heart. But he also had a deep and abiding connection—which began long before he met Joan—with Inez."

I rattled my head. "She's a *lesbian*."

"True enough. But approaching middle age, she wanted a child." Lloyd hesitated, then explained, "Gordon fathered a son with her."

Brody said, "That would be me."

I stared at him dumbfounded. When I could catch my breath, I asked, "How long have you known this?"

"Four years. When Lloyd and I got married, I had to list my father—and *his* birth information—on the license. 'Sperm donor' wouldn't cut it. I needed a name. So Inez told me."

"Why ...," I stammered, "why haven't you *told* me this?"

"Well, Sis, it's not the sort of chitchat you bury in an e-mail."

Lloyd added, "You were never around."

I needed to lie down. It was shock enough to learn the extent of my father's relationship with Inez, but even more disturbing to learn that Brody was my half brother, and worse yet to realize I had come *this* close to humiliating myself by attempting intimacy with him. I should never have agreed to return to Zenithgate that day. I wanted to gather my things and get out.

But I was in no condition to drive. Shaking and queasy, I needed some time alone to close my eyes and calm myself. Crossing the parking court toward the main house, I was tempted to run, but why? At the moment, my only escape from my family's past was not in flight, but in rest, perhaps in sleep.

I entered the house and beelined through the front hall, past the towering ceramic penis, and through the great room. Joan and Inez were still fussing and gabbing in the kitchen as I made my way toward the guest quarters. Joan paused to ask, "Allison dear, could you take a few things out to the table?"

"Not right now, Mom." With a thud, I closed the bedroom door behind me.

I drew the curtains, shutting out the mountain view and the piercing June sunshine. Then I kicked off my heels, wrapped myself in the red plaid blanket, and lay on the bed in a tight fetal curl. Closing my eyes, I felt my heartbeat pulsing in my ears. Within a minute or so, the beating grew fainter, slower. What a day.

What more, I wondered, could possibly go wrong?

And it was barely past noon.

"**A**llison dear? You're missing your own party."

I open my eyes to find Mom sitting on the edge of the bed. I squint at my watch. Nearly one. "Guess I fell asleep."

"Soundly. You were snoring."

I laugh. "Was not." Sitting up next to Joan, I stretch my legs over the edge of the bed and wiggle my toes.

She takes my hand. "I hear you had a talk with the boys."

I look at her. "I was hoping I might've dreamed that part."

"No, sweetie. You needed to know. Sorry it took so long to get it in the open. Back then, I just didn't think you were ready to hear it."

"What makes you think I'm ready *now*?"

"Come on." She stands. "Join the party."

My mouth is dry and sticky. My throat feels raspy. "Was

I really snoring?"

With a chuckle, she leaves the room.

After freshening up, when I stroll out to the deck, the meal is almost finished, but a full plate awaits me, set at the head of the table. Joan is sitting with Inez on one side, Brody and Lloyd on the other. Up on the observation deck, an open tackle box is positioned near the telescope, now equipped with its solar filter, aimed high in the sky.

A kerfuffle of greetings sweeps me to the table. As I sit, Lloyd stands. With a broad, theatrical gesture, he intones, "We've fallen now under your spell, O Venus, goddess of beauty and love!"

Joan and Inez applaud as Lloyd sits again.

But Brody looks confused. "Hey, bub," he says to Lloyd, jerking a thumb over his shoulder, "Venus is *that* way."

Lloyd studies his husband for a moment, then turns to the others wide-eyed. "Good God," he says with a tone of delicious anticipation, "the lad doesn't *know*?"

"What?" says Brody. "What'd I miss?"

Lloyd looks ready to pee his pants. Joan and Inez titter.

Dryly, I tell Brody, "You might as well hear it from me. Back in the hippie era, my parents welcomed their first and only child with the name Venus. I suspect they were drug-addled."

"Nonsense, dear," says Joan. "We named you Venus because you were the offspring of our love."

"Be that as it may," I explain to Brody, "I never admitted to that name, using my middle name instead. When I was old enough, I changed it."

"Cry me a river," says Lloyd. "You're not the *only* one to change their name."

The rest of us share a round of puzzled looks. Joan asks

Lloyd, "*You?* I've known you forever, and you've always been Lloyd Washington."

"We may go way back, Joan, and our friendship is indeed epic, but you haven't known me *that* long. No, this transformation happened in college—in architecture school. I changed my name to Lloyd."

Inez thumps her forehead. "Frank. Lloyd. Wright."

"Really?" says Brody, laughing.

I turn to Lloyd. "All right, fess up. What *was* your name?"

He mimes zipping his lips.

I smirk. "I'll bet it was Percival."

"My name was *not* Percival, Miss Venus."

"Stop that."

Brody says to me, "Oh, come on. I think Venus is a beautiful name. *I'd* use it."

"Yeah, right," says Lloyd with a hoot. "A boy named Venus—that'd go over swell in gym class."

I ask him, "Nasty memories, Percival?"

Lloyd looks away, mumbling, "Yes, actually."

We fall silent for a moment, and during the lull, I poke at my chicken salad.

Then Brody asks Lloyd, "When did you *know*?"

"When did I know I was gay? I guess I knew it all my life, beneath all the denial. But I didn't find the guts to act on it till *you* went away to school, and then came back, all smart and gorgeous—a fresh-minted architect. You drove me nuts. Outright nuts. And you still do. In a good way."

"Wow." Brody kisses his husband. "But that's not what I was asking. I meant: When did you know you wanted to be an *architect*?"

"Hmmm." Lloyd sits back, recalling, "Well, I was never good at sports, not even interested, and for a black kid, that set me apart. I had teachers—coaches, mostly—telling me

I was wasting my 'born talents.' Even then, I found that sort of insulting, as if being black didn't offer much of a future, unless I was willing to play games, literally. But I wanted something else. Something better. And the more I thought about architecture — Frank Lloyd Wright was even in our American *history* book — the more I felt drawn to it. It's big. It lasts a lifetime, or maybe thousands of years. So I boned up with math and art in high school, and once I got to college, I never looked back."

"You evolved into it," says Brody.

Lloyd shrugs. "Yeah."

"Not Brody," says Inez, leaning into the conversation. "For him, it wasn't an evolving interest. It came in a flash."

I set down my fork. "Right. I remember that. The two of you took a trip to Wisconsin."

"We did," says Brody. "Mom and I went to her brother's wedding. I'd never met the Norris family. And her brother, my uncle Ted, was an architect."

"Still is," says Inez.

"And he had a business partner — Mason or Morton or something like that."

Inez tells her son, "His name's Marson. And unless I'm mistaken, *you* were rather smitten with him."

"Mom, please."

"Awww," says Lloyd, "puppy love."

Brody concedes, "Puppy crush, maybe. I was like, *four-teen*. Nothing came of it, obviously, but I did follow through on the career."

I say to him, "Your uncle must be proud of you."

"We haven't been in touch very often. I heard from him last year when he and Marson were preparing a proposal for a big project, a performing-arts center — sounded great. But I saw them just that once."

Inez explains, "I keep my distance from the Norris tribe. Even growing up, I felt like the black sheep."

Lloyd says, "You and me both, doll. *Baa-aa-aa.*" He beams a huge pearly-white smile.

I tense. My hands grip the arms of the chair.

Inez continues, "When I took off for California, that sealed the deal—the emotional distance became physical distance. Which suits me fine."

Joan tells her warmly, "Their loss is our gain. Your home is here now."

I tell them, "But it's not *my* home, at least not anymore. All my life, *I've* felt like the black sheep in this crowd."

"Allison, dear," says Joan, "that's nuts."

"Right—it *is* nuts. Since I was little, you've made me feel like an outcast in my own home."

Inez looks me in the eye. "Then you and I have more in common than you've thought."

"Like hell we do." I rise.

"Be nice, dear," says Joan.

"Allie," says Lloyd, "why don't you sit down and enjoy the day with us?"

Inez says, "There's cake to go with the berries."

With balled fists, I shout, "I don't want *cake!*"

There's a stunned silence. Brody clears his throat. "What *do* you want, Sis?"

"I want to leave, okay? So if we're here to watch the transit of Venus, let's have a look and be done with it." I stomp toward the telescope.

Joan says, "It won't be visible till after three. We've got plenty of time to kill."

Stopping short, I check my watch—not even one-thirty. "Then this trip has been wasted. I need to be on my way before then."

"What?" says Brody. "You just got here."

Joan rises, approaches me, and gestures for me to join her on the striped cushion of a chaise longue near the edge of the deck. Sitting, she tells me, "The trip's not 'wasted.' This party today—it has nothing to do with Gordon's wishes."

I sit next to her. "But the telescope . . . the solar filter . . . what's that all about?"

"Really, Allison—must you always be so *literal*?"

"I try to be, yes."

"The transit today—it's about you. *Your* transit. It's time you found out a few things. We wanted to make it nice for you."

"Oh, it's been 'nice,' all right." I start to get up, but Joan tugs me down again. I tell her, "Do you mind? I need to be in L.A. before traffic gets impossible."

But Joan's hand rests heavy on my knee; she does not remove it.

Brody gets up from the table and steps toward our chaise. "Why the rush, Allie? Big murder trial in the works?"

"Nothing quite that dramatic. The primary is today, and we're counsel for Chester Duggins's campaign. He's challenging Senator Feinstein."

Still at the table, Lloyd asks, "Aren't there like a *dozen* right-wing nut jobs on the ballot for that?"

"They're not *all* nut jobs, Lloyd." Under my breath, I add, "Twenty-three, to be exact."

Joan removes her hand from my knee. "Don't tell me you're expecting a *victory* party."

"Win or lose, I need to be there."

"Well," says Lloyd, "I hope they're paying you plenty. Be sure to collect before the loot runs dry."

"It's a pro bono account. We support the values Duggins would bring to the office."

"Wait a minute," says Lloyd, getting up from the table, moving over to join us. "Duggins? That racist bastard? He's the one who keeps yapping about voter ID laws and a crackdown on immigrants."

"The important thing," I insist, "is that he values fiscal restraint, coupled with a more robust defense budget—which is good for everyone."

Brody asks, "Fiscal restraint and military expansion? How does *that* work?"

"Oh, my God," says Joan, fingers to her mouth. "He's also the one who supports that crazy 'personhood' amendment. Those commercials—'Let's go gunning to protect the unborn.'"

"Men!" says Inez, alone at the table. "They just can't keep their noses out of our vaginas."

Brody and Lloyd turn to her with a grimace.

She adds, "Present company excluded, of course."

No one speaks. A woodpecker flutters in the branches of an oak reaching over the deck. A few acorns drop and bounce.

Joan shifts on the cushion, facing me squarely. Our knees touch. "Allison, sweetie, you're a grown woman, but I'd be remiss not to mention this: I'm a smidge disappointed by some of the company you keep."

"Me?" I stand. "What about this damn freak show you're living with up here?"

Inez's voice lilts from the table: "Seems the apple fell a bit far from the tree . . ."

I point at Inez, telling Joan, "And *her*—you not only tolerate her—you're chummy as can be. After what *she* did?"

"What?" asks Joan, standing. "What'd she do?"

"That bitch did her best to wreck our family."

The woodpecker makes its way to the trunk of the oak

and explores a crack in the bark.

Joan's jaw flexes as she gathers her thoughts. With forced composure, she says, "Allison, dear? Your father and I were married almost four years when you finally came along. Bringing you into the world—it meant everything to us. Everything. That's why we named you Venus."

"I've heard this song before, Mom."

"But it wasn't easy. You see—try as we may—I was infertile. Old Doc Schneider called me 'barren as a brick.'" Joan laughs at the memory. "His bedside manner always did leave something to be desired."

Through a squint, I ask, "You were . . . 'barren'?"

"Still am. It's not a condition that improves with age." With a wry grin, she adds, "Allison, honey. Connect the dots. Far from wrecking our family, that so-called bitch *made* us a family."

After a long, breathless pause, I summon just enough oxygen to ask, in a whisper, "You're not my mother?"

Joan leans very close. I hear a hint of menace in her words: "I'll *always* be your mother, dear."

Inez rises from the table and moves in my direction.

The woodpecker toils overhead, showering us with flecks of bark.

❏

PART 2

SEVEN

A Familiar Face

The prospect of starting over had never felt so real or immediate. This was no metaphorical "new beginning." This was no everyday resolve to shake things up, to broaden his horizons. No, this was a total leap into the unknown—and the plane was leaving in ten minutes.

Brody Norris boarded the Chicago-bound flight in Los Angeles. He'd been upgraded to first class, a good omen, he hoped, for the start of his chapter two. He'd requested a window seat—the better to witness the passing of some two thousand miles as morning slipped into afternoon, separating his past from his future—and that wish, too, was granted. Settling in, buckling up, he wondered if by some miracle the adjacent aisle seat would remain empty for the next four hours, but he knew that this third wish was pushing his luck. It was the week after Christmas, two days till New Year's, and flights were jammed.

He'd never owned a winter coat. Ski jackets, sure, but not a proper topcoat. So last week he splurged (hell, it was Christmas) and bought a cashmere Loro Piana, which was now stowed overhead in a rumpled heap. Other than the coat, he'd brought only a leather messenger bag. Everything else, pared down to the bare essentials, he'd sent ahead. It was a clean break.

Opening the messenger bag, he retrieved his iPad for a

last check of e-mails before takeoff. Finding nothing new, he switched off the tablet and pulled from his bag a glossy, oversize magazine, the autumn edition of *ArchitecAmerica*. Three months old, the issue had already been read, reread, and studied, looking frayed around the edges. The cover depicted a dramatic, sprawling building, a performing-arts center set into the rocky crags of a wooded ravine. A crisp white headline emerged from the darkness of the trees: AT ONE WITH NATURE. Smaller, below it: *Iconic Blend of Form and Function in the Midwest.*

"Drink before blastoff?"

Brody looked up to find a male flight attendant leaning toward his seat with a tiny tray bearing an icy, amber-colored cocktail. A name badge adorned with a sculpted pair of wings identified the crewman as Vega.

Brody grinned. "What's in it?"

Vega winked. "Specialty of the house."

Glancing about, Brody saw that no one else had been served. "Are you sure there's time?"

Vega leaned closer. "I'll hold the friggin plane for *you*, doll." He swirled the tray; the ice rattled. "Here's to ya."

Brody was tempted, but he could hear the engines ramping up. The electricity died for an instant, then returned as the plane switched to its own power. "I'd better wait. But thanks—maybe later."

"Lemme know," said Vega. With a little growl, he added, "I'll be ready when you are." And he swished off to the galley.

Brody leaned his head to the window and saw the catering truck hoisted up to the fuselage, delivering battered aluminum serving carts. The exhaust of jet engines wafted through the cabin with the savory smells of lunch. A wedge of sunshine sliced across his forehead and landed on the aisle seat next to him, still empty. He checked his watch. Dare he believe it? With each passing minute, it appeared more likely he would enjoy some extra elbow room. Perhaps, once aloft, Vega would return, invite himself to sit down, and juice up the flirtation. Not that Brody was interested — he preferred older men — but it would help pass the time.

The catering truck pushed away, and then Vega assisted a stewardess in the rigmarole of closing the cabin door. But the chatter of walkie-talkies interrupted them, and soon the door was open again. One last passenger arrived in a fluster and made a beeline for the empty aisle seat as the door thumped shut and the engines whined louder.

She was middle-aged, ten or fifteen years older than Brody, probably in her late forties. She carried an overcoat and a shopping bag loaded with gifts while towing a wheeled carry-on, packed to the point of bursting. Her face was plain but pleasant. Familiar too, though Brody had no reason to think he might know the woman. Rather, she struck him as a "type" — a teacher, perhaps, or a counselor, a therapist, or someone's mom. Despite her harried entrance, she projected an aura of nurturing.

Vega helped with stowing her things and getting her settled while the stewardess recited the rites of departure. Brody felt a gentle thud as the plane began backing away from the gate. Vega removed Brody's Loro Piana from the overhead clutter and snapped the bin closed. "Let me hang this for you," he said, then disappeared.

Buckling her seatbelt, the woman breathed a raspy sigh of relief. She said to Brody, "Sorry for the last-minute hubbub."

"No problem at all. Glad you made it."

She turned to look at him. "That's very kind of you." Her

eyes lingered on his while the slightest wrinkle of her brow seemed to ask, Do I know you? She said, "Travel used to be such a pleasure."

Brody reminded her, "Getting there is half the fun."

She laughed.

The taxiing plane turned onto the main runway. The engines roared.

As soon as the plane leveled off at cruising speed, Vega returned and took their drink orders. The woman asked for white wine. Brody thought for a moment. "Surprise me."

"Oh, *honey*," said Vega with a suggestive lilt, then moved on.

The woman asked Brody, "Friend of yours?"

"He is now, I guess. But no, we've never met." Brody was about to add, That happens quite a bit. But he stopped himself. It seemed egotistical—telling a total stranger that other total strangers often cozied up to him, as if wanting to know him, trying to curry his favor. It had happened when he checked in at the airport that morning and the gal at the desk had so cheerfully gone out of her way to finagle his upgrade while a long line of hapless other passengers stretched out behind him to the curb.

His seatmate said, "You look familiar. And news flash: you're an attractive man. What I mean is, Do I know you from TV? Or the movies?"

He'd been asked that before. "Uh, no. I'm just a lowly architect."

"Nothing lowly about that."

He shrugged. "It has its rewards—the creative satisfaction—but very little glamour, at least by Hollywood standards."

"Hollywood standards are shallow at best. Enjoy the life you've got."

"I like your attitude."

"I like yours too," she said. "Now, tell me—how do I know you? You have such a familiar face."

He took a long, careful look at her features. "I must admit, as soon as you boarded the plane, I had the same feeling about you."

"Aha," she said. "Then it's not my imagination. Our paths *have* crossed." She extended her hand. "Dawn Forgash."

"Brody Norris." He shook her hand. "Ring any bells?"

"Sorry."

"Me neither. But I get the feeling you might be a teacher. A therapist? Something like that?"

She hemmed. "Nurse."

"A noble, caring profession—I commend you. But I haven't seen many doctors of late, so I doubt if that's the connection."

Dawn explained that she had been a floor nurse at Los Angeles Memorial for the past six years. Brody explained that he had never been there, as either a patient or a visitor.

Vega arrived with Dawn's wine and Brody's surprise, a pink lady, thick and frothy, garnished with a cherry.

"Yum," said Brody, tasting it. "I didn't realize you had a blender on board."

"We don't. Let's just say I can really shake it." He swiveled his hips and left.

Brody and Dawn continued to explore possible venues at which people might routinely encounter one another, absorbing familiar faces—restaurants, grocery stores, gyms, churches, clubs, and such—but they found no common links.

"Then it's a mystery," said Dawn.

And yet, the more they talked, the more Brody was convinced not only that they had met, but that they had spent considerable time together.

The pilot banked the plane gently to the right, announcing that passengers should take a look. Brody turned to his window and was astonished to find, seven miles below, a cloudless view of the Grand Canyon. Sunlight glinted from the golden thread of the Colorado River.

While waiting for lunch, the conversation lapsed as Dawn and Brody became absorbed in their own diversions. She worked at solving a Sudoku, filling in the numbers with a ballpoint pen; he opened his design magazine and began reading its cover story again from the start. After a few minutes, he noticed that she had finished the last square of the puzzle.

"I'm impressed," he said. "Plus, you did it in ink. I've never been able to figure those out."

"Once you get the hang of it, it's just logic, no math. And it's early in the week—they get harder each day." She folded up the newsprint, set it aside, and faced him. "And so, Brody Norris, do you mind if I ask: What takes you to Chicago?"

He blew a low whistle. "It's a long story. You first."

"My story's pretty simple. I have two daughters. One lives in L.A., the other near Chicago. They both have young kids—still at that adorable stage—so grandma does double duty, alternating Christmas and New Year's. The L.A. brood got me for Christmas this year, so now I'm due in Chicago."

"Keeps you on the run," said Brody. "That's sweet of you."

"It's a hassle, all right, traveling over the holidays. But who am I kidding? I love it."

"They're lucky to have you. I never really 'had' grandparents."

Dawn smirked. "That's ridiculous, you know."

"I mean, I never met them. In fact, on my father's side, I didn't even know who they were. Up until a few years ago, I didn't know who my *father* was."

"Sounds complicated."

"Let's just say I had an unconventional upbringing."

With a toss of her hands, Dawn asked, "What's *conventional*? Growing up, nobody feels normal—nobody. Then boom, you're an adult, and everything's still out of whack." She paused before adding, "My husband left me when I turned forty. Classic, huh?"

Brody was tempted to say, That's nothing—my husband dumped *me* at the callow age of thirty-five. Instead, he said, "I'm so sorry."

"Thanks, but I got over it. Life goes on."

"I believe you, Dawn. But I just had a setback of my own. Still dealing with it."

"Oh, dear." She eyed him with a motherly frown of concern. "What happened?"

He answered with a question. "Your husband—he left you for a younger woman?"

"Yes." She grinned. "He joked for years about trading me in on a younger model. And then, sure enough, he did it."

"Same story," said Brody, "except *my* husband never joked about trading me in. Never even hinted at it. But that didn't stop him from doing it. The irony is, he has *kids* my age from an earlier marriage, so I always worried that I might be too young for him. Boy, did I get *that* wrong."

"When did all this happen?"

"We were married six years ago. He's an architect, so we went into business together. For an upstart, our firm was doing great. Then he went all googly over one of our clients, a techie whiz kid, richer than God, still in his twenties. I got suspicious about a year ago; they came clean a few months later. And now? The divorce is final; the business is closed. So I'm picking up the pieces—and starting over elsewhere."

Dawn nodded. "And that's why you're flying to Chicago."

"That's the first leg of the trip. At O'Hare, I change planes for Green Bay. And from there, I'll drive an hour or two—don't laugh—to Dumont, Wisconsin."

Dawn wasn't laughing. Bewildered, she asked, "Why *there*?"

Brody showed her the magazine cover. "Because *this* is in Dumont. It was designed by my uncle and his business partner, who also happens to be an uncle, by marriage."

Dawn noted, "Lots of architects in your family . . ."

"Unusual, yes, but it's not the coincidence that it seems. You see, I've been to Dumont only once before, about twenty years ago, to attend my uncle Ted's wedding. I was fourteen and impressionable and starting to think about the future. My mother and I were there for about a week. I visited Ted's architecture firm and met his partner, Marson Miles. I took it all in, and that was it—I just *knew*, then and there, that I'd found my calling."

"That can happen," said Dawn. "A friend of my mother's was a nurse. I wanted to be like her."

"In retrospect," continued Brody, "it seems downright magical, and a bit scary, how things can click like that. Destiny, I guess. Forks in the road. What if I hadn't made the trip that summer? I have no idea where my life might've led, but there's no reason to think I'd be an architect. Today, I can't imagine otherwise—it's who I *am*."

Though Brody didn't say it, there was something else he could not imagine. What if he had never met Marson Miles?

At fourteen, Brody had already announced that he was gay, but it was still an abstract identity to him, rooted more in self-perception than in erotic attraction. Rarely, for instance, did he fantasize about the guys, let alone the girls, he knew at school. But the moment he walked into his uncle's office and met Marson, he experienced a powerful vibe. It shot from his brain to his groin, signaled the end of his boyhood, and gave him a fiery foretaste of what it would mean to be a gay man.

It would be easy to dismiss Brody's adolescent crush on Marson as a misplaced longing for a father figure, as the predictable outcome of being raised by a single mom, a feminist lesbian who not only accepted, but celebrated, her son's nonconformity. But even at fourteen, Brody was sufficiently self-aware to see beyond the armchair psychology. While his attraction to Marson was real, he understood that it could not be reciprocated. Not only was Brody underage, but Marson was married to his partner Ted's sister, Prucilla, whom the boy found as dislikable as her name. *Why*, he wondered back then, had Marson wed such a woman? Brody's disappointment, however, was countered by insight: he recognized, with sudden clarity, his powerful attraction to older, creative men. It was an attraction that would shape his libido and color his fantasies as he went away to college and then grew into adulthood.

Had it been obvious, Brody now wondered, that Marson had both stirred his young passions and set the course of his career? Did Marson even remember their first encounter, twenty years ago?

"And now I'm going to work for them," Brody told Dawn. He opened the magazine for her. "Miles & Norris is just a small local firm, but they're getting some killer projects, now that Questman Center has made such a splash." He explained how the performing-arts center, completed earlier that year, had garnered both critical and popular acclaim, putting Dumont, as well as Miles & Norris, on the architectural map.

Dawn paged through the story, studying the photos. "I'm no expert," she said, "not by a long shot—but wow—this is magnificent."

Brody nodded. "They're doing great work. And I'm flattered they think I have something to offer."

She closed the magazine. "It's a long way from Los Angeles. Can you handle that?"

"Well, *sure,*" he said.

At least I hope so, he thought.

Somewhere over the Great Plains, passing over the Missouri River and into Iowa, Brody and Dawn finished lunch and settled back, Dawn reading, Brody dozing off.

A while later, Brody awoke to hear Dawn conversing with Vega, who had arrived to clear their trays. Brody listened, eyes closed, as Dawn quietly told the steward, "I hope he's not making a mistake. It could be a serious culture shock."

"A city mouse if *I've* ever seen one," agreed Vega. "What's he gonna do for fun out there in the sticks—make *cheese*?"

With a sputter of laughter, Brody blinked his eyes open and entered the conversation. "I appreciate your concern, but it's not as if I've never seen a *tree* before."

Vega didn't buy it. "Palm trees don't count, handsome. You won't find *those* in Wisconsin. Half the year, you'll be shoveling snow. The other half, you're up to your ass in dead pinecones. Not to mention the mosquitoes—big as sparrows, straight from the depths of hell."

Dawn snickered.

Brody assured both of them, "I'll be fine. Granted, I'm used to the noise and hustle of L.A., but I've also enjoyed a fair amount of quiet, rustic living. My family built a second home years ago, a mountain retreat up in Idyllwild. Snow and pinecones—been there, done that."

Dawn raised her fingers to her lips, as if she'd thought of something.

Vega shook his head. "In Idyllwild, it's a short hop to L.A. But in Wisconsin, you're just plain stuck."

Brody reminded him, "You know what they say: it's not *where* you live, but *how*."

Vega dropped the attitude. "Lotsa luck, doll. I mean that sincerely." And he left with the lunch trays.

Brody lifted his tray table and locked it upright. "He makes a fabulous pink lady, but I wonder if the airline—"

Dawn interrupted, touching his arm. "I *knew* I recognized you."

Brody looked at her hand, then at her face, studying her features again, trying to remember.

She said, "Ten years ago, I was a hospice nurse, working out of Riverside. They sent me up to Idyllwild to care for the victim of an intracranial aneurysm."

Brody caught his breath.

"He'd ruptured in Hemet and was hospitalized in Riverside. The diagnosis was bleak, and the family wanted him to die at home. His name—"

Brody said it with her: "His name was Gordon Harper."

Dawn continued, "He hung on for about ten days. The family was wonderful."

"No, Dawn," said Brody. "*You* were wonderful. I can't believe you're here, sitting next to me. I've thought of you many times. Over the years, we've often talked about you— how grateful we were to have you. I know you were there because of Gordon, but you helped *us* as well."

"I knew he was a professor or something, but I didn't get the big picture till after he died, when I read about it. Good Lord—astrophysics, Nobel Prize—while I was up there at the house, no one ever mentioned it to me. No one tried to impress me with it. He was just Gordon."

"My extended family," said Brody, "they're a free-spirited bunch. Never stood much on ceremony."

Dawn exhaled a wistful sigh. "I spent many hours alone with him, and he had his lucid moments—never would've guessed he was such a big shot. Up till the end, great attitude, great sense of humor. I haven't seen that too much. Most people, if they're cogent, they're mad as hell that they're dying. Either mad or remorseful. But he seemed to have no regrets."

"That was Gordon," said Brody. "He accomplished a lot. Big ideas, big dreams."

Dawn took Brody's hand. "Your father was very proud of you."

Brody hesitated before saying, "Gordon was my father, but I didn't know that till several years after he died."

"To be honest," said Dawn, "I was a little confused regarding who's who up there."

With a chuckle, Brody asked, "Did I mention my unconventional upbringing?"

"You did indeed." She paused, recalling, "You were away when this happened—"

"I was still in grad school, and I had trouble getting a flight back on short notice. There was a storm—"

"And Gordon kept asking for you. He said things about you that I didn't understand. But he made me promise: 'If my son doesn't get here in time, tell him his dad loves him.' And I said, 'Of course I'll tell him. But I'm sure your son already knows that.' And you know what Gordon said? Nothing. He winked at me."

Brody smiled, imagining his father's exchange with the nurse.

"And a few hours later," said Dawn, "you walked through

the door, so I waited outside the bedroom with the other women, to give you and Gordon some time alone. It was nice to know you both had a chance to say whatever needed to be said."

"In fact," said Brody, "not much was said. I just sat with him. It was good to be together."

Dawn patted his hand. "Then I'd better make good on my promise. Brody, sweetheart—wherever your dad is hanging out these days, he wants you to know that he loves you. He said to tell you he was sorry. He wished he could have been more of a father to you. I didn't know what he meant."

Brody squeezed her hand and mouthed a silent thank-you.

Then he lolled his head back against the seat. Just above the threshold of perception, he felt the nose of the plane make a subtle but distinct dip. The engines, which had droned in the background for hours, unnoticed, eased back from their forward rush, softening their whine.

Turning his gaze to the window, Brody watched as the Mississippi disappeared to the west.

The plane had begun its long, slow descent toward Chicago.

❏

EIGHT

Upstaged

They arrived in the concert hall and rushed to be seated mere moments before the houselights dimmed and the conductor strode out to the stage. He paused to acknowledge the applause, then stepped up to the podium, directed a fierce downbeat, and launched the orchestra's brass into a loud, spirited reading of a Rossini overture. What was it — *Semiramide? Thieving Magpie? Barber of Seville?* Marson Miles always got them mixed up.

He and Brody Norris had not even had time to glance at their programs, let alone exchange pleasantries with other concertgoers — which, from Marson's perspective, was the whole point. Although he was an exacting and punctual man ("to a fault," according to his newly estranged wife, Prucilla), he had risked arriving late for the concert in order to avoid chitchat in the auditorium while the orchestra tuned. Dumont was a small town. Everyone there in the dress circle that Saturday night knew each other. Everyone, that is, except for Brody Norris, who had moved to Wisconsin from California only ten weeks earlier. And now, there he sat, next to Marson, in the red velvet seat that had been occupied, during every prior concert that season, by Prucilla.

The music drove forward, a series of themes so bright and hummable, they struck Marson as clichés, bringing to mind the Bugs Bunny cartoons of his youth. As his eyes adjusted to the darkness of the hall, the light spilling from the stage to his lap enabled him to read the printing on the cover of the program, so he flipped it open to the middle page, where the musical works were listed. The overture— ah, yes—it was *Light Cavalry*, not Rossini at all, but Suppé. The pounding hooves should have been clue enough. Scanning through the other works, his eyes tripped on a single word, INTERMISSION. Mingling would be mandatory, chitchat unavoidable.

He needed to get over this. He was a grown man—about to turn sixty, to be exact—and if he had left his wife of thirty-some years for a man of thirty-some years, that was his business. Granted, he was old enough to be Brody's father, but he was also old enough to make his own life-changing decisions without explaining to small-minded gossips. If he could find the strength to redefine himself and change the path of his future, no one else mattered.

Except Brody, of course. The transitions he faced made Marson's pale by comparison. Brody's marriage to another man in California had recently ended in divorce, dissolving not only the relationship, but also the business they had founded together, an architectural firm. So he was now starting over—two thousand miles from the home and the life he had always known—in the employ of the firm founded by his architect uncle, Ted Norris, and Ted's business partner, Marson Miles. A small local practice, Miles & Norris had scored national recognition a year earlier with the opening of Questman Center, the performing-arts complex in which everyone now listened to Franz von Suppé's beloved chestnut of an overture.

The infectious, galloping rhythm had the audience bouncing in their cushy seats as the cavalry rode to the rescue, trumpets blaring. No one was immune—not Mary Questman, the wealthy widow in the front row who had led the campaign to build the center; not Thomas Simms, the elected black sheriff of lily-white Dumont County who sat with his wife, Gloria, in the second row; not the symphony board president, Debbie Jacobson, seated in the third row with her husband and son; not Glee Savage, seated on the aisle, reviewing the concert for the *Dumont Daily Register*; not Marson Miles, sitting fifth-row-center, who had designed the magnificent theater, and not Brody Norris, whose bouncing knee tapped Marson's to the beat of the music.

And that's how it had started, recalled Marson, ten weeks earlier on New Year's Eve, when Brody's knee had touched his under the dinner table. He had met Brody only once before, during a brief visit when the kid was fourteen. So the New Year's dinner was a reunion of sorts as Brody returned to Dumont—and at the crowded restaurant that night, under the linen-draped table, their knees made contact. That simple act, that innocent touch, had changed Marson's life. Or rather, it had clarified something that had been there all along.

Though he had never admitted to anyone, least of all himself, that his three decades with Prucilla had been a marriage of convenience—loveless as well as childless—many in Dumont had suspected the truth, despite Marson's impeccable fidelity. He had vowed not to stray, and stray he did not. But New Year's morning, he initiated the split with Prucilla and took Brody to brunch. That afternoon, Marson was reborn when at last he made love to another man. As the days of his new life grew to weeks, he began spending more nights at Brody's sparse apartment than at the splashy house he had built in the hopes of keeping Prucilla happy, a failed effort. And now, just yesterday, he and Brody had signed the papers on their purchase of a commercial loft in downtown Dumont, which they planned to transform into their first real home.

Prucilla, the wronged woman, had slipped into her new role with surprising ease and well-honed cynicism. Friends said her carping could not conceal an underlying zing they hadn't seen in years. When her gal-pals asked, with delicious anticipation, if she planned to attend the upcoming concert with Marson, Prucilla announced that she'd decided instead to slip out of town and drive down to Kohler, near Sheboygan, for a spa weekend at the American Club.

Which presented Marson with the opportunity he had been both seeking and dreading. It was time, he knew, to go public with his situation, to make it official that he and Brody were now a couple, a social unit. Granted, he didn't need anyone's permission to do what he was doing, but at his age, why be coy? There was neither time nor reason to live a lie. And even if he were inclined to take that path, Brody would have no part of it—the younger man had been open about his sexual identity since adolescence. Coming out seemed to be a non-issue for Brody's generation, and Marson would have to catch up. There could be no shared life with one of them stuck in the closet.

More to the point, Marson felt no shame, so why fear the rebuke of petty intolerance? Far outweighing those fears was the pride felt by Marson: not only had he found happiness in correcting, however late, the true direction of his life, but he had found that joy with a much younger and supremely attractive man. In straight parlance, he had bagged the counterpart of a trophy wife that would be the envy of any like-minded red-blooded male.

And now—with Prucilla packed off to Sheboygan,

wrapped up to her ears in mud and kelp—not only could Marson enjoy the spring concert in Dumont with Brody at his side, putting their couplehood on full display, but he could also drop the bombshell about the loft, sending a very public message that he and Brody had taken a significant step into their joined future.

All that and more, Marson promised himself, could be handled at intermission. Meanwhile, he placed his fingers over Brody's on the cushioned arm between their seats.

Brody turned to Marson with a loving smile.

His eyes glistened in the light from the stage.

Intermission was a long time coming, as the program proved to be a tad ambitious for the local orchestra. The crowd-pleasing overture, played loud enough and fast enough to mask the ensemble's deficiencies, was followed by a lush tone poem from the late romantic era, which proved beyond the reach of the orchestra's limited forces. Worse yet was the centerpiece of the program's first half, the premiere of a new flute concerto by a faculty member from the nearby university. The performance featured the composer as soloist, a lanky woman in a baby-blue gown who stood before the orchestra, bobbing and blowing her way through three lugubrious movements titled "Apocalyptic Dawn," "High Noon of Hydraulic Fracturing," and the finale, "Night Sweats." Its slow, piercing atonalities did in fact cause Marson to break into a sweat. His pants stuck to his thighs; his back burned against the hot velvet of the seat; his hand felt clammy against Brody's, so he slipped it away.

The piece stopped after an indecisive cadence, and at first the audience was unsure if the performance had ended. But when the flutist lowered her instrument and the conductor lowered his baton, the crowd rose in unison with thunderous applause. Surely, thought Marson, the standing ovation was neither warranted nor sincere. Rather, the audience was restless beyond endurance, itching to get up, cool off, and move out to the lobby for intermission.

Shuffling up the aisles toward the doors, everyone glanced at each other with steely smiles, engaging in none of the expected gab: They sure nailed it . . . we can say we heard it first . . . wasn't she fabulous? No, their expressions seemed to ask, Is the bar open?

Once in the lobby, the milling crowd still spoke not of the concert, but of the warmer weather, spring break at the college, travel plans, March Madness. As the grating chatter reverberated in the soaring heights of the lobby, Marson guided Brody to the Founders' Room, a VIP lounge reserved for the center's major donors.

Mary Questman stood near the bar amid a clutch of local notables. Inching toward seventy now—with more riches remaining from her late husband's paper and timber dynasty than she could ever spend on herself—she reigned as Dumont's undisputed grande dame. A benign monarch with a sweet nature, a generous spirit, and a zest for later life, she topped the list as almost everyone's favorite person. Motherly yet childless, she relished her role as loving elder to the entire community.

"Marson dear," she said as he entered, "I'm dying to meet your nephew."

Marson cringed at the notion of doing the things he'd been doing—with his *nephew*. And Mary was technically correct, in that Brody was indeed Marson's nephew— by marriage. That, after all, was their original connection. Brody had first visited Dumont for a family wedding when he was a boy, accompanied by his mother, Inez Norris, who was the sister of both Marson's wife, Prucilla Miles (née

Norris), and Marson's business partner, Ted Norris. With Marson's marriage soon to be dissolved, however, he took comfort in rationalizing that when Prucilla ceased to be his wife, Brody would cease to be his nephew.

The little crowd surrounding Mary parted as Marson ushered Brody forward and made the introductions. "It's great to have some younger blood in the office," Marson told Mary. "Brody's a talented architect. We're lucky to have him."

Mary touched the younger man's arm. "Welcome to Dumont, Brody — how delightful that you've settled here." Then she turned to wink at Marson. "I admire your taste."

Okay, thought Marson — she knows. She might be getting on in years, but she's got the picture and she's no prude, thank God.

Brody told Mary, "I admire his taste as well. Marson talks about you all the time — in glowing terms. He knows his stuff."

"You bet he does!" said Mary with a laugh. "Why do you think I *insisted* he get the design contract for the center?" She didn't need to explain that "the center" was the one bearing her name.

As Brody and Mary continued their banter, singing the praises of the arts and architecture and their impact on the community, Marson reflected on his journey of the past year, since the opening gala and dedication of Questman Center last spring. That night, he had been called to the stage by the mayor. Marson's brief and humble comments were met with riotous applause from the audience seated before him and from the orchestra behind. How often, he wondered, does an architect receive a tribute like *that*, hailed as a hero?

It was embarrassing at first. He attended as many events as he could — theater, music, dance — because he enjoyed the performances and wanted to take full advantage of the splendid new facility, not because he expected the adulation of everyone who recognized him whenever he set foot in the place. During those early months, the fulsome back-slapping, the tributes from the stage, had tempted him to stay away, but Prucilla wouldn't hear of it. She relished the attention, the shared glory, and Marson knew better than to thwart her wishes.

But time had a way of changing things. His hero status had begun to wear thin; when he appeared at recent events, he was seldom acknowledged with anything more effusive than a sociable nod. And on the home front, Prucilla's overbearing presence was at last slipping out of his life and into his past. As if by magic, though, just as his Questman Center laurels began to wilt, Brody had appeared—a new source of pride and promise and emotional treasure. Alexander Graham Bell had left the world with a dubious aphorism: When one door closes, another door opens. Marson had always found those words saccharine at best, delusional at worst. But not now.

Now it was hard *not* to view Brody's arrival as anything less than a triumph of fate, a happy accident that led Marson through a new door, wide open, and set in motion a long-overdue transition—so much better late than never. How could he have risked a tardy arrival at the concert hall that evening? He saw with sudden clarity that the possibility of gossip presented scant danger. A far greater peril lurked in failing to celebrate the moment when he could make his newfound joy known to the world—or at least to the local gentry assembled there at Questman Center.

Marson and Brody! A new life! A new home—they had purchased a loft! He would not announce it from a stage, although he felt like doing so. It would suffice to clear his

throat, to draw the attention of the friends and acquain-
tances scattered around him there in the Founders' Room,
and just say it. A little speech of sorts, and it would be
done. He had prepared no remarks, but he was good on his
feet. He could handle this. He could begin with a dash of
humor. Self-deprecating humor. A classic ploy to win over
an audience, a trick that clicks, as they say —

"Who's that?" asked Brody, leaning close, speaking low.

Pulled from his thoughts, Marson turned in the direction
of Brody's gaze.

"Over there," continued Brody with a subtle jerk of his
head. "The guy with the purse."

Marson snickered. "That's not a *purse*."

"Then it's the biggest man-bag *I've* ever seen."

It was big, all right. And it did look like a purse, thought
Marson. It was a shade too red to pass for oxblood. It had
shiny gold bling for a clasp and more on the strap.

"What's he got in there?" asked Brody. "A change of
clothes?"

"Now, stop that," said Marson, although the bag was indeed big enough to accommodate a clean shirt, a dopp kit,
fresh underwear, and some spare reading material to boot.

"He's been watching us," said Brody. "Seems to be with
his parents. When they're not looking, he peeks over at us."

Right on cue, the guy with the purse, maybe twenty years
old, peeked at them.

Marson explained, "That's the Jacobsons' son. His mother
is president of the Dumont Symphony Association — club
woman extraordinaire — name's Debbie, but everyone calls
her Diamonds."

Brody said, "Not to her face, I hope."

Marson grinned. "No. And her husband is Coach Jacobson, from Dumont High — teaches P.E. and American histo-

ry—coaches football or something. I presume he has a first name, but the kids just call him Coach, and everyone else calls him Jake."

"Appearances can be deceiving," said Brody, "but they sure *look* like an odd couple."

They sure did. Debbie was all makeup and glitz, while Jake, a bear of a man, looked out of place in a cheap, tight suit and skinny tie. His arms and legs stuffed his clothes like links of sausage. And rounding out the unlikely tableau was their son, the lanky, slope-shouldered lad with a purse. His features were delicate, his hair thick and straight and much too long.

Brody asked Marson, "What's with the kid?"

"Nice guy, but always kinda quiet. He grew up as Bobby, then Bob, then Rob. While he was still in high school, he started asking everyone to call him Robert."

"Gay," said Brody with an indifference that matched his certainty.

"Think so?" asked Marson. "I never gave him much thought. He's in college now—must be home for spring break."

Just then, Robert looked at them and, finding them staring back, turned away.

Marson glanced at his watch, not sure how long intermission would last. He still wanted to tell the gathering about Brody and him, about the loft, but a drink might be helpful. He asked Brody, "Can I get you something from the bar? I think there's time."

Brody shrugged. "Wine, maybe. Thanks." And he stepped over to the bar with Marson, where they waited behind another couple, who turned out to be Ted Norris—Marson's business partner, Brody's *real* uncle—and Ted's wife, Peg.

Just as they were about to greet them, a husky voice asked from behind, "Who's your friend, Marson?"

Marson turned to find Coach Jacobson standing in line behind them. As in the past, the architect found the coach's hulking presence discomforting, almost intimidating, though the guy's expression that night looked downright chummy.

"Hi there, Jake," said Marson, shaking the man's huge hand. "I'd like you to meet Brody Norris. Ted's nephew from California. Maybe you've heard—he's working for us now."

Beaming, the coach turned to Brody and pumped his hand. "Welcome to town, Brody. Connie Jacobson—pleased to meet you."

Marson thought, *Connie?* Really?

Through an uncertain smile, Brody replied, "Thank you . . . Connie. The pleasure's mine."

"It's bound to be a big adjustment, moving here. But not to worry—folks aren't as square as you might think."

"So it seems." Brody paused before adding, "Sir."

The coach then spun his attention back to Marson, clamped an arm over the architect's shoulders, stepped him away from the bar, and confided, "Marson, buddy? I don't know how you did it. I mean, living with Prucilla all those years? Hell, *I'd* be ready to switch teams." And he let loose with a spirited guffaw.

At that moment, electronic chimes signaled the end of intermission.

Marson's big announcement would need to wait.

Mary Questman often held an after-party for the concert clique at her home on Prairie Street, and tonight was no exception. The grand old house, a mansion by anyone's measure, could accommodate more than a hundred guests with ease, but these post-concert receptions were typically limited to a few dozen luminaries—conductor, soloist, the orchestra board, top-tier contributors, local press, and anyone else Mary was inclined to invite, including Marson and, by extension, Prucilla. Tonight it was the same old crowd, with the conspicuous absence of Prucilla, nixed by Marson and replaced by Brody.

A gifted hostess, Mary had a knack for gracious entertaining, grounded in an understanding of the needs of her guests. For instance: her vintage nine-foot Steinway, once played by Artur Schnabel after he'd fled Berlin and the Nazis, would not be played tonight, not even in the background, as her guests had already spent some two hours focused on music, which was enough. What's more, they had already sat too long, not speaking, so now they would be free to exercise their pent-up need to mingle and gab. Having rushed through early dinners, they needed hearty finger food. They needed cocktails. And the instant they walked through Mary's door, they were greeted by staff to tend to those needs, to whisk away their coats, to make them right at home. This was a time of elegant celebration, but not formality. For these events, Mary encouraged her guests to circulate at will through the living room, the central hall, the dining room, and even the kitchen, where they clustered and regrouped and clustered again to cap off an evening of cultural enrichment by sharing camaraderie and booze and the latest local buzz.

Few had a better handle on the local buzz than Glee Savage, who'd been reporting for the *Dumont Daily Register* for forty years. Features editor, entertainment critic, fashion maven, survivor—Glee had outlasted the paper's two previous publishers and the digital tsunami that had swept away so many small-town dailies, but not Dumont's.

Marson asked her, "What'd you think?"

She fingered the rim of her martini glass, half empty. Her ruby-red lips curled with a wry expression. "I've developed a working formula for my concert reviews. If it's a rave, I rave. If not, I fill the column with facts—what they played, what the soloist wore, who was there, etcetera. The reader gets the idea, and it saves me from trashing a performance, which seems cruel at the community level."

Marson nodded. "And tonight?"

She set down her glass. "Total attendance was eight hundred seventeen."

Brody entered the conversation: "Then it wasn't just me. That flute thing—the premiere—ouch."

Glee covered her ears and mimed a silent scream, à la Edvard Munch, then laughed. "The 'fracturing' theme was spot-on."

"And perhaps a shade too literal," said Brody.

Glee offered her hand. "Glee Savage. I've been waiting to meet you."

"My pleasure. Brody Norris."

With playful menace, she said, "I know your name. But I *want* your story."

Marson warned Brody, "Confide in Glee, and you've confided to the world."

She smirked. "The world of Dumont, maybe."

Brody said, "But I have no story—well, not much of one. Pretty dull."

"Oh, *honey,*" she said, leaning near, "you're the talk of the town. I run an occasional column under the kicker 'Inside Dumont.' These profiles aren't exposés, just puff pieces. How about it? Let's do lunch."

Brody hesitated. He turned to Marson. "Uh, any thoughts?"

Marson assured him, "You don't need *my* permission. Might be fun—a bit of backyard glory." Then he turned to Glee, suggesting, "If you hold off awhile, there'll be more to write about—like the loft." He stopped short.

"Loft?" said Glee, on full alert.

Oops. Too much too soon, thought Marson. The ink was barely dry on the purchase agreement. And negotiations for his divorce settlement were still at a delicate stage. Although his decision was made and his mind was clear — his future was with Brody — it would not look good for either him or Brody to crow in print about their happy adventure together, at least while Prucilla was still adjusting to an unexpected new reality.

"Glee," said Marson, "some of this may be newsy, but much of it is very personal, and for Prucilla, it's still raw."

Glee touched her fingers to Marson's forearm. "Of course."

"About the loft," he said. "Yes, Brody and I have decided to convert a downtown space into our new living quarters, which may in fact be a first for this town. Once that's under way, you might want to write about it — that's news. And it's yours if you want it."

"Great idea."

"Everything will be resolved soon enough, I hope. But let's keep it quiet till then."

She gave him a discreet thumbs-up. "Promise."

Good, thought Marson. Nothing in print, not yet. But in a sense, the story was already out there. As Glee had mentioned, it was the talk of the town. Which only underscored for Marson how important it was for people to begin hearing the story not through the grapevine, and certainly not through the press, but from him.

He needed to gather everyone together and say a few words that night.

But he needed to find the right moment.

As the party bubbled on and the guests relaxed into a spirit of merriment, they nudged from their collective mem-

ory the period of entrapment during which they were tor-
tured with the strident premiere of the flute concerto.
Two full hours had passed since it was played, and after
the downing of a few drinks, the piece didn't seem half
bad. The flutist was at the party—hard to miss her in that
spangled blue gown. As she mingled through the crowd,
liquor prodded the concertgoers to look her in the eye and
offer congratulations.

"*Loved* the underlying message," said the tweedy director
of the county library system. "Earthquakes in Wisconsin were
unknown before fracking."

"*Precisamente.*" The flutist held aloft a crostino of truffle-
infused pâté, pronged on the tips of her fingers. "Without
a social conscience, the arts are reduced to mere entertainment, to *pandering.*" She popped the food into her mouth.

While the flutist chewed, Debbie "Diamonds" Jacobson
told her, "The board was thrilled. The orchestra hasn't performed a world premiere in ages—if *ever.*"

Coach Jacobson chimed, "It was a *huge* night for Dumont."

Robert Jacobson, meanwhile, had made his way into the
kitchen. Clutching his purse, he approached the bar, where
Marson Miles fingered a gin bottle and weighed the possibility of a second martini.

"Go ahead," said Brody. "I'll drive."

"Too kind of you," said Marson. "That settles it: my love
for you is boundless."

"You had doubts?"

Marson grinned. "Not after last night."

"Hi, guys."

Marson and Brody turned in unison to find Robert standing behind them, peeping over their shoulders.

"Hi, Robert," said Marson. "Enjoy the concert?"

He waffled. "It had its moments."

Marson noticed that the younger man didn't have a drink. "Get you something?"

"No, thanks. I'm fine." Robert ran his fingers through a tress of his long, dark hair and tucked it behind one ear, which was pierced—not unusual for a guy of his age. But rather than a modest, manly stud adorning the lobe, there hung instead a sizable gold hoop of the sort worn by pirates or showgirls.

"Where are my manners?" said Marson. "You've been away at school, so you haven't met Brody yet."

The two men introduced themselves and shook hands.

Marson told Robert, "Brody just moved here from California."

"I've heard all about it," said Robert. "News travels pretty fast."

Marson's eyes slid toward Brody's.

"So," continued Robert, "you guys are, like, *together* now?"

Marson's tongue felt stuck in his throat—he needed to learn to deal with this.

"Right," Brody answered with ease. "It happened sorta fast, but sometimes, you just *know*. I guess we took a lot of people by surprise."

Robert's features twisted in thought. "Not really. Sure, maybe at first. But deep down inside? Not so much."

Marson wondered, What did that mean? Had the town understood all along that his marriage was a sham? Had they known he belonged with a man long before he was willing to admit it to himself? Had everyone been *humoring* him? What if he had never pieced it together for himself?

Brody was gabbing with Robert about college. "I always felt spring break was *way* overrated. I mean, it's supposed to be party time, right? But I always seemed to spend it catching up on class projects."

"I know," said Robert. "I've got a project of my own that needs attention right now." His serious tone implied that the project was more daunting than a twenty-page paper.

"What's your major?" asked Brody.

Robert hesitated. "I need to talk to you guys — I'd really appreciate it."

Marson gave Brody a brief, quizzical look, then turned to tell Robert, "Of course, we're all ears. I hope nothing's wrong."

"Can we" — Robert glanced about the room — "can we find someplace quieter? I mean, more private." The kitchen wasn't crowded, but guests popped in and out, gravitating toward the bar, while Mary Questman's grim-faced housekeeper, Berta, stationed near the back door, supervised the catering staff with hissed commands.

Marson knew the lay of the house well. There were two doors leading from the kitchen to the dining room. One of them, open that evening, provided direct access, with guests passing through it in both directions. The other, near the back of the kitchen, led through a butler's pantry, not in use that night, as the door was closed. "That way," said Marson, directing Robert and Brody with has gaze.

Marson followed as they made their way across the kitchen. Watching from behind, he decided that Brody was right — Robert was gay, no question. Why had he not picked up on this before? Was it because he had naively imagined that Robert's identity was constrained by his role as the coach's son? Or had Robert undergone a transformation since leaving for college? For lack of a better, kinder word, he was swishy. Not just the walk, not just the manner, but the way he dressed.

Marson hadn't noticed the shoes till now — little burgundy slip-ons that looked for all the world like Mary Janes. And Robert wore them with sheer, shiny hose. His shirt was more blousy than tailored, billowing over the waist of his pants. That, combined with the Joan Baez hair, the over-size earrings, and the shoulder bag, led Marson to conclude not only that Robert was in the process of coming out, but that he was having a tough time with the transition, that he had not yet found himself, that his confusion was surfacing in the bizarre statement he seemed to be making with his appearance. Or was something else going on?

Although Marson was still new to the scene, he under-stood that not every gay man could be pegged by his purse, real or metaphorical. He didn't feel that he himself, for example, had a girlie edge. Granted, he may have projected an air of refinement and sensitivity, but where was it written that those traits were off-limits in the male realm? And Brody, he didn't come across as effeminate at all—quite the opposite, in fact. Robert, on the other hand, seemed to embody every silly stereotype that had ever been dreamed up by a jaundiced straight world; all that was missing was a lisp. Which left Marson feeling on very shaky ground.

With their heads already bowed in conversation, Robert and Brody proceeded into the butler's pantry; the swinging door whooshed closed behind them as Marson held back for a moment, wondering what Robert needed to talk about, wondering how he himself could contribute any insights — any clarity — to the gray and murky miasma in which Robert seemed to be floundering. Let Brody handle this, thought Marson. Let Brody lead the way. He's younger.

When Marson stepped into the pantry, Brody was telling Robert, "Sounds like a good choice." Then Brody turned to tell Marson, "Big switch—he's picking up WGS."

A radio station, maybe? Marson was adrift. Stammering, he tried to formulate a question.

Robert explained, "I've switched majors—women's and gender studies."

"Oh?" said Marson with forced nonchalance. "What *were* you studying?"

"Construction management. It didn't seem to fit."

No kidding, thought Marson.

Robert continued, "But I found my *passion* in gender studies. And it was there all along—right under my nose, right there in the catalog. It's made the transition *so* much easier."

Brody told Marson, "Robert is in the process of transitioning from male to female."

Marson gave a thoughtful nod, wondering, Why would he do that?

"I've just started hormones," said Robert. "Surgery is still down the road. Lots more counseling to come, but it's been great, such a revelation—such a *validation,* after so many years."

Marson grappled for something to say: "You've given this a lot of thought, I guess."

"All my life, Mr. Miles. Gender dysphoria—that's what they call it now—often has an early onset, and I was no different. It sounds trite, but I felt like a girl growing up in a boy's body. It doesn't have quite the stigma that it once had, but going through it, it's still not easy."

As Robert continued to recount his journey, Marson marveled at the pace of change, as evidenced by the young man who stood before him. When Marson was a boy, he'd never even heard the word *gay,* let alone *transsexual.* When he was in college, gay rights had at last become a topic within the larger social dialogue, but even then, the prospect of acceptance and assimilation—to say nothing of prideful self-awareness—took a certain leap of imagination. And transgender issues were off the charts altogether. Now, though, huddled there in the pantry, he listened with interest as Robert and Brody's matter-of-fact discussion covered everything from restrooms to gender binaries to preferred pronouns.

Brody asked, "You'll be changing your name?"

Robert smiled. "Robin. I thought about Bobbie, but it seemed too cute."

"Robin," said Marson, trying out the new name. "I like it."

"*Thank* you, Mr. Miles. That's the first time I've heard the name from someone else. Maybe it's time to go public and start using it. You see, I was so excited when Mom told me on the phone about you and Brody. At school, going through this—everyone just does their own thing. But I was dreading spring break—coming home. I've gone through some obvious changes, and let's face it, there's not much of a gay culture in Dumont. So it helps to have role models."

Marson didn't feel like a role model; he felt he'd barely set foot in a new territory that he was still exploring, inch by inch. And he didn't quite understand the connection, psychological or political, between being gay and being transsexual. Was it the kinship in having strayed from the norm, having shared the same prejudices? He told Robin, "You're doing just fine." He thought, You're braver than I am.

"Tonight has to be awkward for my parents, but I'm surprised how supportive they've been."

Marson, too, was surprised. "Your *dad's* okay with this?"

"Totally. He seems to just *get* it—maybe cuz he grew up as a boy named Connie."

They all laughed.

Robin continued, "Mom and Dad, I've put them both through a lot. I should put an end to the whispering, at least for their sake."

Marson said, "Do it for your own sake, Robin."

"I will, Mr. Miles. Thanks again."

If Robin can do it, thought Marson, so can I.

The three of them emerged from the butler's pantry to find Mary Questman fussing in the kitchen with a tray of appetizers. Marson was forever surprised by the ease with which she wore her wealth, never lording her social station over others, content with the joy of being *part* of her community. She asked Berta, "Can you make sure Sheriff Simms gets one of these? He loves the baby lamb chops."

As Berta left the kitchen with the silver tray, Marson said, "You're the perfect hostess, Mary."

She turned. Big smile. "*There* you are. Where have you boys been hiding?"

"Nowhere. Just a little confab to settle some of the world's more pressing issues."

"That's nice." She turned to Robin. "You're empty-handed, Robert. You're old enough to *drink* now, aren't you?"

"Yes, ma'am, just last month. But I'm fine. Could I, uh, possibly use a restroom?"

"Of course, dear." Gesturing, she directed, "Just off the living room, down the front hall."

With a few parting pleasantries, Robin left the kitchen.

Mary began stirring something in a bowl and said with a wistful sigh, "They grow up so fast, don't they?" There was nothing in her tone to suggest that she disapproved of, or even questioned, Robin's unusual appearance.

Is she that open-minded? wondered Marson. I was far more judgmental, yet I'm ten years younger than she is. Plus, "glass houses"—it's not as if I myself haven't raised a few eyebrows.

And that's when Marson understood his kinship with Robin.

Brody was telling Mary, "The Jacobsons seem like a sweet family. The coach sure defies stereotypes."

"He does," said Mary, wiping her hands with a towel. "I guess that's why the kids like him—he doesn't bully them around like a drill sergeant." She paused. With a quizzical look, she added, "They don't win many games, though."

"Mary," said Marson, "I hate to impose on your hospitality, but I wonder if I could ask a favor."

"Anything, love. Anything at all."

"Brody and I have been together only two or three months, but I think . . . well, I think we have a future. And I'm sure some folks have been wondering what's going on, so maybe it's time for me to clear the air. I'm not ashamed of anything—"

"Nor should you be," said Mary.

"Thank you," said Marson. "So if you don't mind, perhaps I could gather your guests for a few moments and, well, I'd like to tell it like it is."

With a playful scowl, Mary eyed Brody. "You good with this?"

"You bet I am."

She gave a decisive nod. "Follow me, boys."

Leonard Babcock, conductor and music director of the local orchestra, was swanning about the living room in his tux, visiting clumps of guests just long enough to absorb their praise, then moving on to the next group. In the year since his arrival, he had trained nearly everyone in town to address him as Maestro.

"Lenny," said Mary, summoning him with a finger wag. When he stepped near, she asked, "May I press you into service, please? Marson here would like to say a few words, so maybe you could make a bit of noise on the piano to get everyone's attention."

"Noise?" He looked horrified.

"Well, *beautiful* noise, of course." Mary whirled a hand. "Like a fanfare or whatever."

"Ah!" he said, brightening. "Yes, I suppose I could improvise a rousing progression of chords—that ought to do the job."

"Maestro?" said the flutist, who was standing nearby. "Would you like a few trills as well? My instrument's in the car."

Sweet Jesus, *no*, thought Marson. The *last* thing I need is a hostile audience.

Mary told the flutist, "That might be gilding the lily, my dear. Don't trouble yourself."

So Lenny Babcock sat down at the Steinway, made a lavish display of cracking his knuckles, then let loose with a thunderous torrent of dominant sevenths that crashed and resolved, squelching the party babble. In awe-stricken silence, everyone turned toward the piano. Guests who had wandered to the dining room and kitchen filed back into the living room.

Mary stepped to the crook of the piano. "Thank you, Lenny." She turned to the crowd. "I hope you're all enjoying yourselves, and I apologize for interrupting the festivities, but our dear friend Marson Miles has something he'd like to say." She stepped aside.

Not knowing if Mary's words were meant as a cue for applause, the crowd played it safe and remained dead quiet.

Grinning, Brody nudged Marson and told him under his breath, "You're on, pal."

Marson moved to the piano and faced the expectant onlookers. "This may be an unusual evening for you." Attempting humor, he added, "I know it's an unusual evening for *me*." No one found it funny. He continued, "In fact, the last few months have been quite remarkable for me, and I'd like to tell you why."

Speaking from the far end of the living room, Marson could look beyond the mass of curious faces and see the center hall receding toward the kitchen. Berta skirted the edge of the crowd with her appetizer tray, now empty.

"Brody?" said Marson. "Could you maybe come here and stand with me?"

"With pleasure." Brody joined Marson at the piano.

Berta turned away and started down the hall toward the kitchen.

Marson told everyone, "Some of you have already met Brody Norris. Many of you have not. But I think it's safe to say that most of you have at least *heard* about Brody."

Down the hall, a door opened, then closed. Footfalls approached the living room.

"This isn't about Brody, though. And it's not about me, not exactly. It's about . . . well, it's about 'us.' You see —"

Berta's scream interrupted Marson as she dropped the metal tray on the limestone floor. The gaze of the crowd whipped away from Marson to peer down the hall, where Berta, mortified, scrambled to pick up the tray and vanish into the kitchen, revealing the object of her dismay:

There stood Robin, dressed in a skirt.

There was no mistaking it. It was not a kilt. It was not an out-there leather "man skirt." No, it was indisputably a real, honest-to-God woman's skirt—calf-length jersey, blood red, adorned with a riotous, asymmetrical pattern of cream-colored pussy willows. It coordinated well with the burgundy flats and made a statement, loud and clear.

Completing the look, Robin had applied some rusty-hued lip gloss and secured her hair behind one ear with a big gold barrette.

"Mrs. Questman?" she said with a note of apprehension, twisting the strap of her purse. "I'm sorry—I think I scared your maid."

A gentle wave of laughter passed through the crowd.

"Nonsense, dear," said Mary. "You look lovely."

After an uneasy silence, Robin asked, "Am I interrupting something?"

Marson said, "Not at all. I was about to share some thoughts with all our friends here, but you go right ahead. Please."

"Ladies first, huh?"

Marson chuckled. "That's right."

"Thank you, Mr. Miles." Robin cleared her throat. "I just wanted to let everyone know, you haven't been imagining things—I've been going through a lot of changes, and there are more to come. Meanwhile, I'm hoping you won't find this awkward or embarrassing. This is a small town. It's my home, and I love it, but I doubt that you've encountered this before. So please be kind to my parents; they need your support as much as I do. They've been just great. I'm so lucky and grateful."

Debbie Jacobson looked very bold and very proud. The coach, beaming, put his arm around her.

Robin continued, "And I need to mention Mr. Miles and his new partner, Brody. Thanks, guys, for listening and understanding and helping me find my way. You're fabulous together—congratulations. As for myself, well, I'm working on it. I'll spare everyone the details, but I think this pretty much says it." Her hands drifted from her blouse to her skirt. "You've known me all my life as Robert. But now?

Now I'm Robin."

As she fell silent, a murmur rippled through the crowd.

Then, with a slow, deliberate beat, Brody started to clap.

Within moments, the entire room was applauding, and Robin began to mingle — among friends. Glee Savage elbowed forward, snapping pictures with her iPhone. She told Robin, "We've *got* to talk."

After a minute or two, as the excitement waned, Mary said, "Now, Marson. What was it you wanted to tell us?"

Marson shrugged. "I think Robin covered most of it."

"Most of it?" said Brody. "I think you've been upstaged."

Upstaged, thought Marson. Delightfully upstaged.

❏

NINE

Crazy Thoughts

The women's writing group formed a loose circle in a clearing among the pines. At six thousand feet, the air seemed forever cool and fragrant, but now, in June, the afternoons began to carry the promise of summer's warmth. Life in the mountain community could be rigorous, but days like these were the glorious payback for a long winter, with its seclusion and its tire chains and its impossible, impassable winding roads.

"Did you see that truck?" asked Margo, getting comfortable in her folding lawn chair. Its straps squeaked as the aluminum frame sank into the matted pine needles. Thirty-five or so, Margo was one of the group's younger members. Her genre of choice was horror.

"The white pickup?" asked Susan, who'd driven up behind Margo. Like many women of her age, pushing sixty, Susan was hell-bent on writing a memoir, pronouncing it "mem-wah," which the others ignored. She'd been married to a black man for more than twenty years, with two children, now grown and gone. This biracial angle would allow her memoir to transcend the usual claptrap about baking cookies with the grandkids. Hers would be a memoir with meat on it.

"That's the one," said Margo. "Big white pickup—Chevy, I think—with all these built-in *toolboxes* or whatever, and overhead racks for *ladders* or whatever, and, and—"

"Guns?" suggested Susan.

"Right," said Margo, bobbing her head with growing excitement. "I didn't *see* any guns, but I'm sure he had them stashed somewhere in that big bad Chevy. And that *hound—"*

"Where did you see this?" said Inez Norris, settling into her chair, stacking papers on her knees in preparation for their critique. Inez was the group's informal leader—"facilitator," as they preferred to describe her role—because they met at her home, a commune of sorts called Zenithgate.

Built some fifteen years earlier by three small families who shared UCLA connections and a taste for counterculture, the rustic retreat near Idyllwild, high in the mountains of Southern California, now served as a permanent home to Inez and to Joan Harper, a widowed potter. But Joan was away for a month, in San Francisco, installing a gallery retrospective of her erotic large-scale ceramics, so Inez was on her own for a while.

Inez didn't mind the solitude; in fact, she loved it. Now in her mid-sixties, she'd paid her dues as an activist and organizer, devoted for decades to social equality in general and women's issues in particular. Having earned her stripes as both a feminist lesbian and a single mother, she could now enjoy the luxury of crusading more with the pen and less with boots on the ground, amassed with her sisters in protest. She had reached a point in life where at last she understood that tranquility was not so much a cop-out as a blessing. And where better to enjoy it than right there at Zenithgate, in the clearing in the woods? It had been used for everything from yoga classes to drum circles. And now it was the meeting place of her writers' group.

Jogging the stack of papers in her lap, Inez repeated, "The truck—where did you see this?"

Margo explained, "It was out beyond your driveway, down by all the mailboxes. He was stopped there when I drove by."

"The property beyond that ridge"—Inez gestured toward the back of the clearing—"it was sold a few months ago. Don't know who bought it, but they must be doing some work." With a roll of her eyes, she added, "It could *use* it."

Susan said, "I saw the dog too, sitting in the truck as it drove away. Looked like a basset hound."

There were many dogs in the surrounding hills. Pets. Watchdogs. Often in the evenings, one of them would hear something and yelp in imitation or warning. Then the chorus would begin, with dogs from scattered properties joining in, calling to each other, relaying the message, which echoed off into the distance. Inez was never sure if the message was one of alarm or if the dogs were just letting loose, singing to the approaching night. She'd noticed of late the addition of a new voice nearby, the distinctive baying of a hound.

"But the *best* part," said Margo, leaning forward with wide eyes, gripping the edge of her seat, "the best part was the *front* of the truck. Did you see it?"

The others glanced at each other, shaking their heads. The group sometimes numbered as many as twelve, depending on the progress of their writing, but today they were down to five.

"On the front of the truck," Margo continued, "on the grill or the radiator or whatever—you know how these yahoos mount animal parts, like antlers, as some sorta trophy or whatever? Well, *this* guy had a *brassiere* strapped across the grill!"

The others shared a gasp of disbelief. "Wait a minute," said one of the women, another of several memoirists in the group. "Are you talking about a protective *car* bra, like they put on sports cars?"

With a firm shake of her head, Margo assured them, "It was a woman's brassiere—you know, with hooters. *Big* ones. And get this—it was *red*. Like a bikini top. The straps were spread from headlight to headlight. Get the picture?"

The picture was so vivid, Inez hugged herself to quell a shiver. What sort of chauvinistic moron would make such a public display of his degrading view of women? If it was meant to be funny, the joke was on him—he was degrading only himself.

"Anyway," said Margo, "it gave me an idea for a story. Remember what Stephen King said: 'Good writing is often about letting go of fear.'"

The group had heard this lecture before, but its repetition always jazzed Margo while concocting new perils for her recurring heroine, named Marguerite.

"Think the unthinkable," she continued, on a roll. "Indulge in crazy thoughts. Set your mind free to break every taboo. Just ask: What might happen to a woman—Marguerite, for instance—if she found herself trapped by a guy with a red brassiere on his truck? What's the worst thing that could happen?" Almost salivating, Margo challenged the group, "Now make it *worse*."

They knew only too well what could, and would, happen to long-suffering Marguerite. There was a common thread to the plots in which she found herself entangled, with the major variables limited to the identity of the perp, his occupation, and his psychosis. Those differences aside, Margo's deranged villains always managed to hit upon the same sadistic fate for their same hapless victim. They would gag her, tie her to a chair, and then, by assorted means, relieve her of her nipples. Or her eyelids. Or both. And the tools employed in performing the excisions were never so merciful, swift, or obvious as a razor. Poor Marguerite — she had long ago exhausted her natural supply of these body parts. In its collective wisdom, however, the critique group refrained from pointing out that the cringe factor in Margo's stories had gone stale. What *else* might she come up with? Better the devil known.

"Well, then," Inez told her with a chipper tone of approval, "it seems you're on your way with a new story." She turned to Susan. "And how's the memoir going?"

"Forty pages this month, so it's moving along now. I finished the birth scene — Hank, my oldest — one of the book's milestones. I was eager to write about it. Any woman's first birth is special, but I think because Hank is both black and white, I loved him all the more. He made the marriage seem so real, so tangible." Susan paused. Single again, was she wondering what had happened to that marriage?

"Plus," said Inez, breaking the lull, "your first was a boy."

Susan nodded. "I didn't want to say that — equality and all — but yes, I was hoping for a son."

One of the other women asked Inez, "How's *your* son doing? Adjusting to Wisconsin?"

"He is indeed. It seems Brody's in love."

"Already? When did he move there — six months ago?"

"Right, just before New Year's. But Cupid wasn't far behind. Brody says his whole life changed that very first week." The details, Inez felt, were a bit complicated to share, at least at that moment. There was no quick way to explain that the object of her son's affections was a man named Marson Miles, who happened to be her sister's husband — but only till the divorce was final. Besides, the group had gathered to discuss their writing, not to trade updates about the amorous exploits of their adult children.

So Inez changed the subject. "I was going to bring you

copies of my latest essay, but it's too late to critique it. Turns out, it's being published in tomorrow's edition of the *Weekly*."

While the others in the group were honing their skills at writing fiction—or sauced-up memoirs that verged on fiction—Inez found it impossible, even in retirement, to retreat from the clashes that had driven her life, so her writing was limited to think pieces disseminated through political journals with a feminist bent. Sometimes, though, she contributed guest editorials to the local paper, the *Weekly Mountaineer*. One such column would appear the next morning.

"What's the topic?" asked Margo.

Inez hesitated. "It's a bit of a stew. I ran into Dorothy, the editor, a few days ago, and she had space to fill, so I cobbled something together from notes I was gathering for several different pieces. It covers the gamut—equal pay, breast cancer, reproductive rights. It's not my best work."

"But we'll all be reading it tomorrow," said Margo. Her lilting tone suggested she was itching for the opportunity to examine a less-polished specimen of their facilitator's work.

Inez understood that the others often found her writing dull—perhaps *dry* was the better word, given its academic style and persuasive purpose—but she'd always prided herself on the logic of her arguments and the precision of her rhetoric. With a chuckle, she asked the group, "Go easy on me, okay? It was a tight deadline."

The shriek of a buzz saw cut through the afternoon stillness.

A hound howled.

Two hours later, as the group was leaving, Inez had grown curious about the noise from the adjacent property. The guy with the truck had been making a racket with a variety

of tools, drilling and pounding as well as sawing, punctuated by the occasional crash of debris. "See you next
month!" Inez called to the other women, who waved as
they disappeared from the clearing and headed out front
for their cars. Inez then turned in the opposite direction,
crossed the clearing, and climbed the grassy ridge at the
rear of Zenithgate.

What a fright, she thought as she peeped over the top.
The adjoining parcel, maybe half an acre, was cluttered
with all manner of junk—rusting equipment of unknown
purpose, tires, a pile of crates as big as coffins, and a couple
of huge fiberglass containers that might have been septic
tanks, dug up and brimming, no doubt, with unthinkably
vile swill. As for the landscaping, it was nonexistent, just
wild growth, survival of the fittest.

The two buildings were in rank disrepair. One of them
resembled a small barn, perhaps intended as a garage or
work shed, but its dilapidated wooden doors, flung wide,
revealed only more junk, piled high within the darkness.
Across from the barn stood the house. It needed paint, its
trim needed fixing, and its roof needed replacing. But the
structure appeared sound, and in spite of the dismal surroundings, the design of the house conveyed a perverse,
woodsy charm, or at least the remains of it.

Inside, unseen, someone was busy—pounding and scraping, pounding and scraping. Then a figure appeared at an
upstairs window and dumped a wheelbarrow through the
opening. Chunks of plaster and chicken wire and lath tumbled to the ground, raising a cloud of dust that floated off
toward the trees. A dog darted out the front door, yowling
at the commotion. It was not a basset hound, but smaller,
a beagle, mostly white, splotched with black. Inez thought
of Snoopy.

Following the dog, a man emerged from the house. Tall and fit, he wore tan work boots, grubby military fatigues, and a camouflage vest. Inez guessed he was in his mid-thirties, about the same age as her son.

The man walked behind the house. A truck door slammed; its engine roared to life. The big white Chevy crept out from the shadows, crunching gravel as it pulled to the front of the house, then backed up to the porch. Its front end afforded Inez an unobstructed view of the reported brassiere, plump and red and brazen.

He killed the engine, jumped out of the truck, and hoisted a contraption from the rear—a tank connected to cords and hoses, plus an armload of fierce-looking attachments. He lugged everything indoors, followed by the dog. Inez heard them trudge up the stairs.

A few moments later, a new sound came from the house, a loud churning, driven by an electric motor. It churned and churned, then came to a sudden stop, as if holding its breath. Inez figured it was a compressor, building up air pressure. After a short pause, *bang* came the first shot—*bang-bang*, a couple more—then a steady, rhythmic series of shots as the guy in the fatigues shattered the alpine stillness with blasts of metal piercing wood. It was a nail gun.

It sounded like a weapon. A horrible, grisly weapon.

Next morning, as usual, the work next door began by seven-thirty, while Inez was still waking up with coffee, lounging on the deck of the main house, enjoying the twitter and rustle of the surrounding woods. But the mood was trashed by the power tools, especially the nail gun, so she moved indoors and cranked up some Pussy Riot—to hell with her misogynist neighbor.

By midmorning, when she had dressed for the day and

turned off the music, the noise next door had stopped. Good, she thought — that cretin must be on his lunch break already. Cold cuts and a pint of Old Crow, no doubt.

She checked her watch. Deciding the mail had arrived, she headed outdoors, following the long driveway to the access road and then down to the main road, where a row of country-style mailboxes served some dozen properties. Recalling that her column was due to be published in the *Weekly Mountaineer*, she quickened her pace as the mailboxes appeared from around a bend. Just as she reached them, the white Chevy pickup came into view, turning from the main road and pulling over.

As Inez opened the latch of the Zenithgate box, the truck came to a stop, its front grill only a foot or so away from her. The big red bosoms — stuffed, pert, and pointy — came within inches of her own. Stepping back a pace, she noticed the truck's vanity plate; the guy's name, it seemed, was Nick. The bed of the truck contained a load of drywall.

"Morning," said Inez as the guy leaned across the beagle, reaching through the passenger window to one of the mailboxes.

Nick glanced at her, nodded, and flipped the box open. He needed a shave.

Inez retrieved her *Weekly*, along with the rest of her mail, and closed the box. She noticed that Nick had also received the paper as he plopped a stack of mail onto the seat and settled back behind the wheel. Since the brassiere seemed intended to invite comment, she said, "That's a nice set of bazookas you've got there."

He stared at her for a moment without expression. Then he started to laugh.

Inez wasn't sure what to make of his reaction. It made her uneasy, so she turned and crossed the road, heading back to the house. What freaked her out, though, was the howl of the dog.

It was howling with laughter. It was laughing at *her*.

That afternoon, Inez tinkered at the kitchen counter, putting away a few lunch dishes she had earlier washed and left to dry. The house seemed empty; Zenithgate felt deserted. Back when the compound was built, there were often seven or eight people staying there, but now she was alone and found it unnerving. Beyond the ridge at the back of the property, Nick's power tools banged and screeched. There was no escaping the noise as it muscled across the clearing and through the open windows with the warm June air.

The *Weekly Mountaineer* was on the dining room table, spread open to the opinion page. Dorothy, the editor, had not exaggerated—she'd had plenty of space to fill, which doubtless signaled the start of the summer lull. As a result, Inez's column was given conspicuous display, with its text set a point or two bigger than normal and a huge author's photo that, while not unflattering, Inez found embarrassing. The headline screamed, ALL SHARE GUILT FOR CRIME OF BREAST CANCER. Dorothy had written that, not Inez, but the column itself, Inez realized with a wave of chagrin, was no better. It was a screed—a ranting, radical feminist screed from a militant old lesbian. Her mission had merit, but her message was off by a mile.

And there it was in print, her bitching and haranguing for all to see, including that lug next door. If he bothered to open the paper, he couldn't miss it, and then he would know the identity of the woman by the mailbox, the dyke he'd laughed at. Even his dog had found her ridiculous.

How had it come to *this*? She'd had a worthy vision, a dream. She'd battled all her life for it. And now? She was

spinning her wheels, wasting time, wasting trees and newsprint with her blather. She was wasting mother Earth's oxygen with her pointless, self-indulgent breathing.

Hours passed. At four o'clock, as usual, the noise from
next door stopped. The guy had knocked off and headed
out to wherever he crashed. As the sun began to slip behind the mountains, the dogs started up. She wasn't sure
if she heard the beagle; it had probably trucked off with
that dimwit.

She didn't eat. She fussed and fumed. The house was hot.
And when at last the long June day surrendered to darkness, Inez went to bed, leaving the windows wide open,
with nothing but the fine wire mesh of the screens to fend
off the forest and the night.

The churning scratched at her consciousness and nudged
her from a restless sleep. A familiar noise. A loud pumping,
driven by an electric motor. Then it stopped, as if holding
its breath. It was the sound of the compressor that powered
her neighbor's nail gun.

It woke an owl, who wondered with a mournful hoot,
Who dares to rouse me from my slumber? Who dares to
rend the fabric of this hot, hot night?

Somewhere, a dog barked. Another laughed.

Crickets chorused raucously, everywhere, from the surrounding woods. Or was that her tinnitus? The doctor had
said it was an inner-ear thing, common at her age, but she
insisted it came from a crick in her neck, from sleeping
wrong, but he pooh-poohed that theory. The quack. She'd
done it again, fallen asleep with her head at a bad angle,
and now the ringing was frenzied. Or was it crickets?
She squinted at the dim dial of the bedside clock—just past
two. Dozed off.

The churning roused her again, then stopped. She curled into a fetal ball and tensed, waiting for the spray of nails to tear through the screens and shatter the big mirror over the dresser. The sheets were damp. She waited for the spray of nails to arrive, piercing not wood, but flesh. Her flesh.

She dreamed of Margo, who lectured the group about Stephen King and told them to think crazy, unthinkable thoughts. What might happen to a woman—an aging feminist lesbian, for instance—if trapped in the woods by a guy with a red brassiere on his truck? A guy with a nail gun? Now make it *worse*.

The churning of the compressor woke her again, then stopped as if holding its breath. Waiting for the spray of nails, she pulled the wet pillow tight over her ears, unable to silence the crickets.

A flash of daylight prickled her eyes as she rolled over to look at the clock—just past nine. With a groan, she kicked her legs free of the tangled sheets. She got up, peed, shrugged into an old bathrobe, and splashed water on her face. Checking the mirror, she confirmed with a wince that she looked like absolute hell.

She shuffled to the kitchen and started a pot of coffee, then strolled out to the back deck. The morning stillness was broken only by birdsong. Odd, she thought. Had her neighbor's juice gone out? How had she managed to sleep so late?

Her thoughts were nipped by the thud of a vehicle's door in front of the house. The neighbor's dog scampered into view, followed by the neighbor himself. The beagle bounded up to her, and she crouched to rub its ears. "Hi, boy. What's your name?"

"That's Snoopy."

"I should've guessed." She stood.

"And my name's Nick."

She offered her hand. "Hi, Nick. I'm Inez Norris."

They shook. "I know who you are, Miss Norris."

"Ah." She lowered her head. "You've read the article."

"Did I ever," he said. "Gosh, what powerful writing."

She looked up, not sure she'd heard him right. He was clean-shaven and smiling. His crisp work clothes had not yet been sullied by the day's labors.

"I will say this," he continued. "It's an important issue — and you take no prisoners."

"I'm so pleased you liked it, but it really wasn't my best work." She tried to do something with her hair.

"Anyway, the reason I'm here. I wanted to apologize for leaving the compressor on overnight — didn't realize it was plugged in when I left. Hope it didn't keep you up."

"Oh, I *may* have heard something, but it was no bother. No bother at all."

"Glad to hear that. I also wanted to make sure you were up and about. Thought I'd let you catch some extra sleep before things get noisy."

"That's so *thoughtful*, Nick. Thank you. I'm fine." She paused. "You're a carpenter?"

"This summer I am — need to get that place cleaned up. Otherwise, I'm a teacher."

Inez smiled. "Good for you."

"Well, Miss Norris, have a great day." He rapped the side of his leg. "Come on, Snoop."

Inez followed Nick and the dog to the front of the house, where the truck was backed into the driveway. She hadn't seen the rear before. There were two pink bumper stickers, both emblazoned with the image of a folded pink ribbon. One said, ASK ME ABOUT BREAST CANCER. The other, FIND A CURE. With a tinge of concern, Inez asked Nick, "What *about* breast cancer?"

"It took my mother. And I have an older sister. Now she's dealing with it."

"I'm so sorry. My best wishes for your sister."

"I appreciate that, Miss Norris. And thanks for all you're doing. There's always hope." He opened the truck door. Snoopy jumped in.

"Uh, Nick," Inez wondered aloud. "About that . . . that hood ornament."

He laughed. "Just a conversation starter. It seems to get people talking."

"It does indeed," said Inez, sharing his laugh.

It had gotten Margo talking. It got Susan and the others talking. It got Inez herself talking. Talking and thinking.

Thinking such crazy thoughts.

❑

At the Club

Old rivalries have a way of mellowing, given enough time. The girlish pains of yesteryear have a way of morphing into a woman's wisdom—the wisdom of lessons learned. As we grow into adults, then pass through the decades, breezing through middle age and trudging into later life, we can sometimes dismiss a past betrayal, chalking it off as the sparring of worthy foes. In a zero-sum conflict, even between equals, one will win and one will lose. Life goes on.

While growing up half a century ago amid the idyllic ravines and moraines of Dumont, Wisconsin, attending high school with the two Norris sisters, Inez and Prucilla, I had no idea what enduring roles those girls would come to play in my future. Inez was the friend who betrayed me. But Prucilla was the one I never liked.

At some level, deep but never quite forgotten, they both would roil the eddies beneath the surface of my life, which ripples with the small-town dramas I've chronicled through thousands of local newspaper stories under a vamped-up byline: Glee Savage.

The same age as Inez, I had known her throughout our school years, and by the time we were ready for college, our friendship was so thick that we enrolled together at Madison—different majors, same dorm.

Prucilla was a few years younger, so I had little interaction with her at school, but I came to know her through Inez, and the more I dealt with her, the less I liked her. As a youngster, Prue was haughty and scheming. As an adult, she was worse. And even though she always managed to bully her way to the center of a large social circle, she had few if any friends.

Meanwhile, at college, my friendship with Inez took a terrible turn when she stole, on a whim, the man I planned to marry. She fled with him to California, and although her burgeoning feminism eschewed marriage, she would later bear his son, named Brody.

Feeling defeated, I moved back to Dumont after graduation and took my first reporting job at the *Dumont Daily Register*, where I have worked for some forty years. Old enough to retire now, I have stayed on the job, living alone.

Prucilla, ever the bad penny, also returned to Dumont after her college years. She has never worked. Instead, Prue married a successful architect. And several months ago, after thirty-five years of marriage, the architect, one Marson Miles, divorced her. Why?

Be still, my beating heart. Marson divorced Prue after falling in love with another *man*, a much *younger* gay man — Brody Norris, son of Prue's sister, Inez. To be more succinct: Marson dumped Prue for Prue's nephew.

As I watched this transpire, I was chagrined to realize how completely I had forgiven Inez, whose transgressions against me were profound, while shifting the full weight of my animus to Prue, who had never wronged me in any meaningful way at all. Rather than sympathizing with Prue for the circumstances of her divorce, I took joy in the liberation of her long-suffering husband. Some might describe my reaction as schadenfreude. The simpler explanation, however, boiled down to female cattiness. Prue was a bitch, and she got what she deserved.

Perhaps distance was the variable that had inverted my judgment of the Norris sisters. Inez had hightailed it to California while we were in college, and I never saw her again, which left only memories of how we had *been*—the deep and loving friendship as well as the double cross. Prue, on the other hand, was *always* around, as if she'd never left. I saw her everywhere, and I watched her age, even as I was aging. Her innate petulance, her sarcasm parading as humor, nulled any chance of joy in a cushy life that should have been the very picture of contentment. So I found it only too easy to transfer any lingering resentment I might have felt for Inez to her younger, abrasive sister.

Ultimately, though, what clinched Inez's redemption was her son's move from California to Dumont. He—or at least someone very much like him—might have been my own child if, as intended, I had married the man who eventually fathered him. This, I admit, was a stretch of logic. There was no escaping that Inez had birthed Brody. But she had raised him well, ushering a remarkable young man into the world, and for that I had to give her credit. Better still, he was now here, *living* here, as if he had been sent home, a gift that Inez deigned to share with me.

In truth, I was no factor whatever in Brody's decision to come to Dumont. An architect in his mid-thirties with a promising career, the son of Inez had moved here to join a long-established local firm cofounded by Ted Norris (Inez and Prucilla's brother) and by Marson Miles (Prucilla's husband). A reasonable setup, perfectly innocent.

But then—when Marson, nudging sixty, discovered true love with Brody and broke out of his closet—the poop hit the fan.

In a far-flung burg like Dumont, this was mighty big news.

I had worn many hats at the *Register*, which was perhaps the key to my longevity in a profession that had known more downs than ups during the last umpteen years. By serving as everything from beat reporter to gal Friday to women's editor to arts reviewer, I had managed to ride out the digital storm. Now, since being elevated to the ranking position of features editor, I was granted total leeway in assigning any story that didn't qualify as hard news or sports—so long as I wrote it myself and shot most of the photos. I was one of the few bones left on a skeleton staff, still shrinking, picked clean of all fat and most meat.

Brody's arrival in town was newsworthy enough—that was a no-brainer—but how to tell the story? That's where it got sticky. It would be impossible to tell Brody's story without telling Marson's as well, since that was the very angle that had the town buzzing.

I had pestered Brody for an interview since his move to Dumont in January. We would run into each other at various social functions, and I would make a pitch to profile him in an occasional column of mine titled "Inside Dumont." He resisted; I persisted. In March, at a house party following a concert by our local orchestra, I tried again. And it was Marson who suggested that I might want to hold off awhile, till after the dust of his divorce settled, when I would be welcome to run a feature on the downtown commercial loft that he and Brody had just bought, which they intended to transform into a home—together.

I loved the idea. It covered all the angles, glossing over their relationship as a given while allowing me to focus instead on the repurposing of the loft, an otherwise urban housing solution that had not yet materialized in Dumont. The feature would devote far more space to pictures than to words, and I planned to include at least one posed shot of the two of them together "at home." This, I knew, would be a piece that could satisfy not only the design-conscious, but also the pruriently curious.

Preparing for the feature, I conducted a background interview of Brody in August, then visited the loft for the first time a few days later. Within a week or so, I had everything I needed. The loft looked spectacular; the pictures told the story with style and clarity. It seemed a shame, though, to waste something so good in the dead of summer, so I held the feature for the first Sunday after Labor Day, after school had started and the town had come back to life.

Everyone saw it. Everyone was clucking. A week or so later, I should not have been surprised when I arrived at the *Register*'s offices, checked my mail, and found an envelope addressed to Miss Glee Savage from Mrs. Prucilla Miles.

Without even opening it, I was irked by her continued use of her ex-husband's surname as well as the title *Mrs*. And I was galled that she addressed me as *Miss*. As a woman in her sixties, I found the juxtaposition of titles tantamount to name-calling—a jilted divorcée dissing me as a spinster.

Overcoming the urge to toss the letter unopened, I carried it to my desk and set it facedown in front of my computer. I removed my hat—a floppy felt cloche, ocher-colored in anticipation of autumn—then sat and drummed my fingers for a moment. With closed eyes, I took a deep, calming breath. Then I slit open the envelope and pulled out the letter.

"Glee dearest," it said, "I read with interest your recent story about Marson's new living arrangements. The photo of him and my nephew standing with the bed in the background had a queer effect on me, and I wonder if we might discuss it. I have reserved a table for lunch at the club next Monday at one. Won't you join me?"

Next Monday at a quarter till one, with my curiosity outweighing my apprehension, I drove out to "the club," understood to mean the clubhouse at Dumont Country Club. I was not a member—small-town journalists don't make that kind of money—but I had been there hundreds of times over the years, either as a guest of the better-heeled or as a reporter on assignment.

The grounds were looking perfect at that time of year, with the summer annuals in riotous full bloom, not yet nipped by the chilly nights. The golf course, built in the 1920s before the wide availability of heavy earthmoving equipment, was designed to the natural contours of the land, punctuated by rocky outcroppings that had been left by a prehistoric glacier. Immaculate fairways, groomed and green, extended off toward the hills as I drove the winding entryway beneath a canopy of oaks. Sapphire splotches of September sky peeked through the matrix of leaves and dappled my windshield with dancing, pristine sunbeams.

My old fuchsia hatchback, a Gremlin built forty years earlier in downstate Kenosha, was conspicuous among the sleek imports in the driveway that circled beneath a soaring porte cochère of fieldstone and timbers. I had bought the car to celebrate landing my first job, back when I started at the *Register*. It was probably now worth little more than scrap, but it was cheap to drive and I had been good to it. Its new retro whitewalls, baby moon hubcaps, and a recent fresh paint job fetched compliments wherever I went.

"That is one sweet ride, Miss Savage," the valet said as he opened my door and helped me out.

I thanked him with a wink, then strutted up the flagstone walkway to the double-doored entrance, swung wide as if I owned the place.

Inside, I skirted the grill room, which was serving the last of lunch to golfers heading out to the links. Then I took a hallway past several empty banquet rooms, arriving at the rear of the clubhouse, where its formal dining room commanded a lofty, verdant view of turf and trees and bitsy distant foursomes of bankers and lawyers at play. On weekend evenings or Sunday mornings, this room would be filled to capacity, but on a Monday at one, only a handful of tables was occupied — by ladies at leisure, some in hats.

"Good afternoon, Miss Savage," said the head waiter. "So nice to see you again."

"Thank you, Victor. It's a pleasure seeing *you* as well." I always felt like a blushing ingenue in his presence. Hispanic, maybe forty, he was not only handsome, but carried himself with a modest dignity and a constant smile.

"Mrs. Miles is expecting you," he said, "but she's running a few minutes late." His English was perfect, with just the trace of a lingering accent — like spice in the icing on some tasty, exotic cake.

"No problem at all," I said. "I'm in no hurry."

"If you'd care to have a drink while you wait, I can show you to a lovely window table." And he began leading me across the room toward the far wall.

Along the way, I noticed Gloria Simms, a tall, striking black woman with a sharp sense of style. The wife of our local sheriff, she was seated at a table with another woman and the Simmses' young son, Thomas junior, known by everyone as Tommy. The lad was adorable in a tiny blazer and dressy wool shorts, quietly occupied with an iPad while the women gabbed.

Victor broke stride and stepped aside to wait as I greeted the table. "Hello, Gloria," I said, approaching her from behind, "what a pleasant surprise."

Turning, she broke into a smile. "Why, *Glee*," she said, rising, offering a hug and a peck. "Do you know Jane Ingram? We're on the library's program committee together."

I did not know Jane, as she was new to town, so Gloria introduced us. Then she turned to Tommy with a good-natured scowl. "Where are your manners, young man?"

He rose at once with the iPad in one hand, extending the other. "Good afternoon, Miss Glee."

I shook his hand, crouching to tell him, "My gosh, you're growing up fast, aren't you?"

"I just turned six."

Gloria added, "He's in first grade now—can you believe it? A few weeks ago, it was tough enough when I dropped him off for a full day of school. Now, every time I think of *college*, I break into tears." She laughed as she dabbed at one eye. "But today's an in-service day, so he gets to have lunch at the club."

I noticed the tablet in his hand. Having assumed he'd been amusing himself with a game of Angry Birds or Space Mutants, I was surprised that the screen displayed a solid block of gray text. I asked, "Are you reading already?"

"Yes, ma'am." He showed me the tablet. "*Stuart Little*. It's about a mouse."

"Oh, that's a *good* one, isn't it?" Amazed, I looked up to tell Gloria, "I don't think I read that till fifth grade."

She nodded. "Tommy was reading before kindergarten—he just took to it. Loves school, too. We're very lucky."

My knees crackled as I rose from my crouch.

Waiting for Prucilla at our table, from which I could observe the entire room, I asked Victor, "Does Mrs. Miles ever drink at lunch?"

"Yes, ma'am. She enjoys a champagne cocktail whenever she's here, day or night."

"That sounds rather nice," I said. "If you'd care to bring two, we'll be ready for her."

"Of course, Miss Savage." The slightest bob of his head conveyed a perfect measure of deference without the theatrics of a lugubrious bow and scrape. He turned to leave, offering a posterior view. *Caramba*.

His retreat led my gaze back to Gloria Simms's table. The Simmses weren't the only black family in Dumont—granted, there weren't many—but they were by far the most prominent, given the sheriff's position in the community. By all appearances, they were a model couple, smart and involved, raising a bright young son. I found it impossible not to wonder what barriers they'd overcome while achieving what most would define as "the good life." I knew the sheriff had grown up in rural Illinois, which gets Southern, fast, as you travel down from Chicago. I'd heard he'd met Gloria in college. Together, they'd come a long way to their present life in central Wisconsin—not the few hundred miles, but the journey from the prejudice they'd doubtless known. And it seemed they'd succeeded at raising Tommy in a protected world that would not allow the experiences of their past.

Their efforts struck me as nothing short of heroic. I removed the steno pad from my purse and made a note to approach Gloria later about an "Inside Dumont" column. For a great many local readers, her story could prove enlightening.

As I returned my purse to the floor, I spotted Prucilla Miles chugging across the dining room. She greeted no one, beelining toward our table. Victor then appeared in her wake, rushing to catch up, holding aloft a small tray that bore the two cocktails.

I stood as she arrived, mustering a cheery "Hello, Prue. It's been too long."

"Ughhh," she said, reaching for my shoulders to deliver a perfunctory air-smooch before collapsing into her chair. "What a hellish morning. André was backed up."

André was the owner of a hair salon downtown on First Avenue. Prucilla was freshly coiffed; her usual helmet of hair now sported an extra coat of lacquer. A harsh aerosol scent drifted across the table. It matched the look on her face, pinched and peeved. Poor thing—kept waiting ten minutes at the beauty parlor. Could she even begin to fathom what the Simmses might have endured while growing up, walking to school, taunted on the streets with epithets, or worse, because of the color of their skin? I told her, "We all have our crosses to bear, but you're a trouper, Prue."

"You'd better believe it," she agreed with a low chortle.

Victor moved up to the table and placed our drinks on fringe-bordered linen cocktail napkins. Delicate bubbles rose through the champagne flutes, sparkling in the sunlight that sliced across our table from the window. I gave the waiter a grateful nod. Prue ignored him, accustomed to being served without needing to ask. She lifted her glass and tilted it in my direction. "Cheers, love."

After we tasted our drinks, Victor placed menu cards on the table, telling us, "We're not very busy today, so it will be my pleasure to serve you myself."

Prue continued to ignore him, so I said, "That will be delightful. Thank you."

The smile. The bob. And he left us.

Watching him cross the room, I leaned to tell Prue with a grin, "I think every woman at the club must have a crush on Victor."

She blinked. "Who?"

"*Victor*, the head waiter. He's been here for years."

She looked appalled. "*I* don't have a crush on him."

"Why not? You're single now. You've got options." Lowering my voice to a suggestive purr, I added, "I don't suppose *he's* single."

"How would I know?"

Laughing, I told her, "For God's sake, Prue—enjoy the fantasy."

Her hair wobbled. "Let's just say he's not my type. If you know what I mean."

I knew what she meant.

Victor was Mexican.

We ordered our meal—and a second cocktail for Prue, but not for me, since I was on an extended lunch break from the office. As we settled back into conversation, another table of women got up to leave. While passing by, Peg Norris stopped to say hello. She was Prue's sister-in-law, married for some twenty years to Prue's architect brother, Ted Norris, the business partner of Prue's ex-husband. Only in a small town like Dumont could such tangled ties evolve.

"Well, *hi* there, Prue," said Peg. "I didn't see you come in."

With airy indifference, Prue said, "I saw *you*, Peg, but your back was to me."

Peg and I greeted each other. Though we'd been acquainted for many years, I didn't know her well because she never had much to say. But she was always pleasant, and she seemed to be a good wife to a contented husband. No kids. Whether that was by choice or otherwise, I had no insights—I wasn't close enough.

She said to Prue, "Ted tells me we're driving to Green Bay to celebrate your birthday next week."

"If we must fête the wretched event," said Prue, whirling a hand, "let it be out of town. Far, *far* from town." She turned to me, explaining, "There's a new restaurant over there I've been wanting to try. A fusion place — French, Belgian, Dutch — ought to be interesting."

"And just the three of us," said Peg with an open smile. "Sounds like fun. See you next week." She waggled her fingers good-bye and disappeared.

Prue paused, as if waiting for the room to be cleared of Peg's presence, then told me, "I don't know *what* Ted sees in her." She crossed her arms.

I shrugged. "They seem happy. Can't ask for much more than that."

"She's mousy." Harrumph.

I couldn't resist noting, "She's still married. Maybe she's on to something."

Prue took the bait. "Or maybe it's because *her* husband isn't homosexual. Maybe that's why Ted hasn't left Peg for someone else."

"Prue," I said, "maybe they just happen to love each other."

With a brusque laugh, she sat back in her chair. "Marson and I were together more than thirty years, and he *never* loved me."

"I'm sure that's not true. Did you love *him*?"

"That's beside the point. You see, Marson was in love with my brother — my heterosexual brother. Marson married me to keep Ted in his life."

I gave Prue a skeptical look.

"It's true," she assured me. "He told me so the day he left me."

I wanted to ask, After three decades together, you hadn't caught on? Instead, I said, "Then I guess it was meant to be. His leaving. I'm sorry — that had to be rough on you."

She sat forward again. "I made out fine. All's well that ends well."

"Financial security is important," I agreed, "but there's also the emotional toll."

She flipped her hands. "Do I look bitter?"

To my eye, she looked plenty bitter.

She continued, "A lesser woman — a *mousier* woman — might be devastated by all this. But I look at it this way: My husband was a closet homosexual, and now he's a practicing homosexual. He recognized his predilections before he married me. I was the best wife I could be, under the circumstances. But in retrospect, I never stood a chance. *No* woman stood a chance. There's not a thing in the world I could've done 'better' to change the outcome. It was his doing, not mine."

Her analysis was spot-on — I recognized that. In fact, I had planned to use the exact same argument to console her and buck her up, but she didn't need it. What surprised me, therefore, was not her logic, but her readiness to claim this argument as her own. Taking it a step further, she seemed to relish the humiliation that any woman might feel if she'd lost her husband to her gay nephew. For Prue, the collapse of a long marriage was no mark of shame or failure; it was a badge of honor, worn with pride.

Or perhaps it was all an act, a sympathy ploy.

She had always craved being the center of attention.

Victor brought our lunch — a hearty shepherd's pie for Prue, a sensible shrimp Louie for me. While enjoying my first bite, I also enjoyed watching Victor's retreat across the dining room, which again led my eye to Gloria Simms. She was the picture of grace and refinement, tending to the needs of her well-mannered child, chatting with her lady friend, forking delicate flakes of salmon from a bed of greens and sprouts. Seated across from me, Prue grunted with hungry abandon as she gobbled at her big meat pie, washing it down with a third champagne cocktail, the glass foggy with smudges from her lips and fingers.

I said, "The Simmses are such a lovely addition to the community."

Prue glanced up from her feeding with a bewildered look, as if I'd spoken Hindi.

"The Simmses," I repeated. "Gloria—she's right over there—and her husband, the sheriff. They add a lot to the town, don't you think?"

"He's affable enough," she conceded.

"True. But just as important, I think it speaks well of the town that we elected him."

"Well, *I* didn't." Prue rolled her eyes. "Competence is more than a matter of skin color."

I felt my temper rise, but kept it in check. I'd heard this kind of racist spin before, attempting to justify prejudice in the guise of a greater open-mindedness. "By all accounts," I said calmly, "Sheriff Simms has done a first-rate job of managing the department."

Ignoring that, Prue continued, "It was the same thing here at the club."

"What was?"

She exhaled a heavy, tired sigh. "Ever since the *eighties*, there's been pressure to integrate the membership."

"Pressure from whom?"

"From the *members*—or at least a faction of them. They felt an all-white club 'looked bad.'" Prue added the air quotes with her greasy fingers.

"It did look bad," I said. "To be blunt, it was embarrass-ing. Granted, I'm not a member, but maybe that gives me a clearer perspective. It looked as if the club was restricted to good ol' boys."

"But we couldn't *find* any" — Prucilla lowered her voice to a raspy whisper — "any blacks." She sliced into the shepherd's pie with her fork.

I glanced at Gloria, then back at Prue. "But the Simmses are members now, correct?"

"Oh, yes." Prue rolled her eyes again. "Right after he was elected, the membership committee was downright *giddy* to snag them. I'm not certain, but I'll just bet the club subsidized their membership. I mean, how would *those* people come up with the dues, let alone the initiation fee?"

I noted, "They're in a better position to come up with it than I am."

"That's not the point."

Genuinely curious, I asked, "What *is* the point?"

"Entitlement." She set down her fork. "The Simmses would expect a gratis membership because they feel entitled."

I set down my fork. Stunned speechless, I sat back in my chair. Feeling queasy, I took a sip of water.

With evident concern, Victor stepped over to the table. "Is everything —"

"Go away," Prue said without looking at him. "Can't you see we're talking?"

"Sorry, ma'am." He left.

Prue gave me a quizzical look. "Glee, love, you look pale. Lunch not up to snuff?"

"I, uh, need to be careful with shrimp."

"Ah" — she chuckled — "I know. Hard to say where they came from. Mexico? Thailand? Yuck, who knows?"

"No," I assured her, "they're fine. Quite delicious." Proving the point, I ate another.

She finished off the potato crust of the shepherd's pie,

then swiped her mouth with her napkin, smearing her lipstick. "The reason I suggested we get together today—I suppose you're wondering."

"In fact, I am." I offered a soft smile. "Something to do with that Sunday piece on Marson and Brody, correct?"

"Yes." She frowned. Her hair wobbled. Then she too offered a soft smile. "It was the picture that made me do some thinking—the picture of them by the bed."

"You mentioned that in your note."

"Let's just say, it drove home the reality. The cold truth. In the final analysis, I realized, their relationship is carnal."

"That's part of it, I presume—good for them—but I'm sure it runs deeper. I've *seen* them together. What they have is wonderful."

Prue ignored me. "And realizing the sordid basis for their attraction, that's when I came to understand what I told you earlier—I never stood a chance. I can't grow what Brody's got. Really, I'm surprised at him. There's a *word* for men like that. Inez should be ashamed, raising him that way."

"Any woman would be proud to call Brody her son." I paused before adding quietly, "I would."

"Hmmm. I suppose you would."

I lowered my eyes to my hands in my lap.

Prue's tone turned jaunty. "So I want to thank you, Glee. Your article, it helped me see the light. It brought the gift of total vindication. But then, I should've expected no less from *you*—from my oldest friend."

Huh? I looked up, wide-eyed, to find her beaming at me, warm and angelic. She leaned forward to reach her arm past the dishes, resting her hand at my edge of the table. Slowly, I raised one hand from my lap, as if sapped by the spell of this witch, and touched her fingers.

"Glee dearest," she said, "let's find what we lost so long

ago. Let's be friends again."

Snapping out of it, I removed my hand from hers and sat back. I wanted to ask, Have you gone batshit? Instead, I crafted a more diplomatic response: "I'm flattered, Prucilla. But we can't very well 'find' a friendship that was never 'lost' in the first place. Nothing has changed between us." Having spoken God's truth, I flashed her a tidy smile.

She leaned back with a happy little gasp, clapping her fingers with childish excitement. What was she imagining? Shopping sprees together? Picnics in the park?

At that moment, every head in the room turned as Victor ignited a copper skillet of cherries jubilee on a flambé cart alongside Gloria Simms's table. The flash of orange light, the smell and crackle of kirschwasser, the glittering sparks—it was a festive bit of culinary theater that would impress even the most jaded of diners. To a six-year-old on a day off from school, it was nothing short of magical. Tommy Simms had abandoned his iPad to watch the spectacle with huge, wondering eyes and a gaze of pure enchantment.

"Just look at him," I cooed. "He was reading *Stuart Little*—reading a novel in first grade—and now his world just got a bit bigger. Have you ever seen such a darling child?"

Prue gave me a knowing look. Speaking from the side of her mouth, she said, "They're *all* cute—at *that* age." She turned away, adding, "If you know what I mean."

I knew what she meant.

Tommy was black.

My thoughts drifted to Inez Norris—my old nemesis, Prue's sister, Brody's mother—who had left Wisconsin some forty years earlier to follow her feminist calling to California. Though I had not spoken to her in all those decades, I had learned from Brody that his mother was still an activist and organizer, fighting the good fight for gender equality. Once my best friend, but long estranged, Inez was a social crusader, while Prucilla, seated across from me, pleading for my friendship, seemed to have no social conscience whatever.

"Perhaps," said Prue, "you could check your calendar when you get back to the office. See if you're available on the twenty-ninth. It ought to be fun." She hefted another heaping forkful of the chocolate cheesecake she'd ordered with an extra dollop of whipped cream.

Not having the luxurious option of an afternoon nap, I'd ordered coffee. Swirling the spoon in my cup, I fibbed, "I'll do that, but I'm pretty sure the date won't work for me." It was a wide-open Saturday.

When Victor dropped off the bill at our table, I took my pocketbook from my purse and told Prue, "Let me help with this."

"Nonsense. I invited. Besides, this is a club—your money's no good here. Marson's is, though." With a coarse laugh, she added, "Part of the settlement. This one's on him."

With drinks and all, it must have been a hundred-dollar lunch, astronomical by Dumont standards. She signed the chit with a careless dash of the pen.

As we strolled out through the main doors together, I saw that my fuchsia hatchback had been parked at the far curb of the driveway where it circled under the porte cochère. The valets had the option of awarding this prime spot as they wished, typically to the richest executive with the snazziest car; other cars were parked out of sight in a storage lot behind a distant berm. But there, front and center, was my old Gremlin—windows spiffed, ready to go.

The same valet who had welcomed me earlier, an earnest Midwestern college guy, asked, "Enjoy your lunch, Miss Savage?" He was dressed like his coworkers in khakis, spotless white tennies, and the club's baby-blue polo.

I gabbed with him for a moment while Prue fumbled in her purse for her parking stub, snapping at another hunky college guy behind the valet podium. I gave Prue a quick parting hug, thanked her for lunch, and promised to stay in touch. As my valet escorted me out to the car, Prue continued to squabble and fuss. "You'll find it under *Miles*," she said. "Mrs. Prucilla Miles."

My valet handed me the keys while helping me into the car. "Love it," he said, nodding his appreciation as he thumped the door closed.

I passed a five to him through the window, thanking him for such royal treatment. "And I wonder if I might ask you a favor."

"Of course, ma'am."

"Mrs. Simms—the sheriff's wife—is just finishing up inside. She'll be leaving soon. Could you possibly bring her car up and have it waiting? Right here, where you parked mine?"

"My pleasure. I'll take care of it right away."

I glanced out the other window, which framed a view of Prucilla at the podium, still making a stink. I started the engine. Turning to my valet again, I fished out another five and handed it to him. "This may seem like an odd request." I cleared my throat. Speaking low, I asked, "Could you manage to keep Mrs. Miles waiting till after Mrs. Simms has driven away?"

He hunkered down to face me nose-to-nose. We shared a conspiratorial grin. Returning the five, he said, "Consider it done."

Then I circled the entryway and drove out through the serene, wooded grounds.

Prucilla shrank in the rearview mirror, barking and bleating.

I punched the gas, goosed the Gremlin, and felt like a million bucks.

❑

ELEVEN

Carpet Queen

November, everyone warned me, would be bleak. Having moved to Wisconsin the prior New Year's, after living my entire life in Southern California, I had never experienced the ugly transition from a bright, crisp autumn to a dark, frozen winter. November teetered at the cusp between the seasons—frosty nights, drizzly days, with dead brown leaves clumped in the gutters and stuck to the sidewalks, tracked everywhere by the soles of my wet shoes.

"We should take a vacation," said Marson Miles, squaring the shoulders of my sport coat, straightening my tie. "Somewhere warm, somewhere tropical. I'd hate to lose you, Brody."

"You're *not* going to lose me," I assured him with a kiss. We stood under the glare of a streetlight outside the senior center where the board of a local museum held its monthly meetings. Around the perimeter of the parking lot, bare trees dripped on the soggy yellow sod. I finger-combed a lock of Marson's damp hair, telling him, "A bit of crappy weather won't scare me off."

We had found each other, had committed to each other, and now we were working every day with each other, as well as living together. I had made the move from California to join the architectural firm that had been founded in Dumont some thirty years earlier by Marson Miles and by my uncle, Ted Norris. Though Marson was more than twenty years my senior—with a grim wife and other small-town obstacles to contend with—we embarked almost at once on a new, shared life that seemed magical, destined for both of us, and instantly right.

When Marson said that evening that he would hate to lose me, I knew he was speaking not only of his love for me, but also of my expanding duties at Miles & Norris. Earlier that autumn, my uncle Ted had lost his wife to a freak illness that dazed the town and left Ted distracted on the job. He went away for a while to work through his grief and get his head together, but his repeated delays in returning to the business made it more and more apparent that he was weighing an early retirement. Meaning that I, Brody Norris, AIA, would in all likelihood step into the Norris role at Miles & Norris, LLP.

So in spite of Marson's suggestion that we should slip away to somewhere tropical and escape the November muck, it was more realistic to assume there would be no vacations for a while. And in truth, it suited both Marson and me just fine that the needs of the office had to take precedence over the more sybaritic pleasures of beaches and mojitos. The firm seemed poised to enter a golden age of important commissions—of artistic significance—and Marson was as thankful for my younger blood as I was thankful for his mentoring.

As we slogged across the parking lot toward the side entrance of the senior center, another car pulled in. The beams of its headlights flashed through the mist, spotting us like fugitives as I reached for the door. Then the driver gave a dainty toot, as if asking us to wait. I didn't recognize the car, a big Lexus sedan decked out with gaudy gold trim; it was brand new, judging by its lack of plates and by the temporary license taped inside the rear window.

"Who's that?" asked Marson. We huddled in a sallow pool of orange light cast by a sodium vapor lamp.

"Hi, guys," said the driver as she opened the door. She stepped out onto the asphalt with a bulging tote bag of whatnot for the meeting. It was Debbie "Diamonds" Jacobson, president of the museum board; she was involved with the workings of nearly every charitable or cultural group in town. Though her name was Deborah, everyone called her Debbie or Deb to her face, while most referred to her as Diamonds behind her back. She was aware of the moniker—and owned it with a modicum of pride.

Her tastes, in a word, were flashy. She wore expensive clothes but had a cheesy sense of style. I liked the woman—a true pillar of the community, always giving back—but it was impossible for me, a trained designer, not to wince at her provincial take on glamour. If it sparkled, she wore it. Hence, Diamonds.

Marson asked her, "Can I carry that for you?"

"Thanks," she said, handing over her tote and giving him a hug. Then she hugged me.

Marson hefted the bag. "Long night ahead?"

"Probably, but I know how to move a meeting along when I need to. I've put you near the top of the agenda, so at least *you'll* get home at a decent hour."

"Most considerate of you. But I'll need to wait for Brody—we rode together."

"Ah." She stepped to the door, which I swung open for her.

Diamonds had exercised her prerogative as president by appointing me to the board a month earlier, filling an unexpected vacancy. The gesture was intended to welcome me to town, but it also had a practical motive, in light of my relationship with Marson. The board was faced with its biggest task in living memory—erecting a new building, a bigger museum—and Marson was their unanimous choice to design it. Which meant that I would be the board's de facto liaison with Miles & Norris during the design and construction phases.

The board consisted of some fifteen members, and this was only my second meeting. Having not yet connected most of the names and faces, I served as a member at large, still learning the ropes. As we entered the building that Tuesday night, about a dozen people mingled and gabbed, warming themselves with coffee from a battered institutional-size urn. The senior center's large rec room had been cleared of its ping-pong tables and exercise mats, replaced with a U-shaped arrangement of banquet tables for the board and a few rows of folding chairs for spectators.

Diamonds asked me to distribute the agenda packets around the table, and while doing this, I noticed the arrival of a fellow board member, Walter Zakarian. A local flooring contractor and carpeting merchant, he was a husky but elegant man in his late forties, never married, who often squired some of the town's prominent widows at formal social events. According to Marson, this was pure window dressing, as Walter was widely presumed to be gay. Walter never let on, and no one could prove anything, but the rumor mill insisted he had a boy or two tucked away somewhere.

Tonight, as usual, he looked dapper in a custom-tailored silk suit, which he had protected from the wet weather with a classic khaki Burberry, worn over his shoulders like a cape. Very much *not* as usual, however, was his deep, bronzed suntan and a blackened left eye, ringed in shades of purple and yellow—a roundhouse shiner, a real beaut.

Diamonds stifled a horrified shriek. "My God, Walter—

what *happened?*"

Ever the gentleman, Marson helped him remove and hang his coat. "What a magnificent tan, Walter. Been traveling?" Hangers clattered on the steel pipe. Umbrellas dripped.

"Just got back, Marson. I have a place down in Puerto Vallarta, a modest time-share. But the town and the seaside, it's wonderful — ever go there?"

Diamonds repeated, "What *happened?*"

Walter turned to her. "Well," he said with measured patience and an edge of testiness, "I had a little accident — obviously."

"Sorry." She drifted to her place at the head of the meeting table and sat.

Walter mustered a quiet laugh, telling Marson, "Damnedest thing. Flying home, getting into my seat, there was this fidgety kid, and I smacked myself on the edge of the overhead bin. A few cocktails helped."

Diamonds called the meeting to order, the roll was taken, and the minutes of the prior meeting were approved without discussion. Diamonds then told the group, "You'll notice I've asked Marson Miles to sit with the board this evening, as we'll have frequent occasion to defer to his opinion regarding construction issues. I know I speak for everyone present: we could not have been more thrilled with his presentation of the preliminary design at last month's meeting. The future legacy of the Dumont Public Museum has never been in better hands." She led the board in a round of applause, which was picked up by some twenty townspeople who had come to watch the meeting.

While I may have questioned Debbie Jacobson's taste in fashion, I had no quibble whatever with her taste in museum design. Marson had risen to the challenge with a dramatic vision for the new structure that rivaled that of Questman Center for the Performing Arts, completed about a year and a half earlier. In fact, the city fathers were so enamored of Questman Center—and the luster that its world-class architecture had brought to the small town—they had allocated additional land for the new museum among the rugged crags and wooded ravines of an erstwhile city park, where the museum could join the theater complex as anchors of a nascent cultural campus. Now there was even talk of a new main library as well. And while I was lying in Marson's arms one night, he had said, "That one's yours, Brody."

So I joined the others in their earnest applause for the man seated next to me, who had not only ignited my life, but inspired the whole town. Most of the locals were still unknown to me, but I had no trouble recognizing two of the faces beaming through the crowd.

Mary Questman, the town's reigning dowager, still sprightly, pushing seventy, had been the guiding force behind building the performing-arts center. Her spunk and her drive, as well as her checkbook, had turned an improbable dream into a reality of stone, glass, and steel—and national acclaim. Somehow, she had managed all this while remaining the embodiment of sweetness. To know Mary was to love her.

And seated next to her, only a few years younger, was Glee Savage, intrepid gal reporter for the *Dumont Daily Register*. With her oversize hats and her bold, informed style and her glossy red lips, she injected our remote Wisconsin burg with a much-needed dose of pizazz. During the course of her long career, she had written countless features, reviews, and profiles, as well as reports on the doings of Dumont's various nonprofits. In short, Glee Savage was the town's recognized voice of all things cultural. And tonight, there she sat, notebook on knee, pen poised.

When the applause ended, Diamonds continued: "Because the building campaign is now our highest priority, you'll see I've moved that item to the top of our agenda, which — "

"Madam President?" said Walter Zakarian. "A point of order, please."

"Yes?"

"I can't help but notice that the press is here tonight."

Everyone looked about, confused by the statement.

"You mean Glee?" asked Diamonds. "Glee's *always* here."

"But unless I'm mistaken," said Walter, "the bylaws stipulate that our meetings are open to the press only when we issue specific, prior invitation."

Diamonds gave him a look that said, Get real.

He explained, "Given the sensitive nature of items under consideration tonight — contracts and such — I object to the presence of the press. I feel Miss Savage should leave."

Marson leaned to whisper to me, "I'll bet it's that black eye. He doesn't want word getting out."

I whispered back, "He should wear a patch." We snickered.

Diamonds told Walter, "We can't ask Glee to *leave*. That would be rude."

"Read your own bylaws," he told her.

Diamonds turned to ask the board's parliamentarian, "Is that really in the rules?"

The old guy's head wobbled as he raised an index finger, thinking. His mouth hung open for a moment before he answered, "I think so. Yes."

Diamonds took a breath, composed herself, then said, "Glee, I apologize. Would you mind?"

In bewildered silence, all heads turned to Glee, who sat ramrod stiff, as if slapped. She placed her purse on her lap, deposited the pen and pad, then stood. All eyes watched as she crossed the room, her heels snapping at the tile floor. She opened the door, looked back at Walter with a pinched sneer, then left, yanking the door closed behind her.

A chorus of throat-clearing attempted to dispel the tension.

Mary Questman rose, telling the board, "Excuse me, please." As she crossed the room, she said to Zakarian, "Really, Walter. You've gone too far." She paused in her tracks to give him a stiff finger-wag. So much for the embodiment of sweetness — Mary looked pissed. Then she went out the door, following Glee into the dank night.

Marson leaned near and spoke into my ear: "A while back, Mary and Walter had a 'thing' going on. Went on for a year or two."

The design for the new museum was far enough along, and had earned such enthusiastic praise from the entire board, that Diamonds had solicited a preliminary bid from Hand of Zeus Construction, which had also built Questman Center. She explained, "There's no question that Zeus can deliver the quality this project deserves. And by starting the process early with them, we'll be in a better position to determine if we're on target with our funding. If not, we may need to go back to the drawing board — or go back to the city." The museum would be built with a combination of public funding and a board-sponsored pledge drive.

A round of thoughtful nods signaled general agreement with her logic. One of the board members, the director of the county library system, asked Diamonds, "Were other builders invited to bid?"

"Not at this point," she said with a shrug. "This is ballpark stuff. But if the numbers look good, we could save ourselves some hassle and commit to move forward with them." She paused before adding, "Or not — that's a board decision, not mine."

The "ballpark," I knew from the prior meeting as well as from conversations with Marson, was seven or eight million dollars. Though not a huge sum by metropolitan standards (I'd designed a Malibu beach house with a heftier price tag), eight million was substantial money in a town like Dumont, even with the city pitching in.

The library director said, "Does our architect have any reactions to this?"

Marson answered, "Zeus is reputable and qualified, no question. And there aren't many builders in the area who could handle this job. But as a matter of professional ethics, I never steer a client toward a particular builder; in the end, that's the client's choice. At this point, the numbers should be able to tell you more than I can."

"Excellent," said Diamonds. She stood and began circling the table with a stack of handouts. "Here you'll find, on Hand of Zeus letterhead, a summary of estimated construction costs."

As she placed the document in front of me, I noticed her watch, a lady's Rolex. The case and bracelet were heavy gold, with the face ringed by—guess what—diamonds. This was no knockoff. It far outclassed her usual costume jewelry, and I had never seen it before.

Deducing that the watch was new, I wondered about her family's circumstances. Her husband was the football coach at the local high school—a good, steady career, but not the sort of job that put your wife in a Lexus with a Rolex on her wrist. Diamonds herself, while plenty active in the community, was not employed, and they had a kid away at college, which could break anyone's bank. The answer to this seeming inconsistency, I reminded myself, lay in the popular consensus shared by most locals: Diamonds hadn't grown up in Dumont, but she had doubtless "come from money."

These thoughts were interrupted as my eye drifted to the bottom of the page before me. The total estimated construction costs were indeed in the ballpark of seven or eight million—but the digits after the eight drove it closer to nine.

"Looks a little high," said the library director with a tone of caution.

"But we're close," said Diamonds. "I'd be quite comfortable proceeding with these numbers—and let's face it, *I'm* the one expected to go begging."

"Hold on," said Walter Zakarian. "It is *way* too early to commit to Hand of Zeus, or even consider it."

"Not if it's the will of the board," said Diamonds.

"For your information," said Walter, "I've done some construction research of my own since our last meeting."

Someone asked, "In Puerto Vallarta?"

"No, right here in Dumont. In my flooring business, I've worked with every contractor in the area, and most of their subcontractors. For the good of the museum, I've called in a few favors, and Badger Stone Builders has agreed to 'work with us,' if you know what I mean. They believe in the community, they believe in the museum, and they think they can put together a nice package—with some of their suppliers and subs—working at a bare minimum above cost."

The library guy asked, "Could they beat Hand of Zeus?"

"Safe bet," said Walter, "but we can't find out unless we solicit their bid and turn over the plans."

I turned to Marson. "Badger Stone Builders—are they any good?"

"Perfectly reputable, been in business for ages. They're qualified to do the job."

Everyone turned to Diamonds. She said, "I suppose I could approach them."

"Debbie," said Walter, "I'm the glue that's holding this deal together. Without me, it'll never fly. Therefore, I'd like to propose a motion: Authorize me to solicit a bid from Badger Stone and to supply them with all the needed construction documents."

"So moved," I said, along with several others at the table.

"Out of order," said Diamonds.

She turned the tables on Walter by invoking the same bylaws that had forced Glee Savage out of the meeting and into the night. Since the matter of a bid from Badger Stone Builders was not on the agenda, it could not be acted on that night; it would need to be placed on the agenda for December's meeting, when it could be debated and voted upon.

But Walter insisted there was nothing to stop him from continuing to schmooze Badger Stone, and he asked Marson if he would accompany him to the building site the next morning to discuss the project with a few of the contractor's bigwigs.

Marson agreed to pick Walter up at his office shortly before nine.

Diamonds rapped her gavel. "Can we return to the agenda, please?"

"Interesting meeting," said Marson with a grin while driving me home.

"Very," I agreed. "After tonight, I'm not sure what to make of Walter Zakarian."

"Join the club. He's been Dumont's mystery man forever. Some call him 'guarded.' I just think he's closeted."

I mulled the situation for a moment. "Those run-ins he had with Glee and Mary made no sense at all. Things got a bit tense with Diamonds too, but I have to side with Walter on that one—why *not* explore competitive bids with Badger Stone?"

"Well," said Marson, "we're doing just that—tomorrow at nine."

"Am I invited?"

He winked. "Need you ask?" Then he said, "Know what else didn't make sense? Walter's story about the black eye and the kid on the plane—it didn't add up somehow."

"Right. It sounded goofy." A thought came to me: "Puerto Vallarta. That's a popular gay destination. I know any number of L.A. friends who go there all the time—some have condos—quite an enclave. In fact, I've vacationed there with them. This is worth a phone call."

So there in the car, I placed a call to a guy named Allan, whose condo I'd visited, and he answered on the second ring. I told him about Walter Zakarian and the black eye, adding, "He owns a big flooring business here in Wisconsin. On his cable commercials, he dresses up as the Karastan King." Allan said he knew of him, but he hadn't been to Mexico in a while. Another friend, however—Justin—was down there for an extended stay, so Allan offered to give him a call and ask a few questions.

When I hung up, Marson asked, "So Walter *is* known among the gay crowd down there?"

"He is indeed. They call him the Carpet Queen."

Marson and I had completed a quick rehab of a loft space in downtown Dumont. Spare but comfortable, it served our immediate needs for housing near the office, but more important, it was *ours*—our first home.

On Wednesday, the morning after the board meeting, which had run late, we hustled to get out the door a few minutes before nine. Because of the logistics of our meeting at the future building site, it made sense for us to pick up Walter Zakarian, whose office was in that direction, and ride out there together. Marson had an SUV, a whopping hunter-green Range Rover, since he had occasional need to visit construction sites. We climbed in, thumped the doors closed, and backed out to the street. We had no sooner left the driveway when my phone rang.

I glanced at the readout. "It's Allan's friend Justin—in Mexico." After a few opening pleasantries, I said into the phone, "Hold on, Justin. Let me switch this to speaker. I'm in the car with my partner, Marson." When the introductions were complete, I said, "Okay, Justin. Tell us about Walter."

"I'm not sure where to start," he said. "Walter Zakarian has been a fixture down here for years. Gay as a goose, of course, but he brags about how he's got everyone fooled at home—yeah, right. He's into the young stuff, so when he comes to P.V., he either buys them in an alley or brings one from home. Week or so ago, he brought a guy from Chicago, a buff bartender named Jimmy Linsky. But you get what you pay for, I guess, cuz Jimmy was tricking up a storm down here, right under Walter's nose. Big blowup in a restaurant a few nights ago. Jimmy finally hauled off and slugged Walter. When they got back to the condo, Walter made a show of calling the cops and throwing Jimmy out on the street—told him he'd have to find his own way home. The pretty boy was broke, natch. Threats were made. High drama. Ugly, but kinda funny too."

After thanking Justin for the insights, I hung up, then said to Marson, "The black eye."

"A reasonable deduction, Sherlock."

When we were a block away from the vast Zakarian's showroom, Marson phoned Walter to say we were almost there, asking him to meet us outside. Walter said he was in the upstairs office and suggested we use the side street, where there was a private entrance.

Within seconds, we parked at the curb alongside the building and waited with the engine running. A few moments later, Walter emerged from a door at the top of a long flight of stairs and raised the arm of his bulky topcoat to wave at us. He closed the door behind him, giving it a shake to make sure it had locked, and started down the stairs.

And then, when he had descended only two or three steps, he tumbled forward, plummeting head over heals — again and again and again — gaining speed until at last his fall was broken by the concrete stoop.

Sprawled facedown, he seeped red on the chalky cement.

From the passenger side of the Range Rover, I bolted out the door and rushed toward Walter while Marson phoned nine-one-one. Crossing several yards of damp, frosty turf that separated the street from the building, I slid and fell, making a mess of my clothes as I scrambled to regain my footing. When I arrived at the cement slab, I crouched over Walter, catching my breath, tempted to turn him over, but figuring he should not be moved. "Walter!" I shouted. "Can you hear me?"

He stirred — not much, but thank God he wasn't dead.

"Don't move, Walter. Marson's calling for help."

He mumbled something.

"Is he alive?" Marson yelled from the car with the phone to his ear.

"Yes," I yelled back. Then I leaned close to Walter's head.

His bloody face seemed to kiss the cement before tilting to one side. He opened an eye to look at me. "Tripped me," he managed to say. "Something tripped my legs."

I looked up the stairway, and high near the top, glinting in the morning sun, a wire was stretched tight across the treads, secured at shin height to the banister posts on both sides.

Marson's car door slammed. "They're on the way!"

As I turned to watch him rushing toward me, I saw a car zip past on the street, barely slowing as it turned onto First Avenue, heading downtown. I knew the car well— an ancient fuchsia hatchback, there was nothing else like it in Dumont.

It belonged to Glee Savage.

By the time the paramedic team sped Walter away to the local hospital, sirens blaring, Sheriff Thomas Simms had already arrived with his police crew, accompanied by their own sirens. A black man with a graceful bearing and a refined workday wardrobe of natty business suits, Simms defied every stereotype of the small-town cop. He had also defied all the odds of rising from the rank of detective and being elected top lawman in Dumont County, where the white-bread demographics were as rooted as the region's timbered past. Earlier that year, not long after my arrival in Dumont, when I first met the sheriff at a chamber luncheon, I had asked Marson if Simms was gay. "No," said Marson, "unless his wife, Gloria, and their little Tommy are parties to an elaborate sham."

That morning at the foot of the stairs, Simms asked us, "And you saw it happen, correct?"

"Yes, Thomas, both of us," said Marson. "We were sitting in the car waiting for Walter, watching as he left the building."

"And he said he was tripped?"

I answered, "Right, Sheriff. Those were his only words:

'Tripped me. Something tripped my legs.'"

Simms already had his crew clambering about the top of the stairs—taking pictures, making notes, checking for footprints. "Too bad," he said, "you can't pull fingerprints from a wire."

Simms then asked if we could come to his office to give signed statements, and of course we complied.

An hour later, we were sitting across from his desk when the police stenographer left the room and Simms's phone rang. He spoke a bit, nodded a lot. After hanging up, he told us, "Walter's in intensive care, but they think he'll pull through. I can't even try to question him before tomorrow, which means I have nothing at all to work with. Ditto for the physical evidence at the crime scene—it yielded nothing." He leaned forward with his elbows on the desk, continuing, "Help me with this. I don't know Walter very well. Can you give me any background that might shed some light on what happened?"

Stalling, Marson asked, "What sort of background?"

"Enemies. Motives. Axes to grind."

Marson glanced at me. I glanced at Marson.

Then we told him about Mexico and the Chicago bartender.

We told him about the prickly confrontations at the prior night's meeting.

And I told him about the fuchsia hatchback speeding away that morning.

Thursday morning, Sheriff Simms phoned to tell us that Walter would be out of intensive care by afternoon and moved to a private room. He asked if we could meet him in the hospital cafeteria, maybe have lunch, and then visit Walter together.

"Just name the time," said Marson, and we settled on one o'clock.

By that hour, the cafeteria's noon rush was over (moving from California, I was forever amazed by how early most Midwesterners took their meals), so we had no trouble finding a quiet corner table where we could talk freely.

Simms, tall and lean, ate a few forkfuls of tuna salad from the wedged tomato splayed open on a bed of greens. He dabbed his lips, returned the napkin to his lap, and said, "The doctors tell me Zakarian was lucky. The padding of his heavy overcoat, in addition to what they called 'the victim's corpulence,' protected his vital organs. And your quick action getting help—that improved his chances a lot. He suffered some serious trauma, so he'll be laid up for weeks, maybe months. But all the brain scans are negative; the concussion wasn't as bad as it looked."

I shook my head. "'Corpulence.' Walter wouldn't like hearing that."

Marson asked Simms, "Have you talked to him yet?"

"This morning, briefly. He was cogent enough to answer a few questions. For instance, he didn't *enter* his office by the outside stairway yesterday—he parked in back and used the employee entrance, went through the store, and took the indoor stairs up to the offices—which means the wire could have been rigged anytime, like the night before. Also, he's the only one who uses those outside stairs; the door is always locked and opens straight into his office. So this wasn't random mischief. The intended victim had to be Walter."

I asked, "Did *he* have any idea who might have done it?"

Simms sat back. "That's where this gets sorta strange. Other than supplying the information I told you about, Walter wasn't very cooperative, and I don't think his crankiness was the result of his injuries or the painkillers. He was plenty lucid, and he seemed far more concerned about keeping things quiet than he was about solving the crime."

With an exasperated tone, Marson said, "That just doesn't make *sense*."

"To Walter's way of thinking"—Simms tossed his arms—"he says that something like this could be 'bad for business.'"

"Or," I noted, "something like this could boot him out of his closet."

After lunch, Simms made a call and learned that Walter had been moved to his new room, so he led us to the top floor of the building, which was quieter than I'd expected, without the typical scuttle of staff in the halls. The guard posted outside Walter's room was not from the hospital's security team, but an armed and uniformed sheriff's deputy—a sobering reminder that someone had tried to kill Walter.

Stepping inside, I was not prepared for the sight of Walter's elaborate traction apparatus. He may have been "lucky," as the doctors had told Simms, but he had nonetheless broken a leg, an arm, several ribs, and had suffered additional fractures from stem to stern. There was very little of him that wasn't bandaged, and the parts still exposed were needled with tubes or wired to monitors. Given the total picture, his black eye looked pretty good.

Both Marson and I mumbled stunned expressions of sympathy.

"How are you feeling, Walter?" said Simms.

Walter managed to roll his eyes. "I've been better."

The sheriff told him, "I understand there was a confrontation of sorts on the night before this happened—at the museum board meeting."

"People don't always agree on everything," said Walter.

"True enough. But are you aware that Glee Savage was seen speeding away from the Zakarian's showroom at the time you fell yesterday?"

Walter shook his head. Monitors bleeped.

Simms said, "So I talked to her last night."

"Don't talk to *her*," said Walter. "She's the biggest mouth in town."

Simms stated the obvious: "She's a reporter. And it turns out, she was running late for a nine-o'clock interview downtown at the *Register*'s offices. It all checks out."

I thought aloud, "Then Glee didn't do it."

"I doubt it," said Simms.

"But now," said Walter, "she knows what happened, right? You handed her a big, fat-ass story, and she just can't wait to plaster this on page one."

"No," said the sheriff, "she doesn't know about it, at least not from me. I don't want to go public with this—yet—because the early stage of the investigation is sensitive, and it would be a mistake to start tipping people off. So I told her that someone had seen her in a hurry and was worried that something might have been wrong. She apologized for speeding, and that was that."

"Good," said Walter. "Just drop it. I'll be fine, sooner or later. And I still have a business to run. So leave this alone."

"First of all," said Simms, "this won't 'keep,' not forever. The *Register* has a police scanner in the newsroom, so even if they missed what happened yesterday, it's only a matter of time before they catch on. But more to the point, Walter: a trip wire at the top of a long flight of stairs is not a prank. In my book, that's attempted murder. Now, if you don't want to pursue this, fine, don't cooperate. But I'm sworn to uphold the law—I can't just walk away from it."

"Take my advice, Sheriff, and don't waste your time.

There's nothing to go on."

Simms turned to Marson and me. "Guys, the reason I brought you here today: tell Walter what you told me."

Marson and I looked at each other, then looked again at Simms.

He added, "About Mexico."

Walter's monitors chattered and blipped with evident panic.

Once they calmed down, Marson and I laid out for Walter what we'd learned on the phone about his recent stay in Puerto Vallarta—the trick from Chicago, the fight, the threats, all of it.

When we finished, Simms said to Walter, "This bartender friend of yours, we need to talk to him. How can I reach him."

"I've no idea."

"Walter," said Simms, "Chicago may be a big town, but it shouldn't take too much digging to locate a gay bartender named Jimmy Linsky."

From his nest of splints and bandages and tubes, Walter gave us a steely look. "Gentlemen, I have nothing more to add to this conversation. If you don't mind, I need my rest."

Knuckles rapped at the door. Simms cracked it open. The guard said, "Delivery for Mr. Zakarian."

Simms opened the door wide, and the deputy brought in a lavish floral arrangement, all white—roses, lilies, orchids, hydrangeas—and set it on a nightstand near the bed. Then the deputy left and closed the door. The fragrance was so thick, it stung my eyes.

"There's a card," said Marson, plucking a small envelope from the bouquet.

Walter, whose bandages made it impossible for him to manipulate anything, said, "Go ahead. Open it."

Marson opened the envelope, looked at the card, and passed it to me. I read it and passed it to Sheriff Simms. He read it, then held it for Walter to see.

Written with a fountain pen in peacock-blue ink, the graceful script said, *You need to be more careful.* And it was signed, *XOXOX, Mary.*

How, I wondered, had Mary Questman known to send flowers?

That evening, we decided to prepare a quiet dinner for two at the loft. The last few days had been unnerving—the testy board meeting, Walter Zakarian's death-defying fall, the weirdness of his refusal to cooperate with the investigation—so we took refuge against the chilly night by staying home and creating a simple meal that featured a comfort-food standby with a decadent twist, lobster pot pie. That, together with a light, elegant salad and a lovely bottle of Pouilly-Fumé, would help us keep at bay the perplexities of wanton malice, at least for a few hours.

Working in tandem, Marson and I assembled the pie and popped it in the oven, then opened the wine and tippled while we arranged our place settings on the granite-topped counter of the center island. Perched on stools, we would dine in the kitchen, huddled with a few candles, gazing out into the cavernous loft we now called home.

We had made little effort to disguise the building's utilitarian past—it had been a retail space, a haberdashery—and we had taken a sleek, minimal approach to its furnishings. Some, no doubt, would criticize our aesthetic as sterile, but to our way of thinking, it represented a clean slate. Having found each other less than a year earlier, we were still in the process of exploring a new life together. We were still defining who "we" were. The surface issue of decorating had no urgency. It could evolve, perhaps in directions that would surprise and delight us. Why rush the journey of discovery?

And now our home was filled with the rich, heady aroma of a pot pie baking and bubbling and browning. As we sat together at the counter—still in our business clothes, without the jackets—our conversation had drifted through a hodgepodge of trifling topics, avoiding the one matter that chafed for attention. Then, while pouring another splash of wine for both of us, Marson ended the moratorium by asking, "You know what worries me most about Walter?"

"Well," I said, loosening the knot of my tie, "it's worrisome that whoever tried to kill him might try again."

"Okay, that hadn't occurred to me"—he scrunched his features in thought—"but what worries me *second* most is the tragedy Walter has inflicted on himself."

I scrunched *my* features. "All right, cupcake. I'm listening."

Marson grinned. We'd been testing pet names for each other, but nothing had stuck yet. He said, "I'm talking about Walter's deeply closeted life."

"Ahhh." I swirled my wine. "And his fear of being outed is obstructing the investigation."

"There's that, sure. But even worse is that he's wasted so many years covering his tracks instead of living a full life. And he's determined to go on wasting whatever years are left. Walter's how old—almost fifty? With any luck, he might have another thirty ahead of him, maybe forty, so why not come clean?"

"He's afraid it'll be 'bad for business.'" I snorted.

Marson gave his head a slow, woeful shake. "Those demons are imagined—who cares if the guy selling you a rug is gay? He's stuck in the prejudices he grew up with." Marson leaned forward on the counter and placed his hand on my arm. "Do I sound like a hypocrite? When I was Walter's age, I was living the same lie. It took me another ten years to finally get it."

I gave him a kiss. "There's a big difference between your story and Walter's. On New Year's Day, when you and I first made love, you told me you'd never had sex with a man before."

"That's true," said Marson, "I swear it. I'd wondered about it since college, but the fantasy always felt forbidden. So I just lived with the pain."

"On the other hand," I said, "Walter has a long history of tasting that forbidden fruit—often and with abandon—but in another country, so the wealthy widows at home won't get wind of it. Now, *that's* what I call a major closet case."

"And what would you call me?"

"A late bloomer." I traced a finger along the inside of his thigh, from the knee up, before adding, "I'm so glad I was around for the deflowering."

The pie burned.

Even so, it was delicious—when at last we got around to eating it, back at the counter, wearing big, fluffy bathrobes. Dropping a single ice cube into my wine, which had lost its chill during our absence, I said, "Mary Questman's floral tribute. What did you make of that?"

"What did it say?" Marson set down his fork and recited from memory the message on the card. "'You need to be more careful.' Such an odd sentiment. You could read it two ways: either genuine concern or a veiled threat. At the very least, it carries a ring of snarkiness."

"But," I noted, "Mary doesn't have a snarky bone in her body."

"No, not the Mary I know."

"Then again, deep down, she might be a psychopath, hell-bent on Walter's demise. If so, that sweet facade could cloak all manner of devilry."

Marson laughed.

I raised a brow. "Just saying—we need to cover all the angles, cupcake."

"If you say so, Sherlock."

Hmmm, I thought. Cupcake and Sherlock—were they starting to stick? "Anyway," I said to Marson, "You told me that Mary and Walter once had a 'thing' going on. Did Walter jilt her?"

"To the best of my knowledge, *she* dumped *him*. Which means: if one of them's grinding an ax, it wouldn't be Mary."

"Depends on why she dumped him. Maybe she thought it was time to get some closure and finish him off." My tone was playful.

Marson understood. "Look, kiddo. We both know Mary isn't capable of that."

Kiddo, I thought. That just might work. Being more than twenty years younger than Marson, I might have found the term condescending—and overly literal. But I knew Marson well enough by now to understand that his spontaneous use of the word carried not a hint of ageism. Or reverse ageism. Coming from him, it conveyed pure tenderness.

Marson continued, "Sheriff Simms flat-out loves Mary, same as everyone else. But he did see the card, and he had the same reaction we did: What did she mean by that?"

"Plus," I said, "how did she know about Walter's accident at all?"

"Right. So this gets touchy for Simms. He needs some follow-up, but even questioning Mary—implying she might be hiding something—could be found offensive. And we don't want Dumont's top lawman offending Dumont's top philanthropist, do we?"

"Nope," I agreed. "She's laid a lot of golden eggs in this town."

"Nicely put."

"Thank you." I got up from my stool at the kitchen island and carried a few dishes to the sink.

Marson followed with a few more. "So Simms asked me to talk to her and try to get a feel for the situation. We're having lunch tomorrow, which ought to be pleasant enough, even under these crazy circumstances. I mean, we're friends."

I was rinsing a plate. "She seems to adore you."

He stepped back to the island to retrieve our wine glasses. "It's mutual. We've known each other forever, but it's Questman Center that really brought us together—getting it designed and built, sharing that dream and watching it rise from the ground. Over the past three years, Mary and I have become soul mates."

"Soul mates," I repeated. "Just like us."

Marson rubbed up behind me and whispered in my ear, "Not exactly."

His robe had flopped open.

So had mine.

Since Marson would be lunching with Mary Questman at her home the next afternoon, I figured that would be a good time for me to meet with Debbie Jacobson. As president of the museum board, Debbie needed to know what had happened to Walter, despite his preference to keep the whole incident hushed up. And as a member of the board, I felt duty-bound to report such a significant development, as Walter had been in the midst of important board business when interrupted by deadly mischief.

Debbie agreed to meet me downtown for lunch at First Avenue Bistro. One of Dumont's better dining venues, it had opened some years earlier as First Avenue Grill, but then someone informed the proprietress that people were tittering about the restaurant's initials, so she modified the name to produce a more fabulous monogram.

It was a crisp, pleasant day as I walked along the main street from the Miles & Norris offices to the Bistro. When I entered through the front door at twelve-thirty, Debbie had just arrived through the rear entrance, which led in from a small parking lot. We waved, then met in the center of the room with the owner, Nancy Sanderson, who showed us to the table often occupied by Marson and me. A prime spot, it nestled between a stone fireplace and the front window, affording a fine view of both the entire room and the noontime bustle on the street.

An earnest and knowledgeable foodie, Nancy recited a few specials, including the soup, clam chowder—no surprise, as it was Friday. She left our menus, then moved to the door to greet new arrivals.

Debbie smiled. "This is *nice*, Brody. We should do this more often." She patted my arm.

I returned the smile. "Couldn't agree more, Deb."

"So." She sat up straight, folding her hands in front of her. "Are you glad you joined the board?"

Tough call, I thought. "Well, sure," I told her, "but I'm afraid the last few days have been less than pleasant."

A quizzical frown wrinkled her brow. "What do you mean?"

I exhaled a deep, breathy sigh. "I assume you haven't heard—about Walter."

"No." She dropped her hands from the table, leaning forward. "What?"

"That's why I thought we'd better have lunch. In the best interests of the museum, you need to know about this. Two days ago, when Marson and I drove over to pick him up at his showroom, he took a terrible fall—from the stairway outside his second-floor office."

Deb was ashen. "*Jesus.* Is he okay?"

"He's alive. And he'll recover, eventually. But he's in awful shape." I ran through the litany of his injuries. "But the *worst* part—"

"There's *more*?"

I lowered my voice. "Sheriff Simms thinks someone tried to kill him."

Deb sat back again, raising a hand to her forehead, retreating from the unthinkable. "Who would *do* such a thing?"

"Simms is working on a few leads, but only one seems promising. Walter had a fight with someone while he was on vacation." I offered no other details. Though I was convinced his life would be better outside the closet, it was not my job to out him by spilling the sultry secrets of Puerto Vallarta.

"A *fight*?" said Deb. "That doesn't sound at all like Walter."

"He's a man of many surprises, I'll grant you that."

Digesting what she'd heard, composing herself, she asked, "Is there anything I can do to help?"

"I'm not the praying type, but that might help. Otherwise, just send good vibes."

She smiled.

"Either way," I added, "keep it under your hat, at least for now. Word is bound to get out, but Simms wants to buy some time during the early investigation."

Nancy then returned to our table, order pad in hand. "Getting hungry?"

Though we had not yet looked at the menus, we made some quick choices, and one of the servers brought iced tea.

Waiting for lunch—Asian chicken salad for Deb, spinach

and mushroom frittata for me — we eased our conversation toward topics more genial than attempted murder.

"How's Robin?" I asked.

"Happy. Doing well at school. Hard to believe she's a senior already." With a soft laugh, Deb added, "But I'm still having trouble with the pronouns. They get stuck in my mouth."

Robin Jacobson had been born Robert Jacobson, whom I'd first met the prior March, during his spring break from college, on the evening he announced his transition to "she."

I said, "She's lucky to have you. Kids in that situation need supportive parents, but too many of them go through hell."

"I can't pretend to fully understand it, but the love, that's unconditional. He's my baby. I mean, she."

"And the transition?" I asked. "Last spring, the hormone therapy had begun. Any more talk of surgery?"

"Full steam ahead," said Deb, sounding brave, looking resigned. "Still in intensive therapy, but the first surgery is scheduled for the week after graduation."

Sounds expensive, I thought. Although progress had been made, not many insurance policies covered gender re-assignment.

As if reading my thoughts, Deb said, "We'll work it out." She paused before explaining, "Growing up, we didn't have much. I know what it means to be deprived of things. There's no way I could deprive Robin of this."

I repeated, "She's lucky to have you."

When lunch arrived, we got back to business and spoke of the new museum plans — tweaks to the departmental al-lotments of interior space, various concerns regarding ex-terior details, the need for computerized perspective draw-ings for final design approval, timing of press releases, and on and on. Deb had a leather-bound notebook open on the table next to her plate and scratched out a checklist as we ate. I took out my iPhone and began typing notes.

After an hour of this, with the meal finished and the check paid, she said, "This was great, Brody. Really productive. Thanks for your time."

"I'm just sorry I had to deliver such awful news—about Walter."

"Ugh." She swung her head. "Poor guy. Hope he pulls through okay." She scooched her chair back.

Taking her cue, I rose, then helped her up.

"Need a ride?" she asked.

"No, but I'll walk you out."

We said goodbye to Nancy, complimenting her on another fine meal, then stepped out through the rear exit.

The parking area off the alley behind the building accommodated some half-dozen cars, with Deb's new Lexus nearest the door. Its golden accents sparkled in the midday sunlight, and I noticed that her temporary permit had been replaced with Wisconsin plates, framed with gold to match the other trim. As we stepped behind the car, she turned to me, recalling, "I've made a few calls to Walter's cell number since Tuesday's meeting, but they never got past voice mail. That alone should've clued me that something was wrong— he never lets messages pile up."

"Well," I said, "at least *that* mystery is solved. He won't be taking calls for a while."

"Talk about lousy timing."

I quipped, "There's a *good* time to wind up in traction?"

She smirked. "Of course not. I meant it's lousy timing for the museum. Walter was trying to patch together some sort of deal with Badger Stone. Who knows? That might've saved the museum a bundle."

I took out my phone to type another note, telling Deb,

"Let me look into that."

She took out her own phone to check for mail. "I doubt if it'll do any good," she said. "Walter told us at the meeting that the whole deal hinged on favors owed to *him*. And now? He's out of the picture, at least for quite a while."

I typed another note.

Deb returned her phone to her purse. We shared a parting hug. Then she got into her car and pulled out to the alley.

As she drove away, the phone in my hand chirped with an arriving text message. It was from Marson. He wrote, "Just finished with Mary. Simms wants to see us. Meet me at his office."

The phone chirped again.

Marson added, "Love you, kiddo."

The sheriff's headquarters was only a few blocks away, adjacent to the county courthouse, so I walked. When I arrived outside Simms's office, a deputy said, "He's expecting you." She opened the door, then closed it behind me. Marson was already there. Both he and Simms stood to greet me as I entered.

"We were just getting started," said Simms, pulling an extra chair over to his desk. I settled in next to Marson, facing Simms across the desk. As the sheriff seated himself, he suggested, "Maybe you should start over, Marson."

Marson turned to tell me, "Mary is so sweet, but that housekeeper of hers—Berta—such an ungainly creature. Impertinent, too. I can't imagine why Mary puts up with her. But I think she does most of the day-to-day cooking, and I must admit, she knows her stuff. Her chicken quenelles were sensational. And that *sauce*—a perfect lemon beurre blanc." He shook his head, adding, "If only she'd stay in the kitchen . . ."

I gaped at him. "What does Berta have to do with Walter's trip down the stairs?"

He shrugged. "Nothing. I was trying to set the scene."

"Okay, got it. Nice lunch. So let's flash forward: Did Mary try to kill Walter?"

"Of *course* not."

"How do you know that?"

The sheriff's eyes slid back and forth, following our exchange.

Marson explained, "Mary was aghast when I told her the extent of Walter's injuries, and she was mortified to realize how unsympathetic her note had sounded. She had no idea Walter's situation was so serious."

Simms asked, "But how did she know about Walter's situation at all?"

"Late Wednesday afternoon—the day of Walter's fall and the day after the confrontation at the board meeting—she phoned Walter at his office. She'd been angry the night before, but had since calmed down, and she called to talk to him about what had happened, wondering what was behind his treatment of Glee Savage. In other words, she was hoping to mediate. What's more, she was concerned about Walter's black eye—curious about what had happened, intending to wish him a quick recovery. But when she called, of course, Walter wasn't there. When Mary identified herself, the guy on the phone must've figured that the revered Mrs. Questman was entitled to more of an explanation than 'he's not in,' so he told her that Walter had 'stumbled on something' and had gone to the hospital 'for observation.' Mary thought he might've sprained an ankle. The huge flower arrangement was meant as a lighthearted joke—to cheer up a friend."

Simms said, "I'll check at Zakarian's and see if anyone can corroborate that phone conversation. If so, that's good enough for me. Safe to say, we're all itching to cross Mary's name off the list." Doodling on his notepad, he slashed through something with his ballpoint.

I asked Marson, "Is Mary now aware that Walter was the victim of attempted murder?"

"No. I told her he fell down the flight of stairs. I didn't mention that he was tripped."

"Good," said Simms. "We're starting to understand the direction of this, but the longer we keep the case quiet, the faster we can move behind the scenes."

Marson said, "It sounds as if you're zeroing in on someone."

I added, "Someone in Chicago?"

Simms hesitated. He glanced at his notepad, then closed its cover. "Okay, guys. You've been terrific—truly helpful. This is for your ears only."

Marson and I gave quick nods of agreement, eager to hear more.

"We found out where Jimmy Linsky works," said Simms. "A bar in the so-called Boystown area. And we've just reached the bar manager, a guy named Bruce. He's a good friend of Linsky, and as a favor, Bruce gave him the bartending job about a year ago when he got fired somewhere else. So Linsky phoned Bruce from Mexico after the fight with Walter, told him what had happened, and asked for an advance so he could buy a plane ticket home. Bruce couldn't advance wages from the bar, so instead, *he* booked the flight for Linsky—with his own credit card. Next day, this past Monday, Linsky phoned Bruce from the airport in Puerto Vallarta to confirm he was on his way, due at O'Hare that evening. So Bruce told Linsky he was scheduled for the Tuesday shift at the bar, starting at four." Simms paused with a Cheshire grin.

Marson asked, "And?"

"No show, no call. Bruce confirmed that the charge for the flight went through on his credit card, but he's had no word from Linsky since. Mad as hell. Hopes we find him."

"Wow," I said. "Linsky goes missing in Chicago sometime Tuesday, and then Wednesday morning, just a few hours north in Wisconsin, Walter nearly tumbles to his death."

"Yes," said Simms. "Wow."

Marson and I had spent far too much time playing cloak-and-dagger that week, at a time when we had plenty of work waiting at the office. Not only did we need to get hopping on revisions of the museum plans, but we also needed to focus on requests that had been made for proposals for several other public projects. With the critical acclaim that had been lavished on Questman Center, the Miles & Norris design brand had acquired sudden cachet. Municipalities large and small, hoping their next big project might be judged a landmark, now thought of us. We could pick and choose our work—a great luxury for any firm, even greater for a small one like ours—but it would take time and study to evaluate the requests and to rank our interest in pursuing them.

Friday night, therefore, we decided to make a dent in our backlog on Saturday. With any luck, the distractions of Walter's attempted murder could be back-burnered over the weekend. We could spend the day together, just us, plotting our firm's future, doing what we loved most. And the office would be quiet—no staff, no interns, no appointments.

The office was quiet, all right. In fact, it seemed eerie.

Downtown on First Avenue—Dumont's main drag—traffic was so light that we were able to park on the street in front of our building, entering around ten and locking the door behind us. In the front reception area, we left the blinds drawn on the street windows, then went back to our respective offices to sift through e-mail for a few minutes before settling into the conference room, where we planned to spread out the proposals.

At my desk, I woke the computer and waited a moment as the messages poured in from overnight. Dozens transferred instantly to the junk folder, which I gave a quick perusal before trashing en masse. Perhaps half a dozen, surviving the purge, remained in my inbox. One by one, I dealt with them, junking a few, saving others, and typing short responses to those that required it. Just as I sent the last of these—*ding*—a new e-mail arrived in the inbox. It was from Diamonds. The subject line: EMERGENCY MEETING.

I opened the message, which had been sent as an e-blast to the museum board and copied to all of its advisers. Then I read through the body of the memo:

> To those of you who may not yet have heard the unfortunate news, I am sorry to report that our fellow board member, Walter Zakarian, has suffered serious injuries as the result of a fall. While his prognosis is encouraging, his recuperation will be lengthy, and it is unrealistic to expect him to perform board duties while tending to the priorities of his health and well-being. I know I speak for all of us in wishing him a complete and speedy recovery. We look forward to welcoming him back.
>
> Meanwhile, for the rest of us, it's business as usual— our most pressing matter being the new building project. As you'll recall from our last meeting, Walter felt he might be in a position to solicit special pricing considerations from Badger Stone Builders. While that

struck me as wishful thinking, it was a direction worth exploring. Due to these recent developments, however, Walter will of course be unable to follow through.

Our best course of action now is to solidify our emerging relationship with Hand of Zeus Construction, which has already invested considerable effort in a comprehensive preliminary proposal. I am therefore calling a special meeting of the board of directors this coming Monday—usual time and place—to consider and approve a single agenda item, authorizing me to execute needed documents with Hand of Zeus.

Please make any necessary adjustments to your calendars that will allow you to attend on Monday evening, as we must have a quorum to proceed with this important work.

With thanks for your anticipated cooperation, I remain respectfully yours,

Deborah Jacobson
President, Board of Directors
Dumont Public Museum

I turned from the computer to see Marson standing in my office doorway. He asked, "You got the memo? What do you think?"

"I think I should call Sheriff Simms."

Simms was also working on that Saturday morning, so I had no trouble reaching him. As we spoke, I forwarded Debbie's e-mail to him, explaining, "When I met with her yesterday, I mentioned that she should *not* go public with the news about Walter—because it could hamper the investigation."

Simms asked, "You think she's trying to do that?"

Instead of a direct answer, I gave him a license plate number, which I read from the notes on my iPhone. "That's Debbie Jacobson's new Lexus. Can you verify the registration?"

"Sure. Why?"

"Just a hunch."

Marson and I found it difficult to concentrate on our intended task that day. As we sifted through the pile of projects in the conference room, the merits of the proposals we attempted to evaluate were sidelined again and again by the intrusive topic of Debbie's ill-timed group e-mail.

"What was she *thinking*?" said Marson.

"If we knew that," I said, "the suspense would be spoiled."

"Wise guy." He pecked my cheek—we weren't accomplishing much.

By late afternoon, after too many hours of this, we'd grown bored, restless, and hungry, so we decided to go home for an early dinner or, better yet, an early cocktail. While switching off lights in the back offices, we heard a rap at the glass of the street door. Together, we stepped out to the reception area.

It was just past four-thirty, and the sun had already set. With the November sky clogged by a thick cover of clouds, the afternoon street scene beyond the drizzled window looked like the dead of night. A tall figure waited outside the door, hunkered in a trench coat. A fist of black knuckles reached forward and again rapped the glass.

"Thomas!" said Marson, swinging the door wide. "Come on in. Let me take that wet coat."

I asked, "Can I get you something, Sheriff? I can start some coffee."

"Thanks, Brody, but don't bother—too much caffeine today."

With a grin, Marson asked, "Social call?"

Sheriff Simms returned the grin. "No. I was hoping to catch you at home, but driving by just now, I spotted your Range Rover at the curb." Tapping his noggin, he added, "I put two and two together."

"And *that*," I said, "that's why you're the detective and we're the lowly architects."

"Don't sell yourselves short. Your instincts have been pretty damn good." Then he moved half a pace closer and lowered his voice. "Got a minute? I have a few developments."

We moved another half-pace nearer, closing the circle. The dim outer office, with its blinds closed to the world, felt hidden and conspiratorial. The sheriff's chest rose and fell, rose and fell. I could hear him breathe. Beneath the lapel of his wool serge suit jacket, I saw the glint of a polished leather shoulder holster.

"We found Jimmy Linsky," he said. "I just talked to him."

Marson said, "You mean he's, like, behind *bars*?"

"No, I talked to him on the phone. And he has an airtight alibi. He's in Mexico—never left. While waiting at the airport for his return flight, he met some hunky guy arriving on the incoming plane. A guy with lotsa bucks. He paid Jimmy plenty to spend the week with him. Checked in together at some snazzy resort that very afternoon. All documented."

Marson thought aloud: "So Jimmy Linsky didn't try to kill Walter. Mary Questman didn't do it. Neither did Glee Savage."

"Right," said Simms. Then he looked toward me. "But I ran the plates on Debbie Jacobson's Lexus, and guess who owns it."

I guessed, "Hand of Zeus Construction?"

"Bingo. Great thinking, Brody. It was just the tip we needed."

Marson's mouth hung open.

I told them, "I just *knew* something wasn't right—the way

Diamonds kept trying to railroad Hand of Zeus for the museum project. Meanwhile, the new car, the flashy clothes. And *then* I noticed she was wearing a Rolex."

With a huff of scorn, Simms said, "She got way more than a *watch*. After we traced the car to Zeus, we ran a check of all their public records, and about an hour ago, we hit pay dirt. For tax purposes, Hand of Zeus publicly registered a charitable scholarship foundation. The record shows that the foundation has received only one application. And they've awarded a full, ongoing college scholarship to that sole applicant—whose name is Robert Jacobson."

"They'll need to change their records," I noted. "Robert is now Robin."

Marson cleared his throat and managed to find his voice. "This started *when*?"

"Three years ago," said Simms, "when Robert started college. Into the fourth year now."

"Good God," said Marson. "Construction of Questman Center began about three years ago. Hand of Zeus built it. And Debbie chaired the building committee."

"Coincidence?" I asked.

"Payola," said Simms.

Simms wondered if Marson and I could ask Debbie to come to our loft on Sunday morning, so I called to invite her over for coffee, under the pretext of discussing changes to the museum plans. Glad to hear that things were moving forward, she said she'd stop by at eleven sharp, as she'd already agreed to drive a neighbor to church. "It starts at eleven," she said on the phone, "but I don't need to stick around."

Hours before her arrival, we awoke to a sunny morning — a blessing, one might say, after such a dismal Saturday — to find news of Walter's calamity as the top story on page one of the *Dumont Daily Register*. The headline covered the full width of the page: ZAKARIAN VICTIM OF MURDER TRY. Below it, a question: *Was it payback for Mexico scuffle?*

Tossing the paper onto the kitchen counter, Marson said, "It was just a matter of time."

"After Debbie's e-blast," I said, "it was just a matter of *hours*. You can't stuff the genie back in the bottle."

The story attributed most of its details to "a source close to the situation," including the fall from the stairs, the trip-wire, the black eye—and speculation that Walter, "a life-long bachelor, may have had an altercation with another man while on a secretive trip to Mexico."

"That had to come from Debbie," I said. "The e-blast came from her, so the *Register* went right to the source."

Marson asked, "But why would she *do* that?"

"I can think of two reasons. First, it directs suspicion down a course that we already know is dead-ended. And second, it robs Walter of sympathy by putting him at the center of a salacious-sounding scandal—scotching his chances of sweet-talking Badger Stone into doing him any public favors."

Marson shook his head with wonder. "Is she that clever?" But no answer was needed. The facts spoke for themselves.

Promptly at eleven, Diamonds pulled up in front of the loft, got out of the Lexus, and entered to our greetings and chitchat. "Poor Walter," she said. "That story this morning—yikes."

And two minutes later, as planned, Sheriff Simms "happened" to stop by. We invited him to join us as we settled into the conversation area near the front of the loft, seated on sofas surrounding a large, low table, where the museum plans had been laid out along with a tray of pastries and the coffee service.

We had not yet finished our first cup when Diamonds idly asked Simms, "Any progress with Walter's . . . problems?"

"Well, Miss Debbie"—Simms had a charming habit of addressing women that way—"let's look at the big picture for a moment. When dealing with a whodunit, it's conventional wisdom that the answer lies in motive, means, and opportunity. In this case, the 'means' was stretching a wire across a flight of stairs, which is baby simple—*anyone* could've done that. And the 'opportunity'—it was an open stairway on a public street, so anyone and everyone had access. Which leaves us with the motive, the 'why.' Would you like to hear about that?"

Diamonds nodded.

And then, step by step, Simms laid out his case—stretching back to the influence peddling when Questman Center was built, leading up to the extreme and desperate attempt to prevent Walter Zakarian from securing another contractor's lower bid to build the new museum. Simms concluded, "The 'why' was good old-fashioned greed."

Diamonds had listened in stone-faced silence. When at last she spoke, she asked Simms, "How did you know?"

The sheriff looked in my direction.

I told Diamonds, "At lunch Friday, when we were talking about the expense of Robin's surgery, you mentioned that while you were growing up, you didn't have much—you knew what it meant to be deprived."

Staring into space, she closed her eyes.

I continued, "But you seem to have pricey tastes, so everyone has always assumed you 'came from money.' Once I understood otherwise, that led to a very different explanation for your new car—and everything else." I paused, then felt the odd compulsion to add, "Sorry, Deb."

Diamonds exhaled a soft laugh of defeat. "Poor Walter. Stupid Walter. He just couldn't leave well enough alone. And now he's screwed things up for both of us."

"Miss Debbie?" said Simms, standing. "Will you come with me, please?"

With supreme understatement, she said, "I don't suppose I have much choice."

He gave her a look. "No."

In the quiet space of the loft, we watched through the street windows as Simms drove away with Diamonds, leaving her Lexus at the curb outside our door. Its fake gold trim gleamed cheap and swank under the November sun, which struggled toward noon, slanting low through tangled branches. The last of a few brown leaves let go, surrendering to a northern breeze. Dry and nipping, it whispered of the coming winter.

Marson asked, "What would you like to do today, kiddo?"

"I dunno."

"Maybe we've already accomplished enough for one day. Anything else would seem anticlimactic. I think we should just stay home."

"Well," I said, "it *is* Sunday. We could roast a big chicken. Or glaze a ham."

Marson traced a finger around my ear. "But we have no chicken."

I grinned. "We have no ham."

❑

TWELVE

The Perfect House

New Year's morning, the house is quiet, save for the lullaby rumble of the furnace. He lies beside me, safe and loved. His belly rises and falls with the slow, contented rhythm of his breathing.

One year ago this morning, we didn't understand that it would be our "first date" when I invited Brody Norris to meet me for a holiday brunch at the club. By that evening, though, my life had changed, turned upside down — beginning a venture into passion and commitment and shared dreams. For me, at the cusp of sixty, the prospect of such a profound twist of later life had seemed all but impossible.

My first clue that this was *it* — that there was a magic about Brody far deeper than the spark of lust — came moments after I joined him at Dumont Country Club that morning. He had arrived a few minutes early and was already seated in the crowded main dining room, sipping coffee, engaged in conversation with the head waiter. Brilliant January sunshine, the first daylight of the year, angled in from a nearby window, reflecting from the white linen tablecloth and glowing through the delicate porcelain of Brody's cup. His sandy hair shone with flecks of gold. His smile dazzled as he gabbed with the waiter, and although I was out of earshot, his lips conveyed words of promise.

As I approached, his eyes brightened and he stood to

greet me. "Hi there, Marson. What a surprise to get your call this morning." He shook my hand, hugged my shoulder.

The waiter said, "Happy New Year, Mr. Miles."

"Thank you, Victor. Best wishes to you, too. I see you've already met Brody." I started to explain that my wife's nephew had just moved from California to Wisconsin, that he was an architect, that he would be joining the local firm I had cofounded with my wife's brother.

"I heard all about it," said Victor. "What wonderful news."

He did not ask after my wife. Had he caught the vibe? Did he sense that, not thirty minutes earlier, I had told Prucilla I wanted out of our abysmally long marriage? Did he guess the fantasies I dared to entertain at that very moment? They featured the handsome sandy-haired architect who was not only *my* nephew—by marriage—but twenty-four years my junior.

"Did you know," Brody asked me, "that Victor here is the father of Victor the parking valet?"

I had known the head waiter for many years, as did everyone at the club, but I did not know any of the parking valets by name—they seemed to come and go. And yet Brody, who had never before set foot in the club, was befriending everyone he met, introducing himself, taking time for small talk, going so far as to inquire about family. The contrast with Prucilla was astounding. Sharing my joint membership for decades, she still refused to address "the help," as she referred to them, by name. Her condescending attitude was so complete, so elevated, she wouldn't even look them in the eye while conversing.

"Why, no," I told Victor, breaking into a smile, "I should've seen the resemblance. Such a great kid—you must be proud of him." Though I hadn't known that one of the valets was named Victor, I had no trouble guessing which one he was.

"Thank you, Mr. Miles. I'm very proud of him." Then he helped Brody with his chair and asked me, "Where would you care to sit, sir? Facing the window or facing the room?"

It was a smallish square table, and the second setting had been placed across from Brody. In his wisdom, though, Victor must have gathered I would prefer sitting closer to my guest. I replied, "Facing the room, please."

With fluid efficiency, Victor moved the place setting, moved the chair, seated me, poured coffee, and left.

"There now," I said. "That's better."

Brody looked into my eyes, grinning. "Couldn't agree more."

Beneath the table, we touched knees.

And by midafternoon, back at his modest apartment, I was in love.

This morning, the loft we call home is quiet, save for the lullaby rumble of the furnace. He lies beside me, sound asleep. The slow, contented rhythm of his breathing reminds me of a purring cat. Like a cat, he embodies a beautiful paradox, both lithe and muscular.

We bought the loft in March, not three months after Brody's arrival. The downtown commercial space needed work to make it livable, and by August—after the ink was dry on my settlement with Prucilla—Brody and I began to get comfortable in our first shared home. The loft offered a quick solution to the needs of our new circumstances, near the First Avenue offices where we worked, but it was never intended as our permanent dwelling. From the beginning, there was an unspoken understanding. I don't even recall which one of us first put words to the idea, making it concrete. We wanted to build a house together. The perfect house.

"The dream house," said Brody. "It'll be a breeze. I mean,

we're both architects."

"But I want *you* to design it," I said while cuddled close to him one night, waiting for sleep. "I'll give you any input you want, but this should be your masterpiece, not mine." I had already designed one dream house—Prucilla's—and had sacrificed every aesthetic principle I'd ever held, all in an attempt to please her, or at least to keep her quiet. Wishful thinking.

For Brody and me, there was no urgency to build a house. We were still finding our way as a couple, still adjusting to the routines of daily life, and at a deeper level, still defining our merged aesthetic.

What's more, we had plenty of design projects to occupy our time, especially since September, when my business partner, Ted Norris, lost his wife of twenty years, Peg, to a sudden illness that stemmed from a bizarre bout of amnesia. His grief was profound and disorienting. Worse, he refused to talk about it, which was not like him at all. Ted then decided to take some time off—in Hawaii—hoping the physical distance might help him also achieve some emotional distance from his loss. He even left open the possibility that he might not come back, that his nephew, Brody Norris, should perhaps begin to assume Ted's role in the Miles & Norris firm. If that were to happen, it would necessitate a good deal of legal mechanics, not to mention the investment required to buy Ted out, so the perfect house was back-burnered. It seemed more a pipe dream than a present priority.

That didn't stop me, however, from exploring a few possibilities behind the scenes. The perfect house would require the perfect setting, and I recalled a bit of land that would fit the bill—*perfectly*.

Mary Questman, widowed heir to a fortune made in

timber and paper, still owned huge swaths of land spreading out from the edge of town. We'd become fast friends a few years earlier when I designed the local performing-arts center that bears her name. One day, while we were out in my SUV, returning from the building site of the theater complex, she asked, "May I show you something I've always found quite pretty?" Following her directions, I drove to a remote section of her property that abutted a preserved prairie, held in trust by a conservancy.

My jaw dropped. What she had described as "quite pretty" I could only describe as breathtaking. Her land was lightly wooded with birches where it opened to the prairie. A stream ran through a rocky ravine, forming a lovely waterfall of perhaps twenty feet where some Ice Age mischief had cleaved upper and lower plateaus. My heart skipped a beat, and I could imagine how Frank Lloyd Wright must have felt on his first visit to Bear Run in Pennsylvania. The similarity of this setting was arresting, and I tried to form a mental image of the vista that might be enjoyed from a house perched on its upper plateau—a prairie view that would never change, never be developed, preserved for posterity. Mary mentioned that although she'd been tendered many offers for the land over the years, she'd never felt right about parting with it.

But all I had to do was ask. When I approached her two months ago, in early November, not only was she thrilled with my notion for its use, but she offered me the land for a song. I protested—albeit mildly—that she was "giving it away," but she dismissed my reticence as "nonsense, dear," so we sealed the deal, then and there, with a kiss on the cheek and a token deposit consisting of the cash I happened to have in my wallet. Done.

A few weeks later, while driving home with Brody from

Thanksgiving dinner at the club, I said, "Let's take a little ride. I have something to show you."

When I stopped the SUV, he got out and approached the waterfall, speechless.

Following from behind with a roll of drawings I'd stashed in the vehicle, I stepped up beside him. "It's ours."

He gave me a quizzical look, and I explained how Mary had sold me the land.

Shaking his head with disbelief he asked, "Know what it reminds me of?"

"Don't say it—that's a tough act to follow." With a grin, I added, "But I know you're up to it." And I handed him the roll of drawings.

"What's this?" he asked.

"A topographical survey of the site. So get busy, kiddo. That is, when you have a chance."

I presumed he wouldn't wait for a lull in our workload at the office. I presumed he'd drop everything for this labor of love. And he did. Night after night, he put in long extra hours, toiling at his computer, asking me not to look.

Christmas Eve, we were invited to dinner at Mary Questman's home—some eight or ten guests, black tie. As it was our first Christmas together, Brody and I had not yet established our traditions, but there at the loft, once we were dressed, with some time to spare before leaving for Mary's, it seemed like the right time to exchange gifts.

Brody had never looked so handsome. A tux will do that. He suggested that I fix us a round of drinks, and as I did so, he retrieved from some hiding spot a long roll of drawings, tied with a lavish red velvet ribbon. With a sheepish smile (good God, he was adorable), he placed his offering on the counter before me.

"Well, well," I joshed, handing him a short Scotch and

soda, "what's this?"

"It's *preliminary*," he stressed, sounding nervous. "You might not care for this at all, and if you don't, I'll start over. But I had this idea, and I wanted to develop it, and now I need some feedback." He inched the roll of drawings in my direction.

Poker-faced, I pulled the ribbon, undoing the bow, allowing the prints to flop open on the counter. The set of large drawings measured some three by four feet. The top page was a detailed three-point perspective — the big picture, so to speak — showing the finished building as it would appear in the wooded setting, as seen from the lower plateau. My eyes widened. Brody had taken a more modern, minimalist approach than I would have guessed. I had assumed he would design something hinting at Wright's Fallingwater, which appeared to have grown from its setting, but Brody had been lured by a different muse. This house was not an organic outgrowth of nature; rather, it was a polished, faceted jewel in the woods. And it worked. It absolutely worked.

I flipped to the next drawing, an overall plan of the main floor. Then the next, the second floor. Then the site plan. Then the structural engineering for the cantilever over the waterfall. Exterior details. Interior details.

"You're not saying anything," he mumbled. "You hate it. And that's okay."

I wondered aloud, "How shall I put this?" Then I demonstrated to him, in no uncertain terms, what I thought of his creation.

I'm a punctual man. It's a point of pride. But I recognize priorities.

We were twenty minutes late for dinner.

This morning, the loft is quiet, save for the lullaby rumble of the furnace. He lies beside me, still sleeping. His restful dreams surface in the slow, contented rhythm of his breathing.

A week has passed since he revealed to me his vision of the perfect house, *our* perfect house. And just last night, another piece to the puzzle of our future fell into place.

It was New Year's Eve, and we were getting ready to go out to dinner, with reservations at the same restaurant where our journey had begun a year ago that night. Last year, there had been five of us at the table, squeezed into a horseshoe-shaped corner booth, but last night, it would be a party of two—Brody and me. Prucilla was out of my life. Ted was somewhere in Hawaii. And Ted's wife, Peg, had died.

As we prepared to leave the loft, debating whether or not topcoats were needed for our drive to dinner, the phone rang. I answered. It was Ted—wishing us a happy New Year, recalling last year's dinner, and delivering news of a decision he'd made.

"I've moved again," he told me. Two months earlier, he had begun his getaway, his retreat from grief, in Honolulu. Finding the city scene less than soothing, he had hopped over to Maui for a while, and then, seeking further solitude, Lanai. "Now," he said on the phone, "I'm on Molokai."

"Isn't that a bit *isolated*?" I asked.

"That's the whole idea, Marson. I like it. A lot."

"I mean, it was a leper colony, right?"

"Not anymore. And guess what. Hard to believe, but I've . . . well, I've *found* someone."

I rattled my head. "On Molokai?"

He wasn't sure of his plans with her—they had connected just recently—but he had decided to stay there, perhaps for good. In any event, Ted would not be returning to Dumont, and he hoped Brody could take over his share of the Miles & Norris partnership.

On Brody's behalf, I asked what sort of terms Ted was seeking for the buyout. His price was realistic. He was leading a simple life now. He wanted out.

We spoke awhile longer, agreeing on various business details, then wished each other happiness before saying good-bye.

Brody and I discussed the phone call while driving to dinner. We hadn't bothered with overcoats, so the heater was cranked high, roaring against the frigid night. I reached across the console to rest a hand on Brody's knee. "This is it. It seems you and I are in business together. Sound good?"

"Sounds great." He rested his hand on mine.

"And if you have trouble with the buyout, don't be bashful. I can help."

Brody patted my hand. After a long moment's silence, he said, "Ted *found* someone? Already? Out there in the middle of nowhere?"

I shrugged. "That's the story. He sounded happy. Good for him." Then I recalled, "While we were on the phone, she came into the room and spoke to him briefly—going out for something, I guess. But I couldn't help thinking, her voice reminded me of Peg's."

Brody suggested, "Maybe that's what attracted him to her."

"Maybe."

This morning, New Year's morning, our loft is quiet, save for the lullaby rumble of the furnace. He lies beside me—sleeping, purring, dreaming.

When we met one year ago, I was mourning the passing of my fifties. Today I'm eager to leap forward into this next phase of my life. With Brody. A year ago, I had lost interest in the ritual of declaring resolutions as the calendar reset itself to January. Today, however, I am brimming with resolve for the year ahead.

Be it resolved: Brody Norris will join me as equal partners in Miles & Norris, LLC, replacing his uncle, Ted Norris. I have known Ted most of my life, and I have loved him since college, when we were roommates in architecture school. I have never dared to confess that love to Ted, let alone act upon it, but it has both nurtured me and agonized me for forty years. Now that he has moved half a world away, I will of course miss him; there will always be that pang. But Brody has compensated for that loss a hundredfold, and we can love each other openly. What's more, Brody's relative youth and manifest talent will help ensure the longevity of the Miles & Norris firm for another generation.

Be it resolved: Brody and I will build the perfect house. It was an unspoken understanding that we would someday get around to this, and now the project is real and tangible, not only because we are discussing it—at length and often—but because Brody has designed it. I challenged him to create a masterpiece, and he has delivered. His beautiful perspective drawing now hangs in the loft, on a wall within sight of our bed. It is the last thing I see at night and the first thing I see upon rising. Sometime within the next four seasons, we will celebrate a groundbreaking.

In the same way that the eventuality of the house was at first an unspoken assumption, there is yet another issue on the horizon that has been little discussed but seems inevitable. Today, I plan to bring it out of the shadows and nudge it forward.

Be it resolved: Brody and I will marry this year. When he moved to Wisconsin twelve months ago, the state had a ban in place that prevented him from marrying me or any other man. But now—*poof*—with the smack of a gavel, it's open season. And it's time.

Brody and I each have the experience of a prior, failed marriage; we are mature enough not to expect the trappings of a fairytale romance. No one needs to "pop the question" on bended knee. But today—call me a sentimental sap—that's just what I intend to do. Last week, I bought the ring.

During a year's worth of frolicking with Brody, I have often fallen to my knees at his service, and vice versa, but the genuflection I have in mind today will be more formal than functional, more solemn than impassioned. I might do it at the club, during brunch, embarrassing both of us. I might do it afterward, when we visit the building site again, ruining my pants in the frosty mud. Or I might wait to do it later, here, back at the loft. But I will do it.

Now I turn my head on the pillow to whisper in his ear, "Good morning."

He stirs. My tongue glides over his eyelid, tasting the crust of sleep on his lash. The mattress quivers as he stretches, lithe and muscular, like a cat.

"Let's get moving, kiddo." I lift the blanket from his shoulder and toss it aside. "We've got a busy year ahead of us."

He smiles, aroused. Eyes still closed, he offers his arms. His lips find mine.

Clinging to each other, we share the same breath.

❏

ABOUT THE AUTHOR

Michael Craft is the author of fourteen novels, including the highly acclaimed "Mark Manning" mystery series, three installments of which were honored as finalists for Lambda Literary Awards: *Name Games* (2000), *Boy Toy* (2001), and *Hot Spot* (2002). Craft grew up in Illinois and spent his middle years in Wisconsin, which inspired the fictitious setting of this book. He holds an MFA in creative writing from Antioch University, Los Angeles, and now resides in Rancho Mirage, California. Visit the author's website at www.michaelcraft.com.

ABOUT THE TYPE

The text of this book was set in Cochin, which is classified as a "transitional" serif typeface, bridging the gap between "old style" and "modern." The font exhibits an unusual synthesis of stylistic elements, a hallmark of the typographical neo-renaissance movement. It was originally produced in 1912 by Georges Peignot for the Paris foundry Deberny & Peignot and was named in honor of the eighteenth-century French engraver Charles Nicolas Cochin. In 1977, Cochin was reworked and expanded by Matthew Carter for Linotype. The font has a small x-height with long ascenders, lending a decidedly elegant appearance to the printed page. Perhaps the most distinctive aspect of the font family is its *playful italic, which adds an appropriate note of whimsy* to the stories in this book.

CPSIA information can be obtained
at www.ICGtesting.com
Printed in the USA
FSOW01n2117261117
41681FS